THE WOMAN IN THE GARDEN

JILL JOHNSON

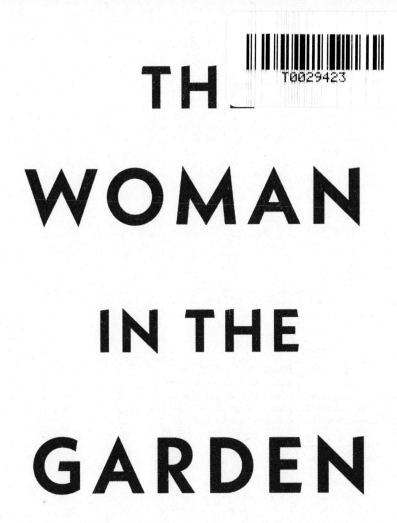

Poisoned Pen
PRESS

Copyright © 2024 by Jill Johnson
Cover and internal design © 2024 by Sourcebooks
Cover design and illustration by Holly Ovenden
Cover image © Genzi/Getty Images
Internal design by Tara Jaggers/Sourcebooks

Sourcebooks, Poisoned Pen Press, and the colophon
are registered trademarks of Sourcebooks.

Published by Poisoned Pen Press, an imprint of Sourcebooks
P.O. Box 4410, Naperville, Illinois 60567-4410
(630) 961-3900
sourcebooks.com

Cataloging-in-Publication Data is on file with the Library of Congress.

Printed and bound in the United States of America
VP 10 9 8 7 6 5 4 3 2 1

For Casper

pretty unremarkable in many ways: neither tall and slim, nor short and overweight. I keep my hair neat in the old-fashioned way—precisely parted with Brylcreem and a tortoiseshell comb—and I take care of my clothes, washing them in the bathroom sink and ironing them on the kitchen table. The cuffs are frayed, the linings are torn, and there are holes in my pockets, but there is no one to see this damage. No one to comment on the greasy stains on my collar or the earthy smell of my trousers, and for this, I'm also grateful.

I like to think I have the faded air of a learned university lecturer, which was indeed once my profession. There's a deep crease between my eyebrows formed by years of concentration, and my large nose is permanently dented at the bridge by my steel-rimmed glasses. I have neither smile nor laughter lines, and there's a natural droop to the corners of my mouth that I suppose some might find unattractive, but my lips are soft and are often pursed in thought.

I'm forty-four years old. I would say my appearance belies my age. I look much older. Sometimes I feel befuddled by the outside world and dread interruption—a cold call from an internet provider, say, or a letter from HMRC. When I'm left to myself, however, my mind is clear and intelligent and focused. It has to be.

Every morning, I put on my protective overalls—slightly too short, so they catch uncomfortably at the crotch—climb the ladder and go through the hatch in my kitchen ceiling. I then begin the long list of daily tasks, carrying them out with extreme diligence.

My routine never wavers. I execute each action following the exact scientific method because, if I don't, there's a viable risk of death.

Over the years, I've learned that the nature of my work requires solitude. I could never forgive myself if somebody got hurt. Better to carry the risk myself and save others from harm. This is the reason I've never employed an assistant or a secretary, and why I've always refused the requests for internships from students who attend the university where I once worked. In the past, I perked up flagging lectures by likening myself to a bomb-disposal expert. One slip and *boom*, it would all be over. Not straightaway, mind. Not like in an explosion where I would die instantly, my limbs torn from my torso and flung across the sand. No. My death would take time, sometimes as long as two weeks, but it would come. There's no doubt about that.

It must be said that I've not always been grateful to be alone. I hadn't planned this life of solitude. At the university, I'd interacted with people on a daily basis. Students, other lecturers, staff. It hadn't been easy. I'd struggled with eye contact, been confused by humor, and was often left exhausted after tutorials. But I'd been prepared to suffer these discomforts for the prize of unlimited access to the lab and greenhouses, and the prestige of the university's name that gave weight to my publications.

It must also be said that I'd not intended to remain single. Once upon a time, there had been someone with whom I thought I would share my life. An attractive, intelligent, witty acquaintance, who'd accepted my peculiarities—perhaps even loved me for them—but, in the end, chose someone else. I try not to dwell on this. What's the expression? 'Tis better to have loved and lost... Better to have experienced that doubt, that ache, that misery... As I said, I try not to dwell on it, but that can take great effort. Better to find other outlets, other distractions.

My father was a keen astronomer. He'd positioned his telescope at his study window, permanently trained on the sky, and would spend hours at night against the eyepiece, murmuring to himself, lost in another world. I'd always been envious of this tool he used to remove himself from his surroundings, to detach himself from the mundane reality of his life. Sometimes, when I was a child, and if Mars or Saturn was particularly bright, he would wake me in the middle of the night and take me, half-asleep, to look through the eyepiece. And I would gaze at the distant points of light, full of wonder. Then we would go to the long table in our Oxford kitchen for an astronomy lesson that would end with a live demonstration of a sunrise.

Father excelled at many things. Some said he was a polymath. But out of his many interests, it was astronomy that I chose to make my own. The same tool I now use to detach myself from the mundane reality of my life and to distract myself when I feel I'm tipping into melancholia. My telescope is nothing like Father's. His was archaic in comparison. Mine is of a very high specification and expensive—paid for with my redundancy money—which I keep among the plants on my roof. Late at night, when I've finished my tasks, I like to look at the stars and the planets and the occasional meteor shower. Like Father, I've become fascinated by celestial phenomena. In many ways, I've come to realize that the incomprehensible vastness of time and space makes much more sense to me than anything that happens in the space and time within which I live.

However, on the nights when the cloud cover is too thick to see the stars, and memories of my lost love threaten to overwhelm me, I put the telescope to a different use. Please be assured, I do this with no ill intent. It began purely as a distraction but soon became a form of social observation. A scientific pursuit, if you will. And as time has passed, my observations have grown into something quite significant. In fact, one day I plan to publish my findings, which is why I've always kept detailed accounts of the activities in a notebook. So far, I've filled twenty.

Behind my block of flats is a communal garden that's separated by a high brick wall from the gardens of the terraced houses beyond. From my roof, I have an excellent view of the comings and goings of the residents in those terraced houses because they're all serviced by large Victorian sash windows. I suppose one could say that at night, each floor of every house is a light box showcasing the activity taking place within, and often, while I sit alone in my garden, I feel compelled to watch those activities—and many times, I've used my telescope to enhance that observation. I've been careful. I'm certain no one can see me, because I've positioned the lens so it can't be seen through the vine-covered railings surrounding my garden. I am a bird-watcher in a blind. Completely concealed.

There's the woman with blue hair and crutches, who habitually shares a packet of biscuits with her dog while laughing uproariously at whatever she's watching on television. There's the bickering couple, who are forever practicing the same four dance moves to a tune I can't hear. There's the young boy sunken into a beanbag chair, playing computer games well past his bedtime, shouting furious instructions into a headset microphone while glugging energy drinks. There's the teenage girl with the long, braided hair; lying on her bed, scrolling on her phone. Always scrolling on her phone. There's the tall, stooping man who never smiles and who stands stock-still for hours, staring at a photograph of a mother and baby on his wall. There's the old woman who lives in a basement directly opposite my flat, her white hair tied into a bun, who shuffles around her garden with a flashlight in the middle of the night, picking up snails and throwing them over the wall.

And finally, there's the beautiful young woman who lives in the flat above the nighttime snail thrower.

Whenever I think of the first day I saw her, I experience a peculiar sensation that isn't altogether unpleasant. She was standing at her open window, her hands resting on the sill. She must have only recently moved in, because I'd never seen her before. Intrigued by this new subject, I'd trained the lens on her face and saw that she was young, perhaps in her midtwenties, with widely spaced, large dark eyes that tilted upward at the outer edge, fine eyebrows, a small nose, and prominent cheekbones.

I could see that she was beautiful, but it was her lips that lifted her above the masses and placed her on another plane: a higher, more dangerous altitude, where only the rarest, most valuable specimens are found. They were so full and red that I was reminded of the improbable bracts of the *Psychotria elata* plant, a specimen of which I kept under a cloche in my greenhouse. Gradually, I increased the focus until her mouth filled the entire eyepiece.

I've always been better with plants than people, and I tend to name people after the plants they most resemble. Father first suggested I do this when I was a child because I found it difficult to recognize faces and remember names. That first day, I looked at those full red lips made huge by the power of my telescope and chose an affectionate nickname for the young woman. Psycho, after my *Psychotria elata* plant. I've never confessed to anyone that there have been occasions when I've been tempted to taste those glossy red bracts, even though I know they contain a powerful psychedelic chemical. And as time went by and the observational study notebooks filled, I could sense I was developing a curious fascination for this woman—a fascination as potent and addictive as her namesake.

2

IT WAS LATE. I WAS IN MY GARDEN. I'D JUST FINISHED COVERING the most tender specimens with horticultural fleece to protect them from the night chill and was settling down in front of the telescope to begin the task of recording the activities of my neighbors when I heard the distant sound of my telephone. This was unusual. I rarely received phone calls. I paused to listen until the final ring, and when I heard the answer machine click to record, I put down my notebook and pen, descended the ladder, walked through the kitchen and along the hallway to my front room. For a moment, I stared at the flashing red light before pressing Play, and the deep voice that came out of the machine shot a bolt of excitement through my body.

Tonight, usual time, usual place. Payment as arranged.

I gasped with pleasurable surprise. This was a long-arranged purchase, my most audacious yet, but I hadn't expected it to be delivered so soon. A rare *Dichapetalum toxicarium*–root cutting found in isolated regions of West Africa, common name "broke-back" because of the sudden seizures and convulsions it causes a few hours after ingestion. This particular cutting was not actually from Sierra Leone. It had been stolen from a botanical garden in Yunnan Province during the long-planned relocation of the parent. If the theft was to be discovered, the technician could go to prison. If the delivery was traced and the provenance proved, I could lose my job—if I still had a job to lose.

I sat down and replayed the message, exhilarated by the prospect of this new package. Some of my detractors might say this was my addiction, toxic plants my drug. But for me, plant collecting was my life's work. I checked my watch. It was 11:00 p.m. With purpose, I went to the hall cupboard, put on Father's full-length waxed coat, lifted the collar, and left the flat.

This part of Hampstead Heath was densely wooded with giant oaks, an understory of beech and, below them, holly, hawthorn, and elder. It was a balmy night, with moonlight enough to see a fair distance along the path leading into the wood. Briefly, I scanned the road ahead and behind, then stepped onto the path. The baked earth was hard underfoot from weeks without rain, and the snap of dry sticks as I crunched over them echoed away into the night. Sometimes the gate to the pergola was left unlocked, but not that night. It meant I would have to go the long way around and squeeze through the gap in the wrought-iron fence. Years before, I'd chosen this secluded area of the Heath for my midnight rendezvous because it was always fairly well populated with people—men—prowling the less conspicuous paths through the trees. I'd never felt any threat from the men. On the contrary, I knew that if anything went wrong, I could attract their attention with a call for help, and so the snap of a twig nearby did not make me spin around. The rustle of leaves did not put me on high alert. I simply continued to walk, my gaze averted, toward the gap in the fence.

It was darker here. The trees denser, obscuring the moon. I ducked down, squeezed through the gap, walked briskly to the wall, followed it to a thicket of ornamental shrubs, and pushed through them. A thrilling energy pulsed through me when I saw that the courier was already standing in the shadow of an alcove, underneath the pergola. He unzipped his jacket to pull out the package, and the exchange was over in a matter of seconds. I let him leave first, waited a few minutes, then made my way back to the path that led to the road. Behind me, twigs snapped and leaves rustled, but I ignored this and quickened my pace. When I emerged from the path, Whitestone Pond was deserted, the surrounding roads silent. I walked to the flagstaff and turned down the hill toward home. The sooner I potted this cutting, the more chance it would have of survival.

It was well past midnight. The high street was all but deserted. I turned onto my road and hurried to the entrance of my block.

The building was silent, so I tried not to make any noise as I climbed the stairs to my flat. I took off Father's coat, put on my overalls, and carried the package through to the kitchen. If I could nurture this tiny cutting into a viable plant, it would be the first time it had been achieved in this country. To say I was excited would not do justice to what I was feeling.

I turned on the overhead light in my greenhouse and looked at the padded courier envelope on the bench before me. Inside, the package had been well wrapped in a thick layer of Chinese newspaper. I peeled this away, glancing at the characters, wondering what they said, until I reached a small metal tobacco tin. I frowned at the mistake. Metal doesn't allow a cutting to breathe. It creates a closed, moist environment prone to the development of spores. A horticulturalist should know this. With a sinking heart, I opened the lid.

The tin was filled with a moisture-absorbing substance, similar to vermiculite, that I hadn't encountered before, and in its center lay the cutting, perfectly preserved. I exhaled with relief. *Dichapetalum toxicarium*, broke-back. In many regions of West Africa, the pulp of its young leaves was traditionally used to dip arrows. Even after all my years of study, the damage such an innocent-looking scrap of vegetation could cause still amazed me.

I filled a seed tray with a mix of compost and horticultural sand, took a pair of tweezers from a sterilizing solution, picked up the cutting, and placed it on a board. I then sliced the cutting into small segments with a scalpel. After dusting each segment with rooting powder, I lay them on top of the compost. I wasn't unaware of the enormity of what I was doing. Each step felt like a sacred ritual and I the high priest. I paused to acknowledge this for a couple of minutes, then shook a sieved layer of compost over the cuttings before finishing with a sprinkle of distilled water. Inhaling deeply, I put the tray in the propagator, closed the lid, and stood back to appreciate my work.

With a satisfied smile, I looked through the greenhouse windows at the night sky. It was beautifully clear. I could see Mars and Saturn. It was the perfect night for stargazing.

I went outside and opened the folding canvas chair that had once belonged to Father; then, taking care not to disturb the plants, I went to the telescope to wheel it into the center of the garden.

But just as I was releasing the brakes, my attention was suddenly drawn by a woman's high-pitched scream.

3

As I panned across the windows of the terraced houses through the telescope, the woman screamed again, so I moved my head back for a broader view in time to see the rear window of the house opposite mine slam shut. I stared at it, then lowered my head back to the eyepiece, adjusted the focus, and saw through the dimly lit window two figures: a woman kneeling, holding her head, and a man standing over her. They were in the rear half of a small room. There was a sofa, an open laptop on a coffee table, a television, and a desk covered with books and papers. I could see right through the room to the windows at the front of the house, and through those to the streetlight outside. For a moment, I marveled at the power of the telescope, then pulled back to focus on the woman. Her long dark hair was falling forward to cover her face. She was swaying back and forth on her knees and flexed feet. But even though the light was low, I knew it was Psycho.

The man was leaning down, trying to see her face, his mouth moving rapidly. Suddenly, he grabbed her hair and dragged her head backward, forcing her face up, and when he raised an arm above his head, his fist clenched, I uttered three words. I hadn't spoken aloud for days, so they came out as a croak.

"Leave her alone."

After a suspended moment, he let go of her hair, dropped his arm, and left the room, and I felt a small victory as I watched him through the front windows on the street outside, walking away. I moved the focus back to Psycho. She was standing now, pushing back her hair, rubbing her hands on her thighs. She walked to the rear window and looked out over the gardens. I adjusted the focus for a clearer view of her face and frowned. For someone who'd just been struck to the floor, she didn't appear cowed at all. If I was to hazard a guess, I would say her expression was one of fury.

I noticed a trickle of blood crawling slowly from her hairline to her cheekbone. She noticed as well because she touched it, inspected her fingertips, and put them into her mouth. My stomach muscles tightened at this, and I released a long-held breath. As if she'd heard me, she looked in my direction, and even though I knew she couldn't see me, I ducked down among the plants, and in so doing, accidentally brushed the back of my hand across a leaf, causing the plant's fine hairs to embed in my skin. Hissing with annoyance, I deftly pulled out the hairs, then took a phial from a leather pouch around my neck and applied some cream. Within an hour, there would be blisters and swelling, but I hoped I'd acted quickly enough to prevent the poison from entering my bloodstream. I crouched among the plants for a further five minutes, cursing my stupidity, then cautiously peered over the railings, but the light was off in the room and Psycho was gone.

4

OVER THE FOLLOWING WEEKS, I OFTEN FELT COMPELLED TO
interrupt a task to look through the telescope at Psycho's window,
a forgotten mist bottle or propagation brush hanging loosely in
my hand, and justified these frequent breaks in my routine as
necessary checks on her safety. She wasn't at home much during
the day but often had visitors in the evening—all men—so after
the attack, I decided to stop observing the other neighbors and
only record these appearances, jotting down the time of arrival,
the duration of stay, and a brief description of their activity. I also
made a detailed study of each man. This I did scientifically, as if
cataloguing the taxonomy, morphology, and toxicity of a plant,
attributing a classification to each of them and giving them the
common name of a poisonous plant. I knew I was not a good
judge of character, but I *did* know plants, and one thing was
increasingly obvious: these men were toxic.

Specimen A. The man with the ridged scar and cowboy boots, who'd hit her and made her bleed the night it all began. She seemed frightened of him but let him into her flat anyway. I named him Castor. Toxicity classification: blood. Fatal.

Specimen B. Perhaps a personal tutor, who sat beside her at her desk, leafing through books and making notes. I noted that she seemed to find these lessons difficult, because she often stood abruptly to pace the room, her arms gesticulating. He touched her a lot when she did this, which I assumed she liked, because at the end of each lesson, they shared a meal. I named him Foxglove and gave him the toxicity classification of neuro-muscular—a group of poisons that attack the brain. Also fatal.

Specimen C. The eccentrically dressed young man with long blond hair, with whom she was always arguing and who spent the entirety of every visit sprawled on her sofa, drinking red wine from a bottle. He always seemed to be in despair, and she always seemed to be shaking her head and rolling her eyes at him. I named him Jimsonweed and gave him the toxicity classification of nerve—a group of poisons that are hallucinogenic and can cause mental confusion, headaches, coma, and eventually death. Fatal.

Specimen D. A muscular young man with dark eyes and an urgent manner. She always seemed to be persuading him to sit down, but he always jumped up again and stood rigidly before her, as if his muscles were coiled too tight. I named him False

Hellebore and gave him the toxicity classification of muscular—a group of poisons that attack the muscles and the organs that rely upon them. Also fatal.

Incidental visitors such as meter readers and deliverymen were named Poison Ivies and classified as skin irritants: nonfatal.

On the fourth Friday of my vigil, I lay in my narrow bed beside the illuminated numbers of my digital clock, my clothes folded neatly on a wooden chair beside the door. I'd lived in my small flat for twenty years. I kept it tidy, dusted and swept it once a month, cleaned the bathroom regularly, and took my bed linen to the launderette when required. I didn't bother my neighbors, and they didn't bother me. They were just abstract subjects I was studying. I certainly had never felt even the remotest inclination to be drawn into their lives. In fact, I could say with confidence that I didn't care about them at all.

But as time went by, I wondered what had changed, because I knew with certainty that I wanted to be drawn into Psycho's life. I wanted it very much. Perhaps I felt a responsibility to protect her, to call the police if Castor attacked her again. Perhaps it was because the telescope had brought her so close that I felt a connection with her. Or maybe it was something simpler, baser. Behind my closed eyes, I pictured her putting her fingers into

her mouth—her full, bloodied lips tightening around them—
and groaned.

Sleep would not come. The image in my head would not go.
It taunted me. Tormented me. I rolled onto my side, my front,
my back and groaned again. In desperation, I turned my attention to my throbbing hand. I'd been diligently administering the
cream twice daily for a month now, but it was showing no signs
of improving. In fact, it was getting worse. A moment before, I'd
been oblivious to the pain; now, it was unbearable. Making me
grit my teeth. Making me sit up, get out of bed, put on my overalls, and go up to the roof.

The folding canvas chair was leaning against the wall. I
opened it, sat, and checked my watch. It was a quarter to three.

The moon was highlighting the myriad leaves, bathing the
garden in a green, almost ghostly glow. I held up my damaged
hand. It looked gangrenous in this light. The cream may have
prevented amputation, but it was neither an antidote nor a cure.
The poison was lodged deep in my epidermis, and there was
nothing to be done except wait for the pain to subside. I rested
my damaged hand lightly on my thigh. It would never regain the
strength it had once had, but it was better to have a weakened
hand than no hand at all.

A light snapped on in one of the houses behind my apartment
block, illuminating the red flowers of the *Mandevilla sanderi*
vine covering the railings. I stretched my neck and saw that the

light was coming from Psycho's front room. The battle between respecting her privacy and checking her safety was over in less than five seconds. I stood and went to the telescope. A naked man was pacing the length of the room, back and forth, with long-determined strides while he talked on a mobile phone. It was Foxglove, the personal tutor. He usually left at ten o'clock. I frowned, then exhaled and did the thing I had promised myself I wouldn't do: I panned the telescope upward to Psycho's curtainless bedroom window.

The room was in darkness. It was difficult to find anything to focus on, so I moved my head back and noticed a dim glow on one side of the room. I put my eye back to the eyepiece and focused on the glow—the light from a small screen. Now that my eyes were adjusted, I could see Psycho sitting up in bed, tapping buttons on a small black Nokia. As she tapped, she repeatedly looked up at the bedroom door, as if worried Foxglove would open it. Then she took the back off the Nokia, removed the SIM card, put the phone into her bedside-table drawer—right at the back—dropped the SIM card into her makeup bag, and lay down.

Immediately, she sat up again and picked up another mobile that must have been on the bed beside her. This was a smartphone, with a large, bright screen that fully illuminated her face. She frowned as she scrolled down the screen, shook her head as she rapidly thumb-tapped a text, then rolled her eyes as she read the reply. She was typing another text when Foxglove appeared at the bedroom door, illuminated from behind by the hall light. Quickly, she slipped the phone under the duvet and smiled. I focused on him. He wasn't returning her smile but was looking from her to the place where she'd hidden the phone. She patted the bed beside her. He didn't move. She watched him a moment, smiling, shrugging, then lifted the duvet, and I caught a fleeting glimpse of one perfect breast.

Flinching, I gasped, jerked my head back, and quickly retreated to the canvas chair. What was I to do now? What was I to do with this new image of her that would torment me as I tried desperately to sleep? I stared at the telescope. Willing myself not to go to it. Forcing my eyes to look at the garden, the rooftops, the stars, anything but the telescope. But in the end, I stood, crossed the roof on leaden legs, and lowered my head to the eyepiece.

The bedroom was softly lit by ambient moonlight from the uncovered window. Just enough to see two shapes in the bed. Two shapes moving rhythmically. With a cry of disgust, I spun away, my skin crawling with revulsion, and hurried down the ladder into the kitchen. Covering my face with both hands, I marched back and forth, bumping into the counter, the table, knowing that what I'd seen could never be unseen.

At the back of a cupboard was a bottle of whisky that had belonged to Father. I don't know why I had it. Nostalgia, maybe. I took it out and put it on the table, thinking that if I drank enough, it could erase what I'd just seen. I picked up the bottle, my hand on the lid. If I drank enough, I might even sleep. I twisted the lid a quarter turn, stopped, tightened it again, and returned the bottle to its place at the back of the cupboard. I knew there would be no sleep for me that night, even if I drank the lot. No. The only way to get through this ordeal would be with the certainty that Foxglove had gone and Psycho was asleep in her bed...alone.

I sat at my kitchen table a further half hour, then crept back up to the roof and put my eye to the telescope. With a sinking heart, I saw Foxglove standing at the bedroom window, looking out over the gardens, but it was dark. He must have only been able to see his own reflection. I shifted the focus and discovered that Psycho was no longer in the room, so I panned out to see a sliver of light underneath a door I assumed to be her bathroom. Even though he repelled me, I forced myself to return the focus to Foxglove. Unlike the others, he wasn't young. He looked to be in his midfifties, his stomach extended, the skin around his upper thighs loose, and there was a graying at his temples. He was standing in a wide-legged stance, scratching his testicles, supremely confident in his nakedness. Then, as he stood before his reflection, he tipped back his head to check his teeth and nostrils, sucked in his stomach, and fussed with his hair. And it was that action that caught my breath because, even though I'd been watching him for weeks, when he fussed with his hair, I finally recognized him.

5

FOR THE FIRST TIME, I'D BROKEN MY ROUTINE AND HADN'T gone up to the roof to begin my daily tasks. Instead, I'd sat through the rest of the night and all of the following day at the kitchen table, still in my overalls. I knew I must attend to the plants but feared that, if I went back up, I wouldn't be able to resist putting my eye to the telescope, and the thought of seeing Foxglove—or, to give him his name, Jonathan Wainwright—again filled me with a desperate kind of dread. I'd been in a state of high anxiety for hours. Not just anxiety, something else I couldn't quite comprehend: a revolving mix of emotions beginning with revulsion, then anger, self-pity, loss, and back to revulsion.

If Psycho were a plant, she would be the finest example of exotic perfection I'd ever encountered, and Jonathan Wainwright, well... He was a filthy pest—always had been. The thought of him contaminating her with his foul seed disgusted and appalled me. Jonathan's notebook was on the table in front of me. It lay open on an empty page, but I couldn't bring myself to log his visit or make a note of his activity. It felt like defilement.

My mind went back twenty years to the first time I met him. He'd taken a liking to a PhD student who was sharing my laboratory at the university, so he seemed always to be hanging about. I'd often return from lectures to find him sitting on a stool, perfectly turned out in a waistcoat and jacket, his initials embroidered onto the crisp white cuffs of his expensive shirt. His elbow on the worktop, his chin resting in his cupped hand, his eyes fixed on her. His inane chatter was infuriating. I couldn't understand why she found it amusing. He was an irritant, a distraction. Most infuriating was the way he constantly checked himself in the reflective doors of the specimen cabinet; the way he fussed with his hair, pushing it back and forth, side to side. The way he was always fishing for a compliment. I couldn't understand why she found this charming or why she encouraged his preening with soft laughter.

But it was when he turned his attention to me that the situation became intolerable. The incessant questions began when he noticed I was working on a study of naturally occurring plant-based hallucinogens and the poisonous effects of overdose: the seeds of *Ipomoea tricolor* and *Anadenanthera peregrina*, the leaves of *Mitragyna speciosa Korth* and *Salvia divinorum*, but in particular my experiments with *Banisteriopsis caapi* and *Psychotria viridis.* At the time, I'd put his interest down to an immature fascination with hallucinogens and, despite his persistence, had steadfastly refused to engage with him.

Closing the notebook, I stood woodenly, walked along the narrow hallway to a photograph of Father hanging on the wall, and stopped before it. Agitated and restless, I rapped on the glass above his face with a knuckle, turned, and walked back along the hallway to the kitchen. The image of the rhythmically moving shapes in her bed had flashed across my mind so many times during the day that I was almost driven to despair. Almost driven to drink. For the second time, I went to the cupboard with the whisky bottle at the back and opened the door. Of all the men in the world, why did she have to choose him? Why Jonathan Wainwright? I stared at the whisky bottle, expelled a heavy breath, and went back to the photograph of Father.

"I don't know what to do. You always knew what to do." When I was agitated as a child, or frustrated, or anxious, Father would take me on long rambling walks through the Oxford countryside to, as he said, "restore equilibrium." Along the way he would point out wildflowers and fruiting shrubs and tell me stories of plant folklore or explain the medicinal properties of each berry, seed, and root. He would teach me the Latin and common names of each plant and test me on identification and usage. Sometimes, when I failed the test and complained that they were just weeds, Father would say there was no such thing as weeds. From the first prehistoric single-cell algae to the trillion-cell mighty oak, all plants evolved to have a purpose. Beneficial or toxic, every plant had a place within the ecosystem, and I would do well to remember that.

I nodded, inhaled deeply, went to the bedroom to take off my overalls, and headed out for a long walk on the Heath to restore equilibrium.

It was a warm evening, and the high street was bustling. Tables outside the many restaurants were full: groups chatted outside the cinema, and every few minutes, a train full of people disgorged from the Underground station. I kept my gaze on the pavement, avoiding eye contact, but as I waited at the pedestrian crossing, my elbow was clipped by someone dashing past. I looked up in time to see Psycho, her long hair swinging from a high ponytail, before she was obscured by a double-decker bus. My heart leaped. I hurried after her, craning my neck around the bus, trying to catch sight of her again, but before I reached the other side of the road, someone else rushed past, the wooden heels of his cowboy boots knocking the pavement loudly. It was Castor. Castor was chasing Psycho. I quickened my pace, but they were sprinting down the high street faster than I had any hope of matching, and he was gaining on her.

"Leave her alone!" I shouted. "Stop that man!"

I broke into a skittering, flat-footed jog, veering back and forth to try and see past the bus.

"Stop him!"

A few people turned in my direction, but most ignored me, and when at last the road cleared, she was nowhere to be seen, and Castor was leaping onto the bus just as it was pulling away.

"Damn it!" I shouted, thumping my thigh in frustration.

All these people crowding the pavements and not a single one had tried to stop him.

"He was right in front of you!" I shouted. "Good God. Are you all deaf or just completely inept?"

Again, people glanced at me, and I glared back furiously. Then I glared after the bus and realized it was pulling into a stop beside the Underground station. I had no way of knowing if she was on the bus, but Castor had been chasing her. Why would he leap on, if not after her? I took a step forward. Neither of them knew me. I could board the bus, watch them both. Alight with her and make sure she reached her destination safely. I paused. But Castor was a dangerous man. What if he became violent? I took a step back. And why should I protect someone who had betrayed me with Jonathan Wainwright the night before?

Paralyzed by indecision, I let out a cry of frustration.

My life's work was to protect the rarest, most valuable specimens. To watch over them with meticulous attention. I was the only person qualified for this task.

I took a step forward. It had to be me.

6

BY THE TIME I BOARDED THE BUS, EVERY SEAT WAS TAKEN, AND people were standing close together in the aisle. I scanned the faces. She wasn't on the lower deck.

Neither was he. Halfway up the front stairs, I was suddenly propelled upward by the unexpected acceleration of the bus and had to grip the handrail to prevent myself from being launched straight onto the upper deck in front of everyone. I took a moment to calm my heart and wedged myself halfway up the stairs so I would neither be flung up nor down by the driver's erratic maneuvers. From this half-hidden position, I could see the legs of the passengers on the top deck and very quickly landed on a pair of cowboy boots. He must have ascended by the rear stairs, because he was sitting right at the back, his legs wide apart, forcing his neighbor up close against the window. There were many more shoes, many more legs, but toward the front of the bus, almost parallel with my face, was a pair of bright-white trainers. Whoever was wearing them had one leg crossed over the other—exposing a slender, sockless ankle—and the suspended foot was tapping the air rhythmically. I craned my neck to look at the underside of Psycho's chin, her neat nostrils, and the long, curled lashes of her closed eyes. She was chewing in time with the foot tapping, and her head nodding was almost imperceptible. Whatever she was listening to was making her oblivious to her surroundings. She seemed completely unaware of me and also of the man at the back of the bus.

On the seat in front of her, a small boy was sitting sideways, his legs dangling into the aisle. He was sucking two fingers and staring at me steadily. I wanted him to face forward so he wouldn't draw attention to me and made an impatient gesture for him to do so. He didn't move.

"Turn around," I mouthed.

He continued to stare, his little legs dangling. I gestured again, more vigorously this time, but still he stared. I glanced at Psycho; thankfully, her eyes were still closed.

"Stop looking," I whispered. "Mind your own business."

Eventually, he pulled his fingers out of his mouth and asked in a loud, high-pitched voice, "*Maman, que fait cet homme?*"

His mother didn't look up from her phone. "*Quoi? Quel homme?*"

"*L'homme rigolo. Là-bas.*"

Funny man? I thought, glancing behind at the empty steps.

Is that small child referring to me?

Without taking her eyes off her phone, his mother scooped up his legs and spun him around to face the front, and I glanced again at Psycho to see that her eyes were open, and she was smiling at him. But when his head slowly turned to look back at me, she followed his gaze, and I retreated quickly downward until I was out of sight.

It was impossible to stay in my hiding place, wedged halfway up the stairs, because there was a constant exchange of people leaving and joining the bus and moving between the upper and lower decks, so I found a small space at the bottom, settled back, and waited. After almost forty minutes, I was taken by surprise as she descended the stairs right in front of me. The bus was full. It was impossible to move out of her way. All I could do was stand still and accept her foot crushing mine, her elbow in my stomach, and her hair in my face as she pushed her way off the bus. And all I could do was the same to the other passengers as I pushed my way after her.

She was ahead of me, moving fluidly along the crowded streets, sidestepping oncoming pedestrians with long, confident strides, and I scurried breathlessly behind, bumping into people, tripping on the curbs, willing her to slow down. She continued this unfeasibly rapid pace to the bottom of Wardour Street and along Old Compton Street, and just as I was about to give up the chase, she turned onto Frith Street and sat at a table outside an Italian café. I was out of breath. I was panting audibly. I'd set out that evening for a long solitary walk through an ancient woodland to restore equilibrium. What I was in fact doing was the exact opposite. I leaned against a wall at the bottom of the road, pulled a handkerchief from my pocket, removed my glasses, and wiped the sweat from my face.

When I put my glasses back on, she was chatting and laughing with a server as if they were good friends. Then, as the server went into the café, she crossed her long legs and lit a cigarette, her gaze fixed high up on the building opposite. I lifted my chin and followed her gaze. She was looking at a window two floors above a jazz club. The thin curtain was drawn, and there was no light behind it. I looked back at her and watched her tilt back her head, purse her lips, and blow a long stream of smoke into the sky.

On the next table, four grinning men were openly staring at her. She gave them a sidelong look, and in response, they raised their beers and laughed and jostled each other. They were leaning toward her, trying to engage her in conversation, but I was too far away to hear. I eyed the empty table on the far side of the men. I could sit at it. Attempt to listen in. But I would have to pass in front of her to reach it. I sidled forward, keeping close to the wall. When I was five meters away, the server returned and looked at the men.

"*Ridicolo ragazzini,*" she said, putting an espresso on the table.

Psycho made a grim expression, knocked back the espresso, and stood.

"Not silly little boys," she said, paying for the coffee. "Men, up to no good."

This was the first time I'd heard her voice. It was deeper than I'd expected and heavily accented, and it sent a thrill through me.

"Yeah. Real men who want to have a drink with a gorgeous woman," one of them said, making them all laugh.

She rolled her eyes, kissed the server's cheek farewell, and crossed the road toward the jazz club. The men were calling for her to stay, pleading with her to have a drink with them. I wanted to slap their faces, but that would have drawn attention. Instead, I watched her go through a small door to one side of the jazz club's main entrance, waited a moment, then followed.

The doorway opened straight onto a staircase. She'd just reached the top as I entered, and I was about to follow when a voice stopped me.

"Ticket, please."

I turned to see a small box office squeezed into an alcove, with a man perched on a stool behind it.

"I beg your pardon?"

"Ticket please," he repeated.

I glanced up the stairs, but she was gone.

"I don't have a ticket," I said, putting my foot on the first step.

"You can't see the show without a ticket."

"I'm not here to see the show. I'm here to see a friend."

"Who's your friend?"

"I beg your pardon?"

"Tell me your friend's name. I'll call them, and they'll come down to meet you."

He picked up his mobile and held a finger over the screen expectantly. I stared at him. He stared at me.

"How much are the tickets?"

"Fifty pounds."

"How much?"

At the top of the stairs, the vestibule opened into a small bar with a few tables and low seating. Colleagues at the university had spoken about these intimate spaces, but I'd never been to one. Beside the bar, a band was playing a slow-tempo type of jazz. The lights were low, the conversations muted. I skirted the edge of the room until I found an empty seat and peered through the gloom, trying to find her. She was standing at the bar, watching the band, who appeared to know her, because they were smiling and nodding at her, and she was smiling and nodding back. After a couple more numbers, she reached behind the bar, took a bottle of red wine, and put it in her bag. Shocked by the audacity of the theft, I looked around to see if anyone else had noticed, but the musicians were lost in their music and the bartender had his back turned. She glanced at the band one last time, then slipped through a door to the left of the bar. I stared at it. There was a sign on it clearly stating "Private." Which meant I was not permitted to pass through it. I stood and edged farther around the room until I was standing in front of it. Then, when I was satisfied no one was looking, I moved my hand behind me, opened the door, and stepped backward through it.

There was a narrow staircase on the other side that led up to the third floor of the building. At the top of this was another door, slightly ajar. I stood near it and heard movement inside, followed by a voice I recognized as hers.

"Bas... Bas... Sebastian."

I took a silent breath and turned my head to look through the gap. There was only darkness inside, but then I heard the sound of curtains opening, and the room illuminated with the orange-red glow of streetlights and neon signs from the road outside. I couldn't see her or the person Sebastian, but I had a fairly good view of the small room, which was crowded with once-grand— now shabby—furniture. A standard lamp draped with a slightly scorched silk scarf dimly illuminated one corner. Threadbare fake Persian rugs covered bare floorboards and, on the mantelpiece above a disused fireplace, a scruffy stuffed seagull in a glass case presided over the room with one beady eye.

An easel angled toward the window supported a cloth-covered canvas. She came into view and walked toward it as if intending to take a look, then stopped and turned around.

I craned my neck to see what she was facing. A body covered with a pale-pink velveteen throw lay prone on a chaise longue. She lifted one corner of the throw, covered her nose, and dropped it again. For several seconds, she stared at the body; then, she lifted the throw again, this time letting it ripple to the floor.

"Sebastian."

I adjusted my position for a better view. The body was wrapped tightly in a floral dressing gown, with orange-tinted sunglasses perched askew and a lipstick smudge that ran from the corner of his mouth over one stubbled cheek. I recognized him straightaway as the young man with the long blond hair. Jimsonweed. So, Jimsonweed was called Sebastian.

She kicked the sole of his dayglow trainers, and the force reverberated through his body. He opened an eye and winced.

"Close the curtains. Too bright."

He scrabbled on the floor for the throw, but she picked it up, folded it, and hung it over the back of a tatty mustard-colored armchair.

"I have alcohol," she said, swinging the wine bottle she'd stolen.

"And cigarettes?"

"And cigarettes." She dropped the packet on his chest and slipped off her jacket. "You look like shit and you stink."

"Thank you, darling." He swung his legs off the chaise longue and shrugged into a seated position.

"What're you doing here?"

"I was in the neighborhood, so I thought I would say hello."

At this, he gasped dramatically.

"Don't say that! Say you were worried about me after I texted you last night. Say you came over to see if I was okay. Don't say *I was in the neighborhood!*"

Exhausted by his outburst, he slumped forward and dropped his head into his hands, and she sat down in the armchair opposite him. I looked at her face. She was showing no emotion that I could detect, as if his outburst had had no effect on her whatsoever.

"So, why did you text me at three in the morning?"

At three in the morning, I'd been watching her through my telescope. I wondered which phone she'd been texting him on: the Nokia or the smartphone she'd hidden from Jonathan.

He didn't raise his head. "Because I was sad."

She watched him a moment, then asked, "You went out after you texted me, didn't you? Even though I told you to sleep."

He didn't answer.

"You reek of alcohol, cigarettes, and sweat. You went clubbing."

Shrugging, he said, "I was sad. You wouldn't come out to play, so I went to Bobo's."

"With the girls?"

"Uh-huh."

She rolled her eyes. "I do not know why you spend so much time with them. They just make you sadder."

He took a lighter from his dressing gown pocket, lit a cigarette, and gazed at the ribbon of smoke coiling upward with a serene expression. She lifted her eyes and grimaced, and I followed her gaze to the sticky, yellow layer of nicotine on the ceiling.

He drew on the cigarette deeply and, through a smoke-wreathed exhalation, said, "Not sad, darling. Melancholic. It's a very different state. It's creative, energizing."

"Energizing?"

"Yes. For artists, melancholia is energizing. We do our best work in this state."

She let out a loud huff, and in response, he stood unsteadily, swayed, crossed the room to a small vanity sink, and pissed into it.

"Do you have to?" she asked, covering her nose.

"Yes," he replied, rinsing the sink with a twist of the tap. "Let's have a drink."

He returned to the chaise longue, unscrewed the lid of the wine, and took a swig. "Ah... Breakfast of the gods. Cheers, Dionysus."

Below me, the band was playing an up-tempo number. I could feel the vibrations of it through the soles of my shoes. It brought my attention back to how my body felt and how tensely I was holding it.. Slowly, silently, I eased myself down until I was kneeling sideways and put my eye back to the gap. She was looking at the easel in front of the window.

"What are you working on?" she asked.

"Nothing of significance."

"Can I see?"

"No."

He took another long swig, and she watched him with her blank expression.

"Let's eat something."

Another swig. "I'm not hungry."

"I did not come here to watch you get drunk, Sebastian. Let us go out for food."

He wiped his mouth with the back of his hand and repeated, "I'm not hungry."

She stood. "Then I am going home."

Standing as well, he lifted a hand to stop her. "Okay. Fine. I'll get dressed."

He was naked underneath the dressing gown, bar a pair of very small briefs, the sunglasses, and the ugly dayglow trainers. I was shocked by how pale and gaunt his body was, enough to wonder if he was suffering from a disease. A pair of brown corduroy trousers was in a pile on the floor. He stepped into them, pulled them up, and tugged on a purple T-shirt.

"I'll eat, then we're going to the pub, okay?" he said. When she didn't respond, he said again, "Okay?"

"Okay. But you have to finish the food, not just play with it."

She picked up her jacket and turned to the door, making my heart leap.

I had to move. Fast. I stood and hurried as quietly as I could down the stairs and through the door into the bar. Breathing heavily, I made for the vacant chair I'd been sitting in before and shifted back into the shadows. One or two people looked in my direction but only briefly. Moments later, she and Sebastian came through the door and passed me on their way to the stairs down to the street, so close that I could have reached out and touched them. I kept my hands very firmly clasped together in my lap and held my breath. Then, when they had sunk out of sight, I stood up and followed.

When I reached the bottom of the stairs, I was surprised again by the voice.

"You're leaving already?"

I turned to the man at the tiny box office. "Yes."

"But the show hasn't started yet."

On the other side of the road, she and Sebastian were talking to the server from the Italian café. I took a step back.

"I told you, I wasn't here to see the show."

"But you paid fifty pounds."

They finished their conversation and were now walking toward Old Compton Street.

"I'm well aware of that," I said, giving him a sharp look. I pulled the ticket from my pocket and handed it to him. "Here. Take it."

"I can't give you a refund."

"Keep it for me. I'll come back another day."

"It doesn't work like that."

But I was already outside, following at a discreet distance.

◞

Old Compton Street was so busy, it was difficult to walk in a straight line. Outside the many pubs, the pavements were heaving with customers clutching their drinks to their chests. It had been a long time since I'd been surrounded by so many people. I was used to my own company, my own space. I was now being buffeted by total strangers shoving me off my path, stopping me in my tracks. My heart was thumping. It was difficult to breathe. If I hadn't committed to this rash mission, I would have fled. Several times, I lost sight of them but soon learned to look out for his swaying blond hair and his arm shooting into the air when he spotted someone he knew. It was as if Soho at night revived him. As if it was the time he came alive. The time when he walked with a square-shouldered, straight-backed strut, so different from the hunched, gaunt figure I'd seen slouched on the chaise longue ten minutes before.

Toward the end of Old Compton Street, they entered a restaurant and I slowed to a stop, wondering if my mission had now come to an end. My intention had been to protect her from Castor, but she was with Sebastian now, with whom she seemed to feel at ease, and they were in a public place. It was unlikely Castor would approach her in such a situation. Besides, in my haste to follow her off the bus, I'd forgotten to see if he'd alighted with us. I'd forgotten to watch out for him while I followed her to the Italian café. I'd forgotten about him entirely. I looked around now, wondering if he, too, had followed her to the restaurant and was standing on some dark corner, keeping vigil. Perhaps it wasn't only her that he was watching. I turned a full circle, squinting at every shadowed doorway. Perhaps he was watching me as well. A shudder ran through me, making me hurry along the pavement and push open the restaurant door that she and Sebastian had gone through only moments before.

It was crowded inside. I scanned the restaurant and found them squeezed behind a corner table, sitting side by side. He looked annoyed, as if the table was too tucked away for his liking. His legs were stretched out, his chair pushed back as far as it would go. He was talking in a voice loud enough for everyone to hear. He was a peacock, displaying his feathers, demanding everyone's attention. There was a slatted partition behind them. Behind that, another table. I signaled to a waiter that I would take it and walked right past them, as close as they had been to me in the bar, but I was invisible. Nobody worth their attention.

I sat facing them so that I could watch through the partition, and although they had their backs to me, I could clearly hear their conversation. When their food arrived, he speared a piece of pasta and studied it for a long while before putting it in his mouth. He speared another, held it aloft, and put it back on his plate.

"You need to eat, Sebastian. You are too thin."

He pushed the plate away, leaned back, laced his fingers behind his head, and stretched out his legs.

"Finish the food, then we will go to the pub."

"It's disgusting. It's making me nauseous."

"You are nauseous because you have not eaten," she said, pulling the plate back. "Come on. Have some more."

He pushed it away.

"Sebastian," she said, pulling it back again. "You are not five years old anymore. You need to start being an adult."

"I am an adult. I haven't needed my fake ID for years."

"I do not mean clubbing and drinking and doing drugs until you pass out. I mean looking after yourself. Sleeping, eating, hygiene." She put his fork in his hand. "Come on. Eat."

"Jesus Christ," he shouted, slamming down the fork. "I don't like this slop, and I don't like you."

I heard her sigh. I saw her head shake. I imagined she was rolling her eyes.

"You used to be so sweet," she said sadly.

"We all used to be sweet," he replied. "And innocent."

There was a long silence that I imagined would have been uncomfortable for most people, but for them it seemed natural, easy. Eventually, she tried again.

"If you do not eat, I will not buy you drinks."

"I can buy my own drinks."

"With what?"

He didn't respond.

"You should not bite the hand that feeds you, Sebastian." At this, he let out an unexpected bark of angry laughter, making me jump.

"What? You're learning idioms, now?"

She turned away, but he leaned toward her, pushing his face close to hers.

"So how are the *English lessons* going with your *tutor*?"

"Sebastian…"

"No. Tell me. I'm interested. You must be learning all sorts of new things."

"Don't…"

He shuddered dramatically and collapsed back in his chair. "Ugh… The thought of that bastard touching you makes me want to puke."

I was intrigued. Sebastian seemed as upset as I was about her sleeping with Jonathan. I wanted to hear more, but a large, unnecessarily loud group had just arrived and were taking an inordinately long time to settle at a nearby table. I swapped chairs to be closer to them, turned sideways, leaned against the partition, and closed my eyes to focus on what she might say next.

"Are you ready to order?"

I jumped and opened my eyes. A waiter was in front of me, pen poised over an order pad. I put a finger to my lips and shook my head.

"Do you need a few more minutes?"

Psycho and Sebastian had fallen silent, aware now that someone was sitting close behind them. I shook my head again, stood,
and quickly left the restaurant. Quickly enough, I hoped, for
them not to notice me.

7

SINCE LEAVING MY JOB AT THE UNIVERSITY, IT HAD BECOME my habit when out in public to keep my gaze averted, avoid eye contact, and converse minimally. Sometimes, I could complete my errands without uttering a single word. This day was different because, as I was returning home from the launderette, I noticed a plant in a café window that stopped me in my tracks. It was a *Dieffenbachia*, the dumb cane—so named because, if accidentally ingested, it causes stinging and burning in the mouth and throat, striking the unlucky victim dumb. I looked through the window to see who could be responsible for putting such a dangerous plant in a public place, and my whole body jerked at the sight of Psycho serving coffee to a customer. My first reaction was relief that she'd managed to evade Castor the night before; the second was pure agitation because here was an unexpected opportunity to talk to her. I could either take it or walk away.

I rarely used cafés because they required conversation with strangers. I also had simple tastes and menus confused me, especially drinks menus, but now I found myself staring at a blackboard covered in nonsensical names for different types of coffee. In my peripheral vision, I could see her clearing a table. I could either take this opportunity to talk to her or I could walk away— but before I could make a decision, she was right beside me.

"Can I help you?"

I glanced at her dark eyes, her soft hair. At her improbable lips. I looked away anxiously, looked back, looked away again, and finally settled my gaze on the blackboard. My heart was pounding. I didn't think I could endure being so close to her for the time it would take to drink a whole cup of tea.

"I'm not here to buy anything. I just wanted to make you aware of the poisonous plant in your window."

"What poisonous plant?"

The cut on her forehead that Castor had given her was red and the skin surrounding it swollen. It was all I could do not to reach out and touch it. At once, the image of her sucking the blood off her fingers rushed into my head. I cleared my throat.

"There, in the window." I glanced around the café. "In fact, there are several poisonous plants in here. It's very dangerous."

She frowned.

"You are an inspector? My boss is not here. You will have to come back another time."

I made a noise that I hoped sounded like reassurance.

"I'm not an inspector, I'm just a neighbor concerned for your safety. That cut looks sore. Does it hurt?"

I lifted a hand, but she moved her head back, stepped away, and folded her arms.

"You are a neighbor? I have not seen you before. I would remember."

A thrill ran through me. "You would?"

"Of course. You have a distinctive look."

I looked down at myself.

"The old man's suit, the short hair," she continued. "Very distinctive. This is what I love about London. We can be whoever we want, right? As long as we do not bother other people with our choices."

If I had imagined how our first conversation would go, it would not have been like this. I cleared my throat again.

"Would you like me to tell you which of these plants are dangerous?"

She took her time to answer. "They are just houseplants."

"They're sold as houseplants, but people have no idea what they're taking into their homes. This one here," I said, nudging the plant on the counter, "is *Spathiphyllum cochlearispathum*, the peace lily. It contains calcium oxalate crystals, which can cause skin irritation, burning in the mouth, and nausea." I pointed through the back door into the café's garden. "The one against the wall there is

Cascabela thevetia, yellow oleander. It contains cardiac glycosides. The toxins in a single seed can kill. In fact, in Sri Lanka, it's called the 'lovers' suicide bush.' I see there are several tables underneath it." I paused. "Shall I go on? I really am concerned for your and your customers' safety, but I'll leave if I'm bothering you."

She pursed her lips and glanced around the café. "Stay. I will make you coffee."

"I don't drink coffee."

"Why? Is it poisonous?"

"Of course. The beans contain caffeine, which is highly toxic to animals. For humans, it affects the central nervous system and can stimulate heart palpitations. But I don't drink it because I don't like the taste."

For a reason unclear to me, she laughed and unfolded her arms.

"I will make you a cup of tea, then. Chamomile is not poisonous?"

"Chamomile is not poisonous," I confirmed.

I left the counter to sit at a table, put my laundry bag on the floor, and rested my hands on the tabletop. If I'd imagined how our first conversation would go, it would have been like this. I looked over at her.

"The trailing plant on that shelf beside you is *Epipremnum aureum*, devil's ivy. It's classified as mildly toxic, but for a child, it's highly dangerous if accidentally ingested. It's good that you have it there and not near the tables."

"How do you know all this?"

"I'm a professor of botanical toxicology. The study of poisonous plants is my job… Used to be my job. I'm, ah, retired now."

"So it is your hobby?"

I considered this. "I suppose it is."

I watched her moving with ease as she prepared the tea, using both hands, performing the task intuitively. She was chewing her bottom lip.

"What's your accent?" I asked.

"Hmm? Brazilian."

"Your English is very good."

"Thank you. I had an English maid when I was a child."

"A *maid?*"

"Is that the wrong word? A helper, then—a cleaner, a nanny, a cook. She was all of these."

"Well, she did a good job."

"Yes, she was good at her job."

"I mean at teaching you English."

She shook her head. "I am not so good at English, but I am trying. At the moment, I am learning idioms. They are very confusing. Some of them make no sense. Every cloud has a silver lining. Barking up the wrong tree. On the house means 'for free,' no?"

"It does, but it's not strictly an idiom."

"Is it not? It sounds like one."

She carried over the tray, put it on the table, and sat down. "So, here is your chamomile tea, on the house."

There were two cups on the tray. This was far beyond my imagination. I picked up the teapot.

"Shall I be mother?"

"What?"

"It means, 'Shall I pour?'"

She raised her eyebrows. "There! You see how confusing English is?"

I lifted the corners of my mouth. I hadn't felt like this in years. Decades.

"What happened to your hand?" she asked.

"An accident," I said, quickly putting my hand under the table. "It's nothing."

"It looks like a snake bite, but I know there are no dangerous snakes in this country. In my country, yes, but not here. What happened?"

"Urushiol damage, from a *Toxicodendron* subspecies."

This made her laugh. "I do not understand that."

"Poisonous sap from a poisonous plant, transmitted via small hairs. My hand accidentally brushed the leaf of a very dangerous plant. My own fault; I was distracted. It was a silly accident."

"You have a very dangerous plant?"

"I have fifty-two."

Without a word, she rose to retrieve her bag from behind the counter. She took from it a tube of arnica cream and squeezed some out.

"Give me your hand," she said, holding out her own.

I considered telling her that arnica would have no effect whatsoever on the wound, but instead I pulled my hand from beneath the table and laid it in hers. Her touch was feather-soft, and her lips pouted as she concentrated on rubbing in the cream. I held my breath and tensed my muscles to stop the trembling.

"I am sorry. I am hurting you."

"Not at all," I exhaled through gritted teeth. I felt light-headed. Breathless. After I'd lost my love, I vowed this would never happen again, yet here I was, trembling like a teenager. "You are a scientist," she said, putting the cap back on the tube. "You do not think arnica will help, but there is a place for natural remedies, no?"

"Yes, indeed there is." I pulled the pouch from under my shirt and took out a phial. "I'm a botanist. Natural remedies are a very important aspect of my work."

She narrowed her eyes. "What is that?"

"An antidote. I carry several with me at all times, in case of emergency."

She sipped her tea and gazed out into the café's garden.

"I think your hobby is very interesting but also dangerous." She took another sip. "It must be nice to be surrounded with plants, though."

"I don't surround myself with them," I said, shaking my head vigorously. "They're kept well away from my living space."

"I am still jealous." She shrugged. "I am house-sitting for the rest of the year. There is a garden, but it belongs to the old lady who lives in the basement. I cannot use it. A garden is the thing I miss the most from my country. This is why I have filled the café with plants." She took another delicate sip of tea. "I have a neighbor with a roof garden. I can see it from my window. It has a vine covering the railings with a red flower shaped like a trumpet. We had the same vine on the fence around my house in Brazil. Even though it makes me sad, I look at that roof garden every day, and every day I wish it was mine."

I couldn't help but be affected by her soft voice, her sorrowful expression. Without a thought, I said, "It's mine." And then my body jolted at the mistake. I picked up my cup, gulped a mouthful of tea, and rushed on, "I mean, I have a roof garden. It could be mine."

She lifted her eyebrows. "Do you live on the crescent?"

"I, um, yes."

I hadn't intended to reveal where I lived and certainly had not intended to reveal my collection, but the young woman was casting a spell.

"So it must be yours because I can only see one roof garden on the crescent. We really are neighbors, then. We should introduce ourselves. My name is Simone."

She extended her hand, and I took it. "I'm Professor Rose." Again, without thought, I added, "Perhaps you might like to visit my garden one day?"

And she smiled and answered, "Thank you, Rose. I would like that very much."

a large silver buckle—and his patterned leather cowboy boots. When he'd tilted his face toward my garden, the light glinting off the lenses of his sunglasses, I didn't duck down. Instead, I'd adjusted the focus until I could see his thin lips ringed with white stubble and the ridged scar running from his temple to his chin. He'd lifted a wineglass, taken a deep draught—spilling some on his chin—and wiped his mouth on his sleeve.

A movement behind him had caught my eye, making me shift the focus over his shoulder. Simone was standing at her kitchen counter, chopping vegetables. While his back was turned, she'd glanced at him, put down the knife, then furtively taken the small black Nokia that was charging on a shelf above her and slipped it into her pocket. His glass now empty, he'd gone back into the kitchen for a refill, then picked up the knife and turned it back and forth in front of her, a sneer on his face. He'd then tossed it into the air and caught it by the handle several times before slipping it into his back pocket and walking into the through-room. After a while she'd followed him and, standing close, had placed a hand on his arm and looked up at him as if in entreaty. Straightaway, he'd gripped her wrist and thrown her hand away. He was shouting. I could see spittle flying from his mouth. He began to pace the floor back and forth, back and forth, as if trying to come to a decision.

But it was when he'd marched toward her, grabbed her arm, and dragged her across the room that I reacted. I'd picked up an empty terra-cotta pot and hurled it into her garden, and the sound of it shattering on the paving echoed between the buildings like a gunshot—making him jerk his head toward the sound, making him let her go and leave the room. She'd followed him, and they both disappeared from view for several minutes, so I focused the lens on the front window until I finally saw him on the street outside, walking away. Several more minutes had passed before she reappeared and went through the kitchen to the top of the steps leading into the garden. There, she'd taken the Nokia from her pocket, sat down, and rapidly hammered the buttons.

I tapped my pen on my teeth, mulling over the memory. Who was he to her? Why did she let him into her house? He must have some kind of hold over her. There must be a way I could find out what that was.

I lifted my eyes, looked through the bay window and caught sight of a man at the bottom of my road. There was something about his manner that seemed odd. He was standing like a sentry, totally immobile, and was dressed in dark clothes, the peak of a baseball cap protruding from beneath his tracksuit hood. I stood and moved closer to the glass for a better view and, as if he'd seen me, he turned his head, causing light to glint off his sunglasses. An unpleasant shiver ran through me. Was Castor watching me? Immediately, I shook my head.

Why on earth would he be watching me? He had no idea of my existence. Unless he *had* seen me following Simone that night in Soho. I looked again and saw no cowboy boots, no large silver buckle, just black trainers, a black tracksuit, and baseball cap. Could it be False Hellebore? Or Sebastian? But why would they be watching me? I sat back down, admonishing myself for my overactive imagination. He was probably just a random man standing at the bottom of my road, minding his own business. I picked up my pen again, but after two seconds, curiosity got the better of me, and I scooped up my keys and left the flat.

Whoever it was, he was nowhere to be seen by the time I reached the end of the road, and I instantly felt foolish as I realized I had no idea what I would have done if he had been there. Neither did I know what he would have done to me. I shook my head and was about to turn for home when a voice cut through my thoughts.

"Rose."

I recognized it straightaway—the rolled *r*, the emphasized *o*. Instantly, all thoughts of Castor, Sebastian, and False Hellebore flew from my mind.

I didn't mind that she called me Rose. On the contrary, I found it charming. There she was, on the other side of the road, her long hair loose, one arm lifted in greeting. There were holes in the knees of her trousers. I didn't understand why she allowed them to be so blatantly on display when I took such pains to conceal mine.

"Rose," she called again, darting through the traffic, moving with the fluidity of an eel. "How is your hand?"

I'd taken to wearing a glove because the sight of my hand seemed to be upsetting to people. I raised it now, turned it, and dropped it again.

"The same."

"Does it still hurt?"

"Not so much."

"That is good, no?"

"Yes, that's good."

She smiled as the silence stretched, and I wondered if it was in fact I who was expected to speak next. I was unpracticed at pleasantries. I had no idea where to begin. She continued to smile until, flustered, my gaze slid to her mouth. In response, she pulled in her bottom lip, moistened and released it.

"You're, um…very lithe," I stammered.

"*Lithe*? I do not know this word."

"Your body…"

I felt suddenly, unaccountably hot.

"Your body is supple. You moved lithely through the traffic just now," I said, running a finger along the inside of my collar.

"Oh, okay… Thank you."

My gaze flicked to her eyes and flicked away again. A second silence, but this time I flailed desperately for a subject to extend the conversation, because I didn't want her to leave. I saw the café across the road.

"You're not working today?"

"No. I only work at the café part-time. Today I have been to university." She lifted the strap of her backpack. "But it was my last day. It is now the holidays."

I exhaled in relief. Here, at last, was a subject I could talk about. "Which university?"

"Southside Arts."

"A fine institution. What are you studying?"

"History of Art."

Of course. That was Jonathan Wainwright's subject. And then I remembered that twenty years before, he'd gone to Southside Arts when he left UCL. She must be one of his students.

"Of course," I said, unintentionally voicing the thought aloud. I frowned at my mistake, but she saw a different meaning. "You think I look like a History of Art student, don't you?" she asked, smiling. "I *know* I look like a History of Art student. Everybody says so."

"Perhaps it's the holes in your trousers?"

This made her laugh—a bright, optimistic sound that was an unexpected joy. The laugh subsided into a head tilt, and she said, "You know, I have been thinking about you."

I'd been thinking about her as well, almost continuously, but I kept this to myself.

"You have?"

"Yes. Every morning when I look through my window, I see the roof garden opposite my flat, and I wonder if it is yours. Then I think if it is, you might be up there eating your breakfast."

"If it is mine, I'm certainly up there every morning, but not eating my breakfast."

She laughed again. "So, tomorrow morning, when I look through my window, I shall send a wave. Although, if it is yours, the railings are so high I doubt you will see it."

I made a guffawing sound, as close to laughter as I had ever achieved.

"Oh, I will see it; I can assure you of that."

Unexpectedly, she stepped forward and laid her hand on my arm, and I looked down at it, momentarily disconcerted by the bitten nails, the dry skin, the disappointing lack of perfection. "And then, one day soon," she continued, "I shall take you up on your invitation to visit your garden."

I looked up in surprise. "I beg your pardon?"

"I shall take you up on your invitation to visit your garden," she repeated.

"No, no. I would never issue such an invitation."

"But you did, the last time we met."

"You're mistaken," I said, shaking my head vigorously.

"You do not remember? In the café? You asked if I would like to visit your garden?"

Instantly, the good cheer I'd been feeling vanished as I remembered making that reckless and unguarded suggestion, but why I had made it was beyond me.

"I do recollect saying that now, but it's impossible."

She moved closer and squeezed my arm. "Please do not say that. I have been looking forward to accepting your invitation."

"Then I'm sorry to disappoint you."

"It is because you do not like me," she said, exhaling sadly. The statement could not have been further from the truth, and I wanted to tell her so.

Instead, I fixed my eyes on the cut on her forehead and said, "It's not a matter of liking or disliking you, it's a matter of risk. The plants are very dangerous, and I'm not prepared to put you in a position of harm."

Illogically, she seemed pleased by this. Her smile returned, as did the head tilt.

"I see. Well, I am prepared to accept the responsibility for this opportunity. I will sign a—what is it called?—*disclaimer*, if you like. And I promise not to touch anything." She pushed her hands into the tight pockets of her jeans. "I have seen your hand, remember? I do not want that to happen to me. I will stand very still in one place, and you can move around, showing me all the interesting things."

I sighed but she persisted, this time in a gentler voice.

"I find you fascinating, Rose. I am so curious to enter your world." She moved closer still and said, in a voice so soft it was almost a whisper, "If you will let me in?"

At once, I was thrown back twenty years to the time when my love had said those very words to me—*let me in*. And I had. I had opened the door and let them in, utterly and completely. If I could do it then, why not now?

9

Opening the door and allowing Simone to pass through felt illicit, exciting, dangerous. She was the first person to enter my flat in the twenty years I'd lived there. Not even a meter reader had stepped over the threshold, and any repairs that had needed doing, I'd done myself. Her eyes were everywhere as she walked down the hall, and when she reached the kitchen, she gasped.

"*Meu Deus!* This is a museum."

I wasn't sure if this was a compliment. I looked around, seeing nothing unusual.

"The lights, the furniture, the dishes," she continued. "Everything, it is from the 1940s and '50s, no?"

That sounded about right.

"It's all from my father's home."

"Are your clothes from your father's home as well?"

I fingered a lapel. "Yes."

"Does he not need them?"

"Not anymore."

She made an unreadable expression. "Do you buy nothing for yourself?"

I thought of the telescope on the roof, which, at that moment, was trained on her rear window.

"Of course. When the need arises."

She moved around the kitchen, trailing her fingers over the furniture, pausing to pick up the teapot, a candlestick, a ceramic vase. She turned on the Anglepoise lamp and turned it off again, picked a basil leaf growing in a pot on the windowsill, crushed it between her finger and thumb, and held it to her nose. I stood in the doorway and watched her. How strange it was, having another human in my flat. How intimate.

As I watched, I noticed she was putting objects back in slightly different positions, slightly different angles, and this caused a sensation of disquiet. I could have been pedantic and reminded her that she'd promised not to touch anything. Instead, I followed behind, putting everything back exactly as it had been.

"Does this bother you?" she asked, moving the pepper grinder a quarter turn to the left.

"Not at all," I said, turning it back.

"I think it does, a little." But she smiled and put her hands behind her back. "How will we go up to your garden?"

My eyes lifted to the hatch in the ceiling.

"Oh, I see. Up a ladder. Can we go now?"

"Not dressed like that. Too many holes. It's not safe. Wait here. I'll fetch you some overalls."

The sight of her in my overalls caused a curious feeling, as if I had some sort of ownership of her now that she was wearing my clothes. Or perhaps it was the other way around.

"Your hair."

"What about it?"

"It needs to be tied up."

She pulled a hair band off her wrist and gathered her hair into a high ponytail. I reached out a hand and said, "You've missed some. Here, let me do it for you."

But she swerved out of my reach, regathered her hair, and coiled it into a bun.

"Okay?"

"Yes. Let me go up first. There may be some preparation required."

I climbed the ladder, opened the hatch, swiftly crossed the roof, and tilted the telescope skyward. She was clumsy as she climbed through the hatch, and when she was standing on the deck, she folded her arms protectively across her chest.

"This is not really a garden, is it? I mean, it is not somewhere to relax."

"No. It's a laboratory."

"And some of these plants can kill?"

"Many of them can kill. Would you like me to tell you about them?"

"Of course. That is why I am here."

Pleased with this, I unfolded the canvas chair and patted the seat for her to sit. It had been a long time since I'd given my Classifications lecture. I took a moment to order my thoughts, then began.

"The plants are arranged according to their classification. There are five sections: muscular, neuromuscular, nerve, blood and skin irritants. If a plant from one group needs more sun or shade than another, I move them throughout the day but return them to their group every night. It seems counterintuitive, I know. You're probably thinking that the plants should be grouped according to their place of origin. Southeast Asian, South American, African in the hottest part of the garden. North American, Northern European in the coolest. But I prefer to group the plants according to their classification, for my own safety." I pointed to the far corner of the garden. "That's the muscular-poisons area. Those plants contain alkaloids that act directly on muscle tissue and induce vomiting, abdominal pain, and muscular weakness. You see that tall plant at the back with the green flowers?"

She turned her head in its direction.

"That's *Veratrum viride*, common name false hellebore," I

continued. "It's highly toxic and, if you accidentally eat it, you can expect cold sweats, vertigo, then a slowing of respiration, cardiac rhythm, and blood pressure until, finally, you die. Generally, people vomit it up before too much damage is done. The root is the most toxic part. In fact, some Native American tribes used the root to elect their leaders. The hopefuls would eat the root, and the last one to vomit it up became the chief."

I waited for the reaction and questions this usually prompted in the lecture hall, but she sat with her hands clasped between her knees, her expression inscrutable. Undeterred, I continued. "Over there on the other side is the neuromuscular group. You recognize the pink one, I'm sure."

"It is a foxglove, no?"

"Correct. Latin name, *Digitalis purpurea*. A harmless-looking plant loved by children's book illustrators, but its leaves, flowers, and seeds contain the cardiac glycoside *digitoxin*, a poison that interferes with the transmission of impulses from the nerves to the muscles, which can cause paralysis."

"It can leave a person paralyzed?"

"Yes, but if the dose is stronger, it causes cardiac arrest. Even with a weak dose, a person can suffer from milder symptoms like appetite loss, nausea and drowsiness, headaches, and abdominal pain. Not nice."

This did elicit a reaction: a deep frown, which creased her brow.

"Is it the only plant that causes paralysis?" she asked.

"No, there are many others. That one over there, with the red berries," I said, pointing out the plant, "is a *Karwinskia humboldtiana* from the buckthorn family, common name coyotillo."

"Coyotillo. It sounds Spanish."

"It is. It's native to the southwestern Americas, so Texas, New Mexico, Mexico, northern Columbia."

"Mexico," she repeated. "Is the poison in the berries?"

"The whole plant contains several *anthracenone* toxins, with the highest concentration in the seeds of the unripe berries. One to three weeks after consumption, the toxin causes flaccid paralysis of the limbs, but if the dose is high enough—death."

"How many for death?"

"Five or six."

"What do they taste like?"

I raised my eyebrows. "I have to admit, I've never tasted one."

"Of course not," she said, hitting her forehead with a palm. "I am sorry. Stupid question."

She pointed to a vine twining up a tripod of bamboo canes. "I think I've seen that one in my country. What is it?"

"It's an *Abrus precatorius,* common names jequirity bean, deadly crab's eye, rosary pea—depending on what part of the world you come from."

"I knew I recognized it. I used to make bracelets with the peas when I was young. What does it do?"

"'Do'?" I asked.

"I mean, what does the poison do?"

"It causes nausea, vomiting, convulsions, liver failure, and then, after a few days, death."

"If it's eaten?"

"No, you'll only get sick if you eat it. It's only fatal if it's injected directly into a vein. The bigger the vein, the better."

I waited for a response, but she sank down in the chair as if asking those few questions had taken all her energy. Something had changed. I couldn't put my finger on what it was. She'd stopped smiling—that much was obvious—but there was something else. This would be the time to ask if she wanted to continue. When I'd worked at the university, I'd undergone training to recognize signs of distress in my students. I'd completed the training but had never put the techniques into action. Mainly because I'd never been totally confident that I recognized the signs. A person smiles or does not. Talks in a reasonable tone or shouts. And, on a simpler level, is hungry or not. Is cold or hot. Is asleep or awake. But a person can also feel love, and this emotion I knew…or thought I did. I shook my head to banish the upsetting thought and pressed on.

"Those beside you are nerve-poison plants," I said, indicating the collection of pots next to her chair. "Plants that directly affect the nervous system. The one with the large white flowers is *Datura stramonium*, common name jimsonweed. All of its parts, but particularly the seeds, contain the tropane alkaloids hyoscine and atropine, which cause hallucinations and seizures. The hallucinations can be frightening, coming on slowly and lasting for several days, but if you take a higher dose, you're likely to develop convulsions, a fever high enough to kill brain cells, and a gradual failure of the autonomic nervous system. Then you'll slip into a coma and die."

She said nothing, which was disconcerting. I was used to hearing groans and gasps from the usual cohort of thrill-seeking students. But she seemed to have lost interest. She sat lower in the chair and was gazing off into the distance. She appeared not to be listening at all. I may have found body language baffling, but I recognized when a student was no longer paying attention. Perhaps the subject was too dry, or there was too much science. She wasn't a botany student, after all; she was just a layperson, literally off the street.

I took a deep breath and attempted to pull her back by picking up a pot and holding it aloft.

"This belongs to the blood-poison group. This one's my favorite because it's a plant that does good as well as ill. *Ricinus communis*, common name castor bean. You've heard of castor oil?"

She blinked and looked at the plant. "Yes, we use it in my country as a laxative."

"So do we, and it has other beneficial properties. In some parts of the world, it's used as a dewormer and can also alleviate the symptoms of arthritis. Cleopatra is even reputed to have used it to whiten her eyes. But"—I put the pot back down—"the seeds contain ricin, which is a highly toxic poison that affects the ability of blood to carry oxygen around the body and hampers the functioning of the circulatory system. If you're unfortunate enough to have ricin introduced into your body, you can initially expect a burning in the mouth, throat, and stomach, then diarrhea, vomiting, and abdominal cramps, followed over the next few days by convulsions, fever, difficulty breathing, vomiting blood, and then hemorrhaging in your organs... Certainly one of the more gruesome deaths. Have you heard of the Umbrella Murder?"

She was now sitting straight up, craning her neck and peering over the railings in the direction of the back of her flat. Quickly, I walked in front of her to block the view of both her flat and the telescope.

"Have you heard of the Umbrella Murder?" I asked again, bringing her attention back to me.

She looked at me. "I think it was the assassination on Waterloo Bridge?"

"That's right. Georgi Markov, a communist defector, jabbed in the back of the thigh by the tip of an umbrella. He developed a fever, had difficulty speaking, began to vomit blood, and eventually died in hospital. The pathologist not only found hemorrhages in almost all of his organs but also a small metal pellet in his thigh. The pellet contained ricin."

Again, I wondered if I should ask if she would like me to continue. I didn't think she was distressed or uncomfortable or any of the other negative emotions my training was meant to have taught me to recognize, but it was clear she was no longer engaged. It was perplexing. She'd been so persuasive on the street, so determined to see the garden. I couldn't help feeling disappointed by her lack of interest, and I have to admit, a little hurt.

"And finally," I announced in a loud voice, "the irritants—the nonfatals that, if you're unlucky enough to find yourself in the midst of, will leave you with a nasty rash. You probably recognize stinging nettle, poison ivy…"

She stood up. "Thank you, Rose. This has been fascinating, but I must go now."

I closed my mouth. I wasn't used to being interrupted mid-flow, but at least this was behavior I understood: forthright and to the point. I nodded.

"All right. I'll see you out."

At the front door, I took the overalls she held out for me and said, "I'll come to the café again soon to show you the rest of the dangerous plants."

She flashed a brief smile and, without saying goodbye, ran down the stairs. I went to the front-room window to watch her walk away. It had felt good to step back into my teaching role, even if only for a brief time, and I'd found a perverse pleasure in selecting the plants I'd chosen to nickname the men in her life. But she'd seemed so unimpressed—bored, even. Was it that young people could no longer be shocked? Had they seen everything on the internet already? Perhaps instead of choosing the nickname plants, I should have shown her the ones that caused the most gruesome deaths. Perhaps I should have focused on the *Karwinskia humboldtiana*, the only plant she'd shown any interest in. Maybe then she would have stayed a little longer.

She was approaching the end of the road, and I pushed my cheek against the windowpane, eking out a few more meters of sight before she would turn the corner and disappear. However, before she did, a man got out of a parked car and unexpectedly took hold of her arm. Immediately, she pulled free and stepped away, but he moved toward her again. I saw sunglasses, a black baseball cap, and knew it was the same man I'd seen earlier. I could see now he couldn't be Sebastian. He was shorter, more muscular. Was he False Hellebore? He pointed back up the road toward my flat, jabbing his arm aggressively, and her arms were gesticulating as they stepped toward and away from each other, as if dancing a furious rumba. Suddenly, he grabbed her waist, opened the passenger door, and bundled her into the car, and, while I watched in horror, he got in beside her and drove away.

10

It had been three days since I'd seen Simone pushed into the car and driven away, and although I'd spent many hours watching through the telescope, she hadn't yet returned home. In that first frantic flash of panic, I'd snatched up the phone and called the police, and they'd given me a crime number and told me to wait for a call once an officer had been assigned to the case. As each day went by and no call came, my initial panic morphed into impatient despair. I knew I should wait and trust that the police were doing their job, but when the hours she'd been missing reached seventy-two, I decided to take matters into my own hands.

The café's door was locked when I arrived but, through the window, I could see a man behind the counter. He looked at me when I knocked and mouthed, "We're closed." I knocked again.

"We're closed," he said as he opened the door.

"I see that. I'm looking for the young Brazilian woman who works here."

"She quit."

I paused. "When?"

"Yesterday. She put a note through the door saying she's moved away and the café's too far for her to travel."

I furrowed my brow at the obvious inaccuracy of this statement. "Are you sure?"

"That's what it said."

He spoke as if he were talking to a child. I pursed my lips. "Did it say where she's moved to?"

"No." He tilted his head and gave me a sideways look. "Are you a friend of hers?"

I didn't hesitate. "I am."

"Then why didn't she tell you she was moving?"

"Ours is a new friendship, but I'm very keen to speak with her."

"You and me both," he said gruffly. "When you find her, tell her I'm not happy. She can't just walk out with no warning like that. And tell her, if she thinks I'm paying her for the days she worked before she left, she can forget it."

There was little point committing this message to memory, so I pressed on. "Do you still have the note?"

After some thought, he went to the bin, pulled out a crumpled scrap of paper, and gave it to me. I scanned it. The handwriting was angular and forward slanting, and there were two spelling mistakes of simple words, which was odd for an under-graduate student.

"This may seem an unusual question, but do you have any other examples of her handwriting? An order pad, perhaps?"

He sensed a change in the conversation.

"We're paperless. Everything's touchscreen. Why? You don't think that's her writing?"

"I'm not sure. I need to see another example—but did you not think it strange she didn't ring to say she was leaving?"

"Yeah, I did. No one writes on paper these days. It's archaic."

Again, my brow furrowed. I wrote on paper every day. "May I keep this?" I asked.

"Sure. And listen…" He seemed embarrassed. "When you find her, could you let me know?"

❧

I turned onto Simone's road, scanned the houses, and rap-idly realized that finding hers would not be as simple as I first thought. Every facade looked the same: the same flagstone front steps and wrought-iron fencing around the basement-light wells. The same floor-to-ceiling sash windows. The only differ-ence was the colors of the front doors, which, of course, I hadn't been able to see through the telescope. From the position of her house, I knew it must be approximately halfway up the road. I closed my eyes and visualized what I'd seen through her front windows, and the branches of an ornamental cherry tree came into focus. I concentrated on this. Red, papery, peeling bark. Long, dark-green ovate leaves. Most definitely a *Prunus serrula*, possibly the Tibetan variety, but it was difficult to tell without blossom. I opened my eyes and looked to where I thought the tree should be, and there it was, outside number 29.

There was no response to the doorbell or to my knock, and when I peered through the front windows, all was still. I knocked again—louder this time—opened the letter box, and called her name, rapped on the glass of the front window and then banged on the door with the flat of my hand.

"Can I help you, sir?"

I pushed up my glasses, peered down into the light well at an old woman with dark eyes and white hair pulled into a tight bun leaning out of the basement window, and recognized the night-time snail thrower.

"I'm sorry. Can I help you, *madam*?" she corrected.

"I'm looking for the young Brazilian woman who lives here. Do you know her?"

"I do."

"Do you know when she'll be home?"

The old woman disappeared but quickly reappeared again through a door underneath the front steps.

"I ain't seen her since last week, and it ain't like her to go away without telling me." She paused to assess me with her dark eyes. "You a friend of hers?"

"I am."

"Are you Rose?"

There was little point in correcting her. "Did she mention me?"

"I heard her mention your name. My name's Susan, but everyone calls me Susie."

I doubted I'd call her anything at all.

"When did *you* last see her?" she asked.

I considered telling her about Simone's abduction but decided against it.

"The same as you. Last week."

"Ain't she picking up your calls neither?"

This is where the friend claim slipped slightly. "I don't have her number."

The old woman pulled a mobile from the bulging pockets of her housecoat and paused.

"You're definitely a friend of hers?"

"I am," I said again, with confidence. "We recently shared a pot of tea in a café, and just three days ago, she stopped by to visit me at home."

I looked at the phone in her hand, expectantly.

"You've got an honest face, I suppose," she said, holding the phone at arm's length and prodding the screen with an arthritic finger.

"Thank you, but could you write it down? I don't have a mobile telephone."

She raised an eyebrow and went inside, and I descended the light-well steps to her front door.

"Actually," I called into the gloom, "while I'm here, would it be possible to gain access to your garden?"

"Already tried her back door," she called back. "But you're welcome to have a go, if you want."

I stood at the top of the metal steps, peered through the back-door window, and rattled the handle. I could see a carton of milk on the counter, unwashed dishes, a light on above the oven, fruit flies hovering over a bowl of bananas. A small black Nokia charging on a shelf and two framed, very simple embroideries on the wall next to a blackboard covered with a handwritten shopping list.

"Where are you?" I whispered. I put my shoulder to the door and pushed, but it didn't move. "What's happened to you?"

I let go of the handle and sat down on the top step where she drank coffee every morning. It felt strange being in the place I'd spent so many weeks watching. I looked up at the railings of my roof garden and confirmed that it really was impossible to see through the vine. If I'd been absolutely certain of this, I would not have retreated so carelessly the first time I saw her, I would not have brushed against that leaf, and I would not have this ruined hand. I took off the glove. My hand was darker in color and, after a tentative sniff, had a distinct odor. I took a phial from the leather pouch and scooped out some cream.

"I've made tea," the old woman said, placing a tray on a garden table. "Join me?"

For a moment, I reflected on the fact that I'd spoken to more people in these past few weeks than I had in the entirety of the past year, and also that it was turning out not to be as arduous as I'd always feared. Very carefully, I pulled on the glove and walked down the steps.

The old woman gave me a piece of paper with Simone's number written on it in a wavering scrawl. I folded it and put it in my jacket pocket, along with the note from the café.

"You know, you gave me a shock when I first saw you on the stairs," she said, handing me a teacup. "I thought you was my Stanley come back."

"Stanley?"

"My husband. He died nine years ago. He had a suit just like that. Wore it every day."

I smoothed the fabric of my trousers. "I'm sorry for shocking you."

"That's all right, dear; it was a nice shock." She took a sip of tea. "My Stanley was so particular about his suit. He never once took his jacket off in public. Even on a hot day like today."

"Nor do I."

She looked at my chest.

"Like to keep them covered up, do you? Don't blame you. They're more trouble than they're worth." She took another sip. "If you don't want the kiddies, that is."

I was momentarily thrown by the observation and, frankly, shocked by such audacity from a complete stranger. My breasts had no bearing whatsoever on my decision to wear the suit.

"I'm aware some people find my choice of attire unorthodox, but I wear the suit because I find it comfortable," I said sternly. This wasn't true. It was very uncomfortable. It was too big in the shoulders, too tight across the hips, the arms were too long, and I was constantly having to tuck the cuffs under. No.

The only reason I wore the suit was because it had belonged to Father.

The old woman shrugged. "Wear whatever you like, dear. Ain't for me to judge. As my Stanley used to say, 'Different strokes for different folks.'"

Simone would like that one, I thought, then flinched, shocked by how easily I'd been distracted. I wasn't here for a cup of tea and a chat. I was here to find Simone. Suddenly, a thought struck me.

"Wait," I said, standing and running up the stairs. I held the note from the café against the backdoor window and looked from it to the shopping list on the blackboard, comparing the handwriting. It was totally different.

It was an hour before a police officer arrived at Susan's house and less than a minute for the misunderstanding to come to light. I wanted to take him straight up to Simone's back door, but he planted his feet in a wide-legged stance in Susan's kitchen, pulled out his notepad, and flicked it open.

"I see you've already been in contact with us, Ms. Rose. The duty officer's given me a crime number for you."

"Professor," I corrected.

"I'm sorry?"

"Professor Rose."

He looked at his notepad. "Ah."

"I rang three days ago, and I'm still waiting to hear back from the assigned officer."

"I'm sorry to hear that. We're very short-staffed, but I'm sure you haven't been forgotten."

"Has an officer been assigned?"

He flipped a few pages. "I don't have that information for you right now, but I'm sure you'll get a call soon."

I didn't often shout, but this man seemed so ignorant of the urgency of the situation that I couldn't help myself.

"The young woman's been missing for seventy-two hours. How long does a person have to be missing before you get around to returning a call?"

He looked up from his notebook with raised eyebrows. "I wasn't aware this was a missing person case. I have this as a report of a suspicious incident involving a car."

"Involving a *kidnapping*," I corrected. "On Tuesday the twenty-first, at 6:15 p.m., I phoned immediately to report that I'd witnessed the young woman being pushed into a car and driven away."

"She's been kidnapped?" the old woman cried.

I glanced at her quickly, then turned back to the officer.

"Good God, man. Are you telling me no one's looking for her?"

"I...um, need to call the station."

"Yes, you do. But first, follow me." I handed him the note from the café and marched into the garden. "That's a note she allegedly wrote to her boss, but look." I went up the steps and pointed to the blackboard. "That's her handwriting. As you can see, they're totally different."

The officer cupped his eyes and peered through the window. "How do you know that's her handwriting?"

"Because she lives alone."

"How do you know?"

"Because we're friends, but if you need confirmation,"—I pointed to Susan's door—"ask her."

He jotted something in his notebook.

"Someone," I said, "wrote that note to her boss to stop him

from looking for her, and I believe it was the man I saw pushing her into his car."

"Where did she work?"

"In a café on the high street."

He wrote this down. "What's the owner's name?"

"I don't know."

"How long did she work there?"

I made a noise of impatience. "These are questions for the owner, not me. Now, we need to break down this door."

He looked at me with alarm. "We're not going to do that, madam."

"Come on, you're right here."

He took two steps down, and I threw my arms in the air.

"This is disgraceful! A woman has been missing for seventy-two hours. She could be inside. She could be injured."

His radio crackled and he turned away to speak into it.

"I have to go back to the station. Something urgent's come up," he said, descending another step.

"Something more urgent than abduction?" I shouted.

"An officer will call you soon, and you can discuss gaining access to the property with them. Do we have your mobile number?"

I let out a cry of exasperation. I knew what he was. He was a *Dicentra spectabilis*, common name bleeding heart: timid, almost fragile appearance but with a toxicity that causes seizures. I sniffed in a deep breath and exhaled slowly.

"I don't own one. You have my landline number."

He was backing down the steps, already at the bottom, but before he left, he said, "Then I suggest you go home and wait for our call."

Moments later, Susan came outside and stood at the bottom of the steps. She sighed loudly, stooped to pick up a large stone, and held it out to me.

"Take it. I don't think she's inside. I would've heard something, but maybe you'll find some clues."

I looked at the stone in her outstretched hand. "I'm not a detective. I wouldn't know where to start."

"You couldn't do worse than them useless police."

I considered the consequences of breaking and entering. The last time I'd had dealings with the police was after the incident at the university that had caused my redundancy. I hadn't enjoyed the experience then and would rather it not be repeated. My mind went back to that interview room, that table. The two police officers sitting on one side, my solicitor and I on the other. It had taken a full year to recover from the shame. Perhaps the dread I was feeling now was an indication that I hadn't recovered after all. I pushed up my glasses.

"It would be breaking the law."

"I'll take the blame, say it was an accident. What're they going to do to an eighty-five-year-old, eh?" She lifted the stone higher. "Come on, dear. It's heavy."

The door was secured by two bolts, easily reached through the broken window, making it only a matter of seconds before I was standing in the kitchen. I took a moment to appreciate where I was as a tingle traveled across the back of my neck and down my spine to my heels. I put a hand on my fluttering stomach and looked around. One of the walls had a wide opening into the rear half of the through-room. I could see the sofa and the desk covered in books and papers. I was about to go in when I became aware of the old woman's wheezy breathing behind me and turned to see her at the top of the steps, clinging to the handrail. I didn't want her there. I wanted to be in Simone's flat—surrounded by Simone's possessions, breathing Simone's air—alone.

I pushed a stool out onto the small landing at the top of the steps. "Sit here and wait for me… And don't touch anything." I then walked through the opening and went to the middle of the room. After a moment's hesitation, I knelt down. This was where Castor had struck her. I flexed my feet and rocked my weight back and forth as I had seen her do and looked at the floor. There were three small dark circles on the boards, possibly blood. I touched one with a finger, expecting it to be wet, then stood and went to the window. This was where I'd first seen her face through the telescope's lens, seen the blood on her fingers, watched her put her fingers into her mouth.

I turned away. The desk was a jumbled mess of papers and

reference books. Not at all how a student should be conducting their studies. A book about Frida Kahlo was on top of a pile of art books. I tipped my head to read the spines: Georgia O'Keeffe, Françoise Gilot, Lee Miller, and, at the bottom, Dorothea Tanning. Photographs of women were pinned to a corkboard behind the desk. The artists, I assumed. I knew I was ignorant when it came to art. In fact, most subjects were a mystery to me if they bore no connection to botanical toxicology. There were several notes pinned to the corkboard that were further confirmation that the café note had not been written by her; Simone's handwriting was small and neat and devoid of spelling mistakes. I read one: *possible titles—Artists in the shadow—Only ever the muse—Female artists and their famous lovers.* The titles meant nothing to me. I stepped around the desk and leaned in to take a closer look at the photographs, studying each woman in turn: black-and-white portraits in the attire and hairstyle of their time. Serious women with serious expressions, gazing into the distance.

From this side position, I looked again at the pile of books and noticed something inserted into the bottom one. I squatted and looked closer. The corner of a folded piece of paper was protruding from the book's pages. Very carefully, I held it with a finger and thumb and pulled, and, like in a game of balancing bricks, the pile of books wobbled, then settled. I unfolded the paper. An address was written on it in a looping, barely legible scrawl, obviously not Simone's handwriting. I blinked and read it again, thinking I must have made a mistake.

"32 Grange Ro—"

"You all right, dear?"

I jumped at the old woman's voice, scrunched up the paper, and pushed it into my pocket.

"Found anything yet?"

Susan was standing in the kitchen.

"I told you to wait outside."

She laughed and her dark eyes sparkled.

"I gave up doing what I was told years ago. One of the best things about getting old is you can pretend you're deaf." She picked up the bowl of bananas.

"No, don't touch anything."

"They're rotten. I'm going to chuck them. We don't want the place overrun with fruit flies, do we?"

I sighed. The old woman was being as troublesome as the hairs of a *Rudbeckia hirta*, a perennial prairie plant with yellow petals: irritating but harmless.

"Black-eyed Susan," I mumbled.

"What's that, dear?"

"Nothing. Go back and sit on the stool. I'm going to look upstairs."

There were two rooms upstairs, one bedroom at the rear of the house overlooking the gardens, the other at the front. Both doors were open, and when I reached the landing, I glanced into each. The bedroom at the front was empty apart from a bed with a bare mattress. The one at the rear was Simone's. The bed was unmade, and clothes were scattered haphazardly over the floor, chair, and dressing table. I found the untidiness unsettling, but I took a deep breath and stepped into the room.

A mirror was propped against the wall at the back of the dressing table, with a lipstick kiss in one corner. This was perplexing. I could not fathom why she would kiss her own reflection. Several necklaces with various crucifix designs hung over the corners of the mirror, and among them was a rosary.

"Catholic," I murmured.

A bag bursting with makeup compacts and lipstick canisters lay on its side, its contents spilling onto the tabletop. Next to it, a hairbrush clogged with long black hair. Next to that, a pink padded bra. I eyed it with curiosity.

I turned around. A double bed was pushed against the wall next to the window, the duvet and pillows disheveled. Beside it, a cluttered bedside table. A silk camisole lay on the pillow. I resisted the urge to touch it and nudged the bathroom door open with my foot. There was nothing of significance that I could see, apart from the presence of two bottles of shower gel, two shampoos, and two conditioners, one perfumed and one unscented. I thought this odd for one person until I remembered Jonathan: the man washing off his mistress with unscented soap before going home to his wife. I shuddered with disgust and turned away.

As far as I could see, there was nothing here that could lead me to her, and I was about to return downstairs when the camisole caught my eye. Like a fish eyeing a lure, I was drawn toward it, and when I was there, I hooked it by a strap, lifted it to my nose, and inhaled. It was the headiest scent I'd ever encountered. Shades of exotic fruits: papaya and rambutan, incense, and something acidic I couldn't identify. Furtively, I looked around the room as if expecting to be caught, then crushed the camisole into a ball and pushed it into my pocket.

The old woman was sitting on the sofa when I came downstairs, the bowl of bananas beside her and one of Simone's art books open on her lap.

"Anything?" she asked.

"There's no sign of her. Nor is there any sign that she intended to go away."

"You said you saw her being pushed into a car?"

"I did, and I'm sorry if that was distressing for you to hear."

"Can't deny it. It really was. She's a lovely girl. I always tried to look out for her. I feel terrible right now." She shook her head. "Just terrible."

I recognized that feeling of impotence.

"Hopefully, the police will start doing their job now and she'll be home soon. And talking about getting home, I must go. I don't want to miss their call."

The old woman slid the book off her lap and hauled herself

upright. She picked up the bowl and went through to the kitchen but stopped at the top of the steps.

"Now, don't be a stranger. I need to know what's going on just as much as you do."

"Of course. I'll drop by when I have news."

"You do that. Come by anytime. Day or night," she said, hugging the bowl against her soft belly and beginning her shaky descent. "And remember, don't you worry about the broken window. I'm taking the blame."

I was about to follow when I saw the Nokia on the shelf. It probably contained vital information. I should leave it for the police. I stared at it for one second, two, then crossed the room, picked it up, and put it in my pocket.

*

I made my way home past front gardens tastefully planted with aesthetically pleasing flowers—many of them poisonous—turned onto my road, put my hand into my pocket for my keys and was shocked to feel the camisole. I had no idea now why I'd taken an item as intimate as an undergarment, but the silk felt soft against my fingers. Almost reassuring. I squeezed it and pulled out the keys.

The moment the door to my apartment block opened, I knew something was wrong. I paused at the bottom of the stairwell and lifted my face. Perhaps it was the unexpected breeze, but there was definitely something out of the ordinary. Slowly I climbed the first flight of stairs, stopped, and sniffed. I'd recognize the odor of compost anywhere, and this was definitely it. Suddenly gripped by dread, I rushed up the remaining three flights to my landing and found my front door wide open.

"Oh, please, no," I cried, my voice echoing around the stairwell. For a split second, I hesitated on the threshold, then rushed through the door, along the hall, and into the kitchen to see the ladder lying haphazardly on the floor below the open hatch.

"No, no."

Straightaway, I picked up the ladder, positioned its end in the hatch, and hurried up, and what I saw when my head emerged made my heart stop.

11

FROZEN PARTWAY THROUGH THE HATCH, I STARED AT THE devastation. Every container had been upended, their contents scattered, and destroyed plants and compost littered the rooftop as if flung about in a frenzy. It wasn't just the shock of seeing the destruction that made me clasp a hand to my chest; it was the repercussions of what could happen to the vandal. And if they had accidentally taken plant matter away with them, what could happen to whomever they came into contact with. This was more than a disaster. It was a potential catastrophe.

Across the wreckage to the greenhouse, I could see the *Psychotria elata* plant undisturbed inside, and through the greenhouse, the telescope untouched. It was strange that they hadn't taken the most valuable item in the garden but also confirmation that this wasn't a burglary. This was a determined act to destroy the garden. I never cried—not even over a broken heart—but right then, there were tears fogging my glasses.

"Who did this?"

Logic dictated that it could only have been one person, but it couldn't have been that person because she'd been kidnapped. In front of me was a *Karwinskia humboldtiana* berry and beside that, another. In fact, there was a trail of them from the position the plant had been to the hatch. I scanned the garden, looking for the destroyed plant, but it was nowhere to be seen. On the kitchen floor, at the bottom of the ladder, were a few more berries, and I realized that it had been a burglary after all, because whoever had done this had stolen the *Karwinskia*. In a state of high anxiety, I half climbed, half fell down the ladder, staggered along the hall, picked up the telephone, and called the police.

I didn't return to the roof but sat at my desk, calculating all the possible variations of damage the *Karwinskia* could do in the wrong hands. So absorbed was I that when the doorbell rang, it made me leap, and it took a moment to compose myself before I could go to the intercom.

"Professor Rose? It's DCI Roberts."

I gasped. Detective Chief Inspector Richard Roberts, to whom, the last time we'd met, I'd given the nomenclature Ragweed. Latin name: *Ambrosia artemisiifolia*. A tatty specimen that releases a highly allergenic pollen dust, causing watery eyes, scratchy throat, sinus pain and swollen, bluish skin beneath the eyes. Irritating in the extreme. It was shocking to hear his voice after all this time. I closed my eyes and let my head fall against the wall.

"Professor? Are you going to let me in?"

I hesitated, then, with a trembling hand, pressed the buzzer on the intercom system. Downstairs, the door clicked open, then slammed shut with a bang, like a gavel falling.

He took his time walking up the stairs, but I was grateful because it allowed my racing heart time to calm. On his way, he paused on each landing, and I could hear his heavy breathing even before he came into sight. When he reached the bottom of the final flight, he looked up.

"Hello, Professor. Long time no see."

At the sound of his voice, I was transported back to that interview room with DCI Roberts sitting opposite me, his detective sergeant next to him and the pages and pages of evidence on the table between us.

"You haven't changed," he said.

I couldn't say the same for him. He looked markedly older. His hair was grayer and thinner, his skin sallow, and he'd put on a lot of weight. In fact, I was willing to bet he was really quite ill. I put my hand in my pocket and squeezed Simone's camisole for reassurance.

"I wasn't expecting someone so senior," I said in a clipped tone.

This made his thick, unkempt eyebrows lift. "Oh? Who were you expecting?"

"The officer I met earlier today. I don't recall his name. I assumed he'd been assigned to the case."

"Well, it appears this has become a little more complicated, so I thought I'd pop along myself." He began the final flight, watching his boots as they advanced one step at a time. "The officer you met this morning was James Hannah, and he has indeed been assigned to the case as my detective sergeant." He reached the final step and smiled the thin-lipped smile I remembered so well. "I won't shake your hand. I know you don't like to. May I come in?"

"You're not wearing crime scene overalls."

He looked down at his dark-blue suit, the same one he'd worn on every occasion I'd seen him in the past. Tatty then. Even tattier now.

"I wasn't aware I had to."

I huffed out a breath. "I explicitly told Bleeding Heart—your detective sergeant on the phone—that overalls were required."

"I'm sorry, that instruction didn't reach me."

Tutting with annoyance, I said, "I suppose I shall have to lend you a pair."

"Thank you. You're very kind."

"It's not a kindness."

He smiled and peered around me into the flat. "Shall we go in?"

The thought of this man in my home was unconscionable. I knew I'd have to allow a policeman in at some point, but I would rather it be any other policeman than this one. I sniffed in a breath and stepped aside.

"This is a rum do, isn't it?" he said, walking past me. "I must say, I thought all this"—he made the quotation-mark gesture with his fingers—"*poisonous plants* business was over a long time ago."

I gritted my teeth but didn't reply.

In the hall, he stopped in front of the photograph of Father, and I looked from the cop to the photograph, wondering what had caught his attention. It wasn't a particularly well framed shot. I'd taken it with Father's Kodak camera when I was eleven. He was sitting at the long table, reading a well-thumbed copy of Dostoevsky's *The Idiot*. There was a chaos of papers and pencils, books, and newspapers on the table. Unwashed dishes, a globe, a muddy boot, an old-fashioned abacus, a human-anatomy model, a riding crop, a dissected mole, an egg timer, and a bowl of rotting plums. He was wearing a tweed suit and steel-rimmed glasses. His hair was neatly combed back and precisely parted. He may not have noticed the mess in the house, but he was always particular about his hair.

"So, this is the notorious Professor Herbert Rose," DCI Roberts said. "This photo looks like it could've been taken a hundred years ago."

Notorious? I thought.

"Is this where he homeschooled you?" He turned to face me. "Was that your classroom?"

Notorious?

DCI Roberts lifted his eyebrows but didn't press me for an answer.

"Where shall we go? In here?" he asked, walking into the front room and sitting on the sofa. I hovered in the doorway.

"Please sit down," he said.

He was patting the sofa beside him. I crossed the room and sat at my desk. He was silent. I could feel his eyes appraising me. Possibly even assessing my mental health. I kept my gaze on the carpet.

"So, to clarify," he began. "This is not just about the destruction of a poisonous plant collection but also the suspected abduction of a woman. Is that correct?"

I looked up. "Are you looking for her?"

He cleared his throat. "Before we go any further..."

"I'm very worried," I interrupted. "About Simone—the young woman. Very worried."

He lifted a hand to stop me. "Before we go any further, I need to see your Poisonous Substances License."

I flinched. This wasn't what I was expecting.

"I don't have one. The garden isn't open to the public, it's a closed collection."

He consulted his notebook. "And yet you informed us that the woman was involved in an incident with a car after visiting your garden."

Anxiety crept into my chest, making me grip the fabric of my trouser leg. I'd completely forgotten I'd mentioned Simone's visit. "She's been the only visitor, and it was controlled. She stayed in one place and didn't touch anything."

"But—there's always a 'but,' isn't there?" he said with that thin-lipped smile. "Even a single visit by a member of the public is a breach of the Poisonous Substances License, which means you've fallen foul of the law…again."

"The last time wasn't my fault," I said quickly. "Was it?"

"No."

He made a humming sound in the way he had in the interview room when he wasn't satisfied with an answer, and I turned away, in the way I had, to avoid his eyes, which crawled over me like spiders.

"We never did get to the bottom of that, did we? I mean, *really* get to the bottom of it."

I flicked a quick glance in his direction. "Why are you dragging this up again?"

"Because here we are, one year later, in the similar situation of a poisonous-plant exposure involving your collection, and not only are you in breach of the Poisonous Substances License, but you don't even have one."

Father once said that the more you ignore the past, the more you become trapped by it. I didn't want to "get to the bottom of it." I wanted to forget it had ever happened, yet here I was, teetering on the edge of the snare that had been set long ago. And there DCI Roberts was, waiting for me to step in it. I stood abruptly.

"The license breach is an aside, which I will accept the consequences for another time, but there are more pressing issues. A woman has been kidnapped. A note has been forged to stop anyone looking for her, and someone has forced her to reveal the whereabouts of my garden so they can steal a very dangerous plant."

He narrowed his eyes. "You know this as fact?"

"No. I know it as logical supposition. And the logical consequence of the theft is the high possibility that someone or some people are going to get hurt and quite possibly die."

He closed his notebook. "That's a dramatic statement, Professor, and I know you're not one for drama. Putting the suspected abduction to one side for the moment, what I don't understand—and please excuse my slow-wittedness—is why anyone would go to the trouble of vandalizing a garden if the intention is to steal one plant. Why not just steal it?"

I hadn't wanted to reveal this so early, but there was no avoiding it. I pushed up my glasses.

"Because I think more than one plant was stolen, and until I do a full inventory, I won't know how many. I also think it was the thief's intention to destroy the garden so completely that I may never know."

DCI Roberts pulled in his lips while he considered this and twiddled his pen, moving it from finger to finger like a magician's coin. I remembered the pen twiddling from the interview room. It had unnerved me then, and it was unnerving me now. He was watching me closely. I knew this even though I hadn't looked directly at him, since he'd stepped inside the flat.

"Perhaps you could get me those overalls now?"

I gave him the ones Simone had worn. They were too short in the leg and arms, and he couldn't fasten the buttons across his large belly. When we went into the kitchen, he eyed the ladder with apprehension.

"I'll go up first and call when it's safe for you to follow," I said, slipping on a pair of shoe protectors. "When you come up, stay on the ladder, and don't touch anything."

The sight of the garden almost brought fresh tears, but I held them back, stepped onto the roof, and cleared plant debris away from the area around the hatch. DCI Roberts climbed the ladder slowly, but eventually his head appeared.

"I see what you mean," he said, breathing hard and peering around the garden. "This is a mess, isn't it?"

"As I said," I said.

"Which plant do you know was stolen?"

"The *Karwinskia humboldtiana.*"

"*Karwinskia humboldtiana.* Interesting," he repeated, mispronouncing the words. Soon, his eyes came to rest on the greenhouse. "Why didn't they touch the plants in there?"

"They're only seedlings. Too young to have developed toxicity."

"So they knew what they were doing." He tilted his head. "What about that gaudy one with the massive red lips?"

I didn't like his choice of words.

"It's not poisonous," I said, opening the greenhouse door and picking it up. "Although it does contain a psychedelic chemical. I don't have it for that reason, though. I have it because it's a particular favorite of mine."

"It looks obscene to me." He tilted his head the other way. "I see you have a Celestron CGX-L Equatorial."

I followed his gaze to the telescope.

"Fourteen inches?"

"Yes."

"HD?"

"Yes."

"Always wanted one of those, but it's too big for my little balcony." He paused, then added, "Too expensive as well, for a policeman. You're a keen astronomer?"

The question was irrelevant. Why else would I have such a high-specification telescope?

"The meteor shower last week must have looked spectacular," he added.

He was wasting time when he should have been asking more pertinent questions. Questions about the garden. Seconds went by before I realized he was waiting for a reply.

"I didn't see it."

His thick eyebrows came together. "You have a Celestron, and you didn't watch the meteor shower? What a waste." He made the humming sound. It seemed an eternity before he said, "Well, then. Thank you, Professor. I've seen enough."

All he'd seen, all he'd been interested in, was the telescope.

Where were the pertinent questions? "Is that it?" I asked.

"For now. I have a couple more stops to make before I head back to the station."

"What stops?"

"The necessary ones."

Infuriated by this obfuscation—so typical of him—I glared at him, and in return, he smiled and said, "Goodbye, then. I'll be in touch, Eustacia."

I flinched at his use of my first name. He'd used this tactic to rile me many times in the interview room, but this wasn't the interview room. This was my domain.

"I'll wait to hear from you then…*Richard*."

He gave me the thin-lipped smile and descended the ladder, and I watched the bald circle on the top of his head as he struggled out of the tight overalls. When he left the kitchen, I stood still and listened. He was taking too long to leave. No doubt he was looking in the bathroom, the bedroom, perhaps the front room again. I remained still, breathing softly, until I heard the front door close; then I unfolded the canvas chair, sat, and held the *Psychotria* plant on my lap.

As I sat there, my mind went back to the incident at the university the year before that had gotten me in so much trouble. I still didn't understand how it could have happened. I'd run my lab with absolute precision, kept it meticulously clean. Could account for every scrap of vegetation, every phial of poison in the locked specimen cabinet. Every test tube, petri dish, pipette. So how the *Karwinskia*-toxin contamination had happened— and as I'd said over and over and over again in that interview room—I have absolutely no idea.

12

TEARS THREATENED, BUT NOT FOR THE DESTROYED PLANTS; I was mourning the twenty years it had taken to collect them. Two decades of research, investigation, and negotiation. The interminable wait while the package was transported from remote corners of far-flung countries. Handing the envelope of cash to the courier in the alcove below the pergola on the Heath. The breathless anticipation during the walk home. And then the thrill of opening the package, never knowing if the root or cutting had survived the journey: the careful snip of the string, the unraveling of the paper, the brushing aside of damp sawdust, the peeling open of the cotton wool. In all my forty-four years, I'd never found anything to match the ecstasy of finding a green shoot or a plump white root and knowing what dangers those insubstantial scraps of life were capable of.

Now it was destroyed, never to be replicated. Not as a

private collection, anyway. There was too much bureaucracy now. Tighter border controls, stringent license requirements. Officious busybodies like DCI Roberts sticking their noses in. The garden was all I had. Tending the plants, my sole purpose. I'd lost everything else: Father, my love, my job, my reputation, the use of my hand, and now Simone. All the precious things gone. I was sniveling. It was pitiful, but I didn't care. Let the mucus and tears fall unchecked, because there was no one left to see. A vine lay wrecked at my feet, its tendrils bent and broken.

It was *Abrus precatorius*, common names jequirity bean, deadly crab's eye, rosary pea. It had been a particularly difficult plant to keep alive, and I remembered the feeling of elation after it had finally produced pods, when I split one open to find the peas safely cocooned within. I looked down at it now, my tears falling in fat drops, and bent to pick up a crushed pod. I cradled it, then split it open and emptied the peas into my palm. Seven of them. Seven perfect little red peas, each with its own distinctive black dot. Gazing at them, I let out a sob, then wrapped them in my handkerchief and put them in my pocket.

The *Psychotria* was still on my lap. I hadn't realized I'd been rubbing the red bracts so vigorously that I'd released some red juice. I lifted my hand and watched the liquid run down my fingers. I knew what it contained. I knew its effects, but I needed some time. A brief moment to be in a place without grief, heartbreak, or loss. A place without any emotion at all. I looked at the red juice, then put my fingers to my mouth and licked them clean. The taste was bitter but not unpleasant and produced the same sensation as biting into a sloe berry, as if all the moisture had been drawn out of my mouth. I pulled in my cheeks, swallowed and licked my lips, then snapped off one of the plant's plump leaves, put the broken end into my mouth, and sucked on the juice oozing from the wound.

After this, I lost track of time. I don't know how long I sat sucking thoughtfully on the leaf but, gradually, I became aware of the distinctive football-rattle chatter of a magpie. It was standing on the railings, less than a meter away. It hopped to one side, stopped, and cocked its head, one eye fixed on me.

"Salute him."

I started. It was Father's voice, distant and wavering. I scanned the rooftop, and slowly he materialized in our garden in Oxford, sitting on the canvas chair I was sitting on now, wearing the suit I was wearing now.

"Salute him."

"What are you... How are you?" I asked. "Why are you here?" I reached out a hand and it passed through him.

"I was called."

"Called?"

"Come on, Eyebright, he's on his own. One for sorrow. Salute him. Chase the sorrow away."

In thrall, I lifted two fingers and touched my temple, and he smiled.

"Who called you?"

"Who do you think?" he asked, his outline shuddering and blurring.

My voice was small, almost childlike when I answered, "Me? Was it me?"

But his form was shivering, dissolving until I could scarcely make him out.

"Can't stay, Eyebright. Got to go… Got to go now."

"No. Don't leave me… Stay… Stay with me."

Blinking, I watched him dissipate and disappear, and my breath caught so painfully that I had to press my chest hard with both hands. How cruel. How heartless of him to leave me again.

The football-rattle sound filled my head, pulling my attention back to the magpie. Its eye was still fixed on me as it cocked its head. I stared at it, then, after a moment, cocked mine in the same direction. It cocked its head the other way. I did the same.

"What are you trying to tell me?"

Something important. Something vital. Perhaps it knew who'd stolen the *Karwinskia*. Maybe it knew where Simone was. I stood very slowly, put the plant on the chair, and took a step toward it. It hopped to the left. I took another step. It hopped again. If I stretched out a hand, I would touch it. I stepped forward, and it soared away over the rooftops.

I may have been standing a long time by the railings, staring at the heat haze shimmer over the rooftops, before I caught movement in the garden opposite. Looking down, I saw DCI Roberts and Susan talking at the bottom of the garden steps. She was pointing up at Simone's back door and shrugging, presumably explaining the broken window, and he was looking at the door, his hands in his pockets, his shoulders hunched. I imagined him making the humming sound as he climbed the steps, paused at the top, entered the kitchen, and disappeared from view. I imagined him not believing a word Susan had said.

I squinted but couldn't see him through the open door. For a second, I hesitated, then stepped carefully over the plant debris, tilted the telescope down, and lowered my head to the eyepiece. The blurred bulk of DCI Roberts was in the front room, standing at the desk. I adjusted the focus and watched as he put on a pair of latex gloves. He picked up one of the art books, flicked through it, put it down, and stepped close to the corkboard to peer at the photographs. He walked to the front window and looked out onto the street, then turned and walked to the rear window. In the middle of the back half of the room, he stopped, squatted, pulled out his phone, and took a photograph of the floorboards, then he stood and went through the door into the hall.

I moved the telescope to focus on the bedroom window. It took longer than expected for him to climb the stairs. On entering the room, the first thing he did was cross it to sit on her bed. Seeing him on her bed—his dirty, tatty clothes touching the place where she laid her body—was repugnant.

"Get off," I growled, but he stayed where he was, his head turning back and forth, taking in the room. After several minutes, he pulled out his phone, repeatedly touched the screen, and put it to his ear.

"Get off," I said, louder this time, and he stood and went into the bathroom.

I moved away from the eyepiece for a broader view. Susan was climbing the steps to Simone's kitchen. She opened the fridge, took out several items, turned her head toward the through-room, and hurried back to the steps. I put my eye to the telescope in time to see DCI Roberts walking out of the bedroom. Susan was taking an eternity to walk down the steps with her loot.

"Hurry up," I whispered as she made it into her flat and DCI Roberts simultaneously appeared at the back door.

He didn't descend the steps straightaway but stood on the landing with his hands in his pockets, looking at the gardens on either side. From this distance, I could see his full outline. He was a portly figure, like a Hitchcock silhouette: no discernible neck, round shoulders, large belly. I adjusted the telescope to focus on his face and was momentarily distracted by the clarity. I could see every blemish, every wrinkle, the cut on his neck where he'd nicked himself shaving, the hairs growing out of his nose. And then his eyes lifted to my garden, and even though I knew he couldn't see me, it seemed that he was looking directly at me. For the first time, I looked into his blue eyes—at the web of veins in the whites, at the gray Arcus Senilis rings around the cornea—and frowned. He was making the expression he'd made many times in the interview room. The one I couldn't read. I moved away from the eyepiece, stood upright, and watched him pull his phone from his pocket, lift his arm in the direction of my roof garden, and take a photograph.

I'd read accounts of people being visited by deceased relatives when under the influence of DMT. They wrote of mind melds with ancestors so ancient that they weren't even communicating in the same language. There was no comparison between these experiences and the brief time I'd seen Father on the roof. Nor with the psychedelic iridescent visual displays they described when they closed their eyes, and Father slowly dissolving into mist. For me, the effect of the drug came slowly, starting pleasantly, with a full-bodied feeling of well-being so that it no longer mattered that my garden had been destroyed, or that Simone had been kidnapped, or that DCI Roberts was back in my life. I'd painstakingly arranged Simone's camisole on my desk, along with the scribbled address, the Nokia, the note from the café, and the phone number that had taken me straight to voicemail a hundred times, making sure each item was perfectly aligned.

I was now stroking the camisole from the neckline to the hem, over and over, muttering to myself as I did so. Intellectually, I knew the chemical was having a perception-altering effect on the neural circuits of my prefrontal cortex, yet I also knew it was imperative that I meticulously stroke the silk with the flat of my hand, until every last crease was gone.

Suddenly, the Nokia beeped an abrupt text alert, and my attention was diverted from the camisole as easily as a child is distracted by a new toy. I tried to read the blurred screen where it lay on the desk, then picked it up and held it at arm's length.

Where are you? I'm worried

I screwed up my face.

"I'm here, where I always am," I said, bringing the phone close to my eyes. It beeped again, and I dropped it on the floor. I put my hands on my thighs, leaned down, and stared at it, waiting for it to do something else, then tilted my head to read the screen.

Text me

"Okay," I said, with absolute conviction that it was crucial I follow this command, even though I had no idea how. I picked up the phone, pressed the largest button, and guffawed when the screen lit up. There were many small icons on the screen, the most obvious being an envelope with the word *messages* underneath. I pressed the large button again, and a red square appeared around the envelope. I pressed again, and a list of messages appeared, the top one being the most recent.

Text me

"Just a minute," I said, studying the buttons.

On closer inspection, I could see tiny letters next to the numbers: *ABC* to the right of the 2, *DEF* on the left of the 3, and so on to the end of the alphabet. I may have been a technological Luddite and under the influence of a psychedelic hallucinogen, but I wasn't stupid. Very rapidly, I fathomed how to double- and triple-click the numbers until I had written, *Qwertyuiopasdfghjklzxcvbnm.*

"Ingenious," I said, gazing at the screen.

I held the delete button and watched the letters disappear one by one, then began again.

Simone is unable to reply may I take a message

Several seconds went by while I waited for something to happen, and when nothing did, I pressed the large button again. The phone vibrated, and my text moved to the top of the messages list.

I stared at the screen, waiting for a reply, until I forgot what I was doing and picked up the note with the address: 32 Grange Road, N16. What was she doing with this? Surely she wasn't planning on going there? The mobile beeped and I snatched it up.

Who is this?

Without hesitation, I replied, *The professor.*

I waited. And waited. And was then suddenly consumed by a ravenous hunger. I left the phone on the desk, went through to the kitchen, and straightaway saw that the hatch was still open. If some plant matter was to blow through it, the kitchen would be contaminated. I'd already carefully collected the scattered *Karwinskia* berries and had secured them in a phial, but a rogue leaf fragment could cause untold damage. I took hold of the ladder, but my foot missed the bottom rung, causing me to fall with such a heavy thump that the windowpanes shook.

"Damn it!" I cried, rubbing my face where it had caught the edge of a chair.

I stood up and adjusted the ladder position a little too vigorously, and the end slipped and crashed onto the oven. It took two more attempts to close the hatch, and when I'd finally succeeded, the effort left me exhausted. I glanced despondently around the kitchen, unable to muster the energy to prepare a meal, then made a decision that was completely out of character. I picked up my wallet and left the flat with the intention of dining alone in one of the restaurants on the high street.

It was a good thing no one was around to witness what felt like a gentle float down the stairs, my feet hardly touching the ground, but what in reality was a slip and slide down four flights, accompanied by several crashes into walls. Or my confusion when I finally emerged from my building to see that it was dark outside. I was sure it had only been minutes since I'd seen DCI Roberts standing at the top of Simone's steps, and I was also sure that had been in the morning.

"Curiouser and curiouser," I said. Then, humming a tune, I set off for the high street.

13

THE INSISTENT SOUND OF A DOORBELL WAS DISORIENTATING. Habitually, I woke at dawn, but the digital clock on my bedside table was reading ten o'clock. Never in my life had I slept until ten o'clock. The doorbell rang again, loud and long, and it was a few minutes before I realized it was mine. I sat up abruptly—causing a surge of dizziness—rubbed my face, and immediately winced at a bolt of unexpected pain. Tentatively, I touched my left eye and was surprised to feel swelling. I stood and went unsteadily to the bathroom. In the mirror, my eye was swollen almost to a slit, the skin around it purple-brown. I gently prodded the swollen skin and tried to recollect how this had happened. The doorbell rang again.

"All right. I'm coming," I muttered, going to the intercom. "Yes?"

"Professor?"

My stomach leaped at the sound of DCI Roberts's voice. "Have you found Simone?"

"Not yet."

Then plummeted. "Why not?"

There was a silence before he answered, "Because these things take time. I need to speak to you. Can I come in?"

"No. It's not convenient."

I heard a sigh.

"This is police business. I need to come in."

"Not at the moment."

"Professor Ro—"

I hung up, returned to the mirror, and stared at myself in consternation. My memory of the night before was patchy. I had stronger recollections of feelings than actions: well-being, confidence, purpose, but I couldn't remember how I'd gotten the black eye. I closed my eyes and concentrated on the sequence of events. I remembered sitting on the roof and watching DCI Roberts until he left Simone's flat. From then, the specifics were hazy.

There was a knock on my front door. I tutted. One of my neighbors must have let him into the building.

"Professor Rose? Open the door."

I turned on the taps for my habitually shallow bath and went into the kitchen to prepare porridge. There was another knock, louder this time.

"I said, not at the moment," I shouted. "I'm busy. Come back in an hour."

"This isn't a social call."

I measured a cup of oats, two of water and tipped them into a pan. He knocked again.

"Open the door, or one of my officers will open it for you."

I went to the bathroom and turned off the taps.

"I've given you fair warning."

Then I opened the front door to find DCI Roberts standing alone on the landing.

His eyes opened wide as he took in the men's pajamas, my unkempt hair, and when they came to rest on my face, his thick brows knitted.

"What happened to your eye?"

"I'm trying to recall."

"And your hand?"

I put it behind my back. "An old accident."

"Old? I didn't notice it yesterday."

"I was wearing gloves. Will this take long?"

"I need you to come to the station."

"Is this concerning my garden or Simone?"

"Please get dressed."

The thought of going back to that station filled me with dread. I cast around for a reason not to.

"I'll be happy to comply with your request, Chief Inspector, but I have to bathe and eat breakfast first. My routine has already been disrupted this morning, and if this is not rectified…" I paused to choose the correct words to describe the disruption this would cause. "I won't be able to concentrate on anything for the whole day."

He passed a hand over his face. "We'll pick some breakfast up for you on the way."

"I never eat food that I haven't prepared myself."

There was a standoff of sorts while he stared at me and I stared at the wall behind his head, until eventually he said, "All right, but would you do me a favor first? Would you look out of your front window?"

I glanced into the front room and walked to the window. Down below, on the pavement outside my building, DS Hannah was talking into his radio. Behind him, a scene-of-crime van was parked in the bay closest to my block. Its back doors were open, and two people in hazmat suits and face masks were standing next to it.

"What's happened?" I asked.

"This morning a man was admitted to the Royal London Hospital with symptoms of poisoning. The medical staff contacted us straightaway and put him into quarantine."

"What's the poison?"

"We're waiting to hear back from the lab, but Forensics needs to take samples from your roof in case there's a match with the plant you reported as stolen yesterday. So if you could 'rectify your routine' as quickly as possible, it would be much appreciated."

I turned around sharply. "Why didn't you tell me about the poisoning immediately?"

He lifted his hands, palms upward, then let them drop to his sides.

"Because, to be frank, Professor, experience has taught me that you must be treated with a certain degree of...sensitivity."

"What on earth are you talking about?"

"Well, you can be—how can I put this—unstable when upset."

"For God's sake, man. I'm not an invalid!" I shouted. "This is obviously a matter of urgency. You should've told me straight-away. Wait downstairs while I get dressed."

I hurried to my bedroom, pulled off the pajamas, and threw them onto the bed. If the poison was from one of my plants, it would be my worst fear come true. I'd warned him this might happen, but all he'd been interested in was the telescope. I put on yesterday's shirt and the suit, and ran to the bathroom to fix my hair. Outside in the stairwell, I could hear the forensics team talking as they walked up to the flat, so I gave my hair a cursory pat and headed for the door, but as I was about to go through it, I caught sight of Simone's items spread out on the desk. The forensics team was approaching the final flight. I looked down at them, then ran to the desk, quickly snatched the Nokia, and put it in my pocket.

DCI Roberts turned off the high street and parked outside the imposing yellow-brick police station. I opened the passenger door and looked up at the building, seeing the multitude of tall, thin windows, each divided with eighteen panes of glass, as barred cell doors. Since my last encounter here, I'd avoided this neighborhood so as not to be reminded of that traumatic episode. I shuddered at the awful memories and nervously pushed up my glasses. My hair wasn't sitting correctly because of my haste in leaving the flat, my armpits were itching, my shirt was uncomfortable, I was hungry, and all these things were threatening to push my anxiety past manageable. I sniffed in a deep breath, got out of the car, and waited for DCI Roberts to lead the way.

"I will not go into that interview room. I want to make that clear. I'm here to assist with your enquiries, not to be interrogated."

He stopped halfway up the steps to the arched entrance and looked down at me.

"We can use my office."

Even from the doorway, the odor of wet dog was

overwhelming. I looked around his office expecting a hound to be lounging on its bed, but there wasn't even a bed.

"Take a seat," he said.

My nostrils flared at the sight of the stained, worn office chair, but reluctantly I crossed over to it and perched on the edge.

"So," he began, drawing out the word, "we find ourselves one day after your poisonous-plant collection was vandalized with a man in hospital having been poisoned."

I pursed my lips.

"It could be coincidence of course," he continued. "He might have accidentally eaten rat poison or something."

"What are his symptoms?"

"He can't move."

"Axonal degeneration in the motor nerves? Flaccid quadriparesis?" I asked.

He put on his reading glasses, opened a file on his desk, read the first page, and looked at me. "I'm not sure whether to be impressed or suspicious that you know the victim's symptoms so exactly."

"I'm a professor of toxicology. It's my job to know these things. Is he on a ventilator?"

"He is."

"So you've not been able to interview him." I paused to think. "Several poisons could have caused his symptoms."

"But given that the *Karwinskia humboldtiana* plant was stolen from your garden yesterday—"

"You could be looking at attempted murder," I finished for him. He closed the file and put it to one side. "Indeed."

"How long has he been presenting with these symptoms?"

"His wife told us he'd been off work for the past week, although she didn't believe he was ill. But then, wives rarely believe their husbands are ill." He offered me a thin-lipped smile, but I ignored this irrelevant aside.

"You want me to analyze the samples from my garden and compare them with the victim's blood results," I said. "Is the lab here or in another facility?"

"We have technicians for that," he said, lifting a hand. "But I can expedite proceedings."

I pulled the leather pouch from inside my shirt and selected a phial. "We don't have to wait for your team to collect samples. I have some *Karwinskia* berries here."

His eyes flew open. "You carry them around with you?"

"Not as a matter of course. These were scattered over my roof and kitchen floor after the break-in. I had to collect and contain them."

"And keep them around your neck?"

I looked down at the phial. "I can see that may seem strange."

"Not strange, Professor."

He hummed out a breath, took an evidence bag from his desk drawer, shook it open, and held it out to me.

"Why am I here?" I asked, dropping the phial into it.

"I think you already know the answer to that."

I gave him a quick searching glance, then it struck me. He didn't want me to assist at all. He'd brought me here to remove me from my flat so his forensics team could look for evidence. I touched the outside of my pocket and felt the Nokia.

"Good God. The nightmare has begun again," I moaned, standing up. "You think I'm implicated."

"Calm down. I just need to know where you were between the hours of nine and eleven last night."

"This isn't happening."

"Believe me, I wish it weren't happening as well. Sit down."

I went to the door and opened it. "If you want to speak to me, you'll have to come to my flat. I'll not come here again unless you place me under arrest."

He stood, put his hands on the desktop, and leaned his weight on his arms.

"Professor Rose, you know full well I can hold you in custody for twenty-four hours without charge—longer if necessary—but I'm not going to do that. All I want is an answer to my question so I can eliminate you from my inquiries."

"Eliminate me?"

"Yes. Now please, sit down. I'll repeat the question: Where were you between the hours of nine and eleven last night?"

I remained where I was and patted my hair. "I was asleep in bed, obviously."

"Why 'obviously'?"

"Because I'm an early-to-bed, early-to-rise person. I have been since I was a child."

"You told me your routine was disrupted this morning. Would you mind telling me how?"

"I woke uncharacteristically late."

"Why?"

"I don't know."

"How did you get the black eye?"

"I don't recall."

"You didn't have it when I left you yesterday, so it must have happened in the late afternoon, evening, or during the night."

"I told you, I don't recall how it happened. I wasn't feeling myself. I'd had a very upsetting day."

I knew it would be unwise to tell him that I'd been under the influence of dimethyltryptamine, and therefore my recollections could not be relied upon.

"Perhaps you went for a walk?" he suggested.

"These don't sound like questions to establish my alibi. They sound like insinuation. Do you really think I'd go for a walk in the dead of night to poison a complete stranger?"

He sat down, folded his arms, and rested them on top of his large belly.

"That's just it, Professor. He's not a stranger. You know him. And so does your old friend Mary Spicer."

14

DCI ROBERTS DETAINED ME AT THE STATION UNTIL HE GOT the call to say the forensics team had finished at my flat. I refused his offer of a lift home, preferring to walk off the unpleasant experience rather than prolong it while trapped in a car with him. If I'd known it was his intention to get me out of the way so his forensics team could comb the flat for evidence, I would have stood my ground and demanded a search warrant. But then, I should have remembered his preference for underhanded tactics.

I consider my intellect to be above average, yet I'd long accepted that I'd met my match with DCI Roberts, because he followed an unscientific process of thought, based on what he called *hunches* and *gut feelings*. Concepts I couldn't begin to fathom. Many times in the interview room, I'd not been able to read the direction he was taking me or spot the psychological tricks he was playing or the subtle traps he was laying, and many times I'd found myself floundering in a confusing scenario he'd invented that seemed always to point the finger at me. He was doing it again. Why did he refuse to tell me who'd been poisoned? Why disclose that I knew him, then not reveal his identity? And why mention Mary Spicer? What did she have to do with this?

It'd been a shock to hear her name spoken aloud after all these years. Especially by a police officer. I thought of the photograph album I kept in my desk drawer at home. It was well thumbed and tattered from the countless times I'd looked at it. Even without it open before me, I could visualize every page. The photographs were of dunes, beaches, seascapes. A wooden cabin surrounded by clumps of marram grass. Two bicycles lying in the sand, a picnic hamper. Close-ups of sea thistle, sea kale, sea breeze, yellow-horned poppies, valerian, and then, the first photograph of Mary Spicer: a visiting PhD research student from the University of Edinburgh. There were photographs of Mary sitting on the sand, smiling at the camera. Another of her standing beside her bicycle, eating an ice cream cone outside a quaint village shop. Mary gazing at a stained-glass window inside a country church. And on the last page, the photograph taken by a passerby, of us standing together on the beach, her in the pale-yellow dress, me in the sky-blue one. The wind in our hair, the sun on our skin, beautiful in our youth. Father had never been one for taking holidays. He thought them a frivolous waste of time and, as a consequence, so did I. However, that short weekend by the sea with Mary had turned out to be the best holiday of my life. It was also the only holiday in my life. I reached Gordon House Road, but instead of turning for home, I continued up the hill and joined the Heath at the tennis courts. Very quickly I remembered why I never came to this side of the Heath. It was overpopulated and noisy, nothing like the silent, solitary routes I'd forged over the years. All around, children shouted, dogs barked, and groups of young people played confusingly discordant music. There appeared to be some kind of ramshackle athletics competition taking place on the running track, and when a starter gun fired, I leaped in fright. And when the crowd began to scream encouragement at the runners, I covered my ears and quickly changed direction. There were quieter parts of the Heath. It would just take a while to reach them. I quickened my pace, squeezed through a long line of people snaking away from an ice-cream van, dodged the picnics and football games crowding the flat ground below Kite Hill, and joined the path that led to the top.

Up ahead, a small girl was running down the path toward me, one windmilling arm propelling her faster. She was out of control. It was inevitable she would fall. Everybody could have seen that, but her parents were strolling behind, oblivious. As predicted, she tripped, landed with a thump, and slid a meter along the tarmacked path before coming to a stop directly in front of me. After a stunned silence, she let out a high-pitched scream and her parents lurched into action. The father scooped her up, held her close, and repeatedly told her that she was a brave girl while the mother blew ineffectually on the girl's skinned knees. I watched this strange behavior, thinking this was certainly not how my father would have responded had I injured myself as a child. Then, wincing at the phenomenal sound the child was producing from such a small body, I stepped past them and continued on my way.

As I walked, two thoughts occurred to me. One: Why had he picked her up and held her close when the most expedient way to bring a cessation to the tortuous noise she was making would be to attend to her wounds? Two: Why had he repeatedly told her she was a brave girl when she quite patently was not?

It was quieter at the summit. I sat on a bench and took a long sweeping look at the London skyline, picking out the landmark buildings and noticing how close together they seemed from this perspective. It was clearer up here than in the fume-clogged air of the city but still oppressive. A gust of hot wind lifted my hair. I brushed back my fringe and wiped my forehead with my handkerchief. The summit was fully exposed to the sun, creating a prickly kind of heat, made more uncomfortable because I hadn't bathed that morning. I glanced around, furtively checking that no one was watching, and quickly removed my jacket.

Behind me, kite flyers were silently absorbed in the meditative motion of tugging, releasing, and tugging the string. Guided by their palpable calm, I filled my lungs, blew the air out in a long, slow stream, and tried to clear my mind so I could dissect the conversation with DCI Roberts. At first, he'd been dismissive when I'd suggested a connection between Simone's abduction and the poisoning, but then he'd begun to deliberately obfuscate and use suggestion as manipulation. It was a tactic he'd employed before. When I'd pressed him on what progress he'd made in his search for her, he'd even cast doubt on her very existence, saying that all he'd been able to confirm was that she was not on the electoral register, didn't pay council tax, and didn't have a driving license or mobile phone contract registered to her address. Also, that Southside Arts had no students in their History of Art course called Simone.

When I'd reminded him that she must have appeared as a phantom to Susan and the café owner as well, he'd frowned and moved on to his next gambit: that the woman calling herself Simone had not in fact been abducted but had entered the car voluntarily and was driven away by a friend. This, I strenuously refuted. I knew what I'd seen. But perhaps he was right about one thing: Perhaps she didn't exist as the person she presented herself to be. Maybe she wasn't a History of Art student from Brazil. Maybe she was someone else entirely.

Something thumped against my leg, breaking my train of thought. I looked down to see a football roll a few inches and come to a stop beside my shoe. A small boy came running but pulled to an abrupt stop a few feet away. He looked from me to the ball and pushed his hands into his pockets. I looked from him to the ball and back to him, wondering why he didn't come and pick it up. When his eyes filled with tears, I understood. He was frightened of me. I looked at myself through his eyes and saw a wild-haired woman wearing men's clothes, a single black leather glove, a baggy gray shirt with sweat circles at the armpits, and glasses perched askew above a bruised and swollen eye. I must have looked terrifying to a small child. With effort, I lifted the corners of my mouth, kicked the ball toward him, and said, "There's a brave boy." To which he snatched it up and fled.

But I was wasting time. I shouldn't be in the park, playing with small children. I should be looking for Simone. With purpose, I stood, folded my jacket over my arm, and set off in the direction of Susan's house. If anyone had any information on Simone, even if seemingly unimportant, it would be her.

On the way, I stopped at a corner shop to buy flowers. I wasn't sure why. I'd never bought a gift before—but then, I'd never turned up at someone's house unannounced before either. As I was paying, I noticed a receipt on the floor next to my foot. I picked it up and read it. It was for a meal from the night before. Briefly, I wondered if it was mine and had fallen out of my wallet, but it couldn't have been mine, because it listed two large glasses of merlot, which I would never have drunk, because I didn't drink. I could have dropped it again, but I abhorred littering, so, after folding it neatly, I put it in my pocket.

When I arrived, Susan made several considered blinks as she took in my appearance, then put a finger to her lips and beckoned for me to follow. In the kitchen, she pointed at the ceiling and whispered, "Listen."

I put the flowers on the table and tilted my head. There. Soft footsteps on the floorboards. My heart leaped.

"Is it her?"

"No, it's her friend. He arrived just before you. Let himself in with a key. He's just come downstairs."

Was he False Hellebore, Sebastian, or Jonathan? Not Castor.

He wasn't a friend. "Describe him."

"Broke. Depressed. Hates everyone."

"No, what does he look like?"

"I don't know. I never see them. Just hear them."

The sound was clear, as if it were only the floorboards

separating us, and I wondered if he could hear us whispering. It sounded as if he was looking for something on Simone's desk. There was a scrape of a chair and a crash as something fell to the floor, the shuffling of books and papers, footsteps moving across the ceiling toward the kitchen, drawers and doors opening and closing, the scratch and crunch as he stepped on the broken glass.

And then a voice, as clear as day, that I immediately recognized as Sebastian's.

"It's not here—there's been a break-in, there's glass everywhere… I know what a Nokia looks like, darling, it's not here—I'm sure—no—I'm leaving now—yes, see you later."

Again, I touched the outside of my pocket for the Nokia, and with a jolt, the memory of the text exchange I'd had the previous night came rushing back.

There was a slam so forceful the building shook, and I ran to the old woman's front door in time to see Sebastian's legs walk past the railings. By the time I was up on the pavement, he was already nearing the corner. I could have called out, but instead, I stood in the road and watched the swish of his long blond hair and his slim-bodied, loping walk as he turned the corner and disappeared.

"Go after 'im." Susan was standing behind me, panting from exertion. "Find out who he was talking to."

"It's too late."

"It might not be if you hurry. Here, give us that." She took my jacket and gave me a push. "Quick, before you lose 'im."

It was too hot to run. Sweat had been trickling down my back and pooling above my belt since the climb up Kite Hill, but I broke into a flat-footed jog and didn't stop until I'd reached the end of the high street. Sweating heavily and puce-faced, I looked up and down, wondering which way he'd turned, and caught his swaying blond hair farther down the hill. I lost him again in the throngs of tourists at Camden Lock Market but pushed on until I reached the crossroads. Here I stood, swiveling back and forth, scanning the roads behind, up ahead, and to each side, looking for his hair above the other pedestrians, oblivious to the expressions of distaste on the faces of the people passing by and the wide berths they were giving me.

Unexpectedly, he stepped through a shop door immediately in front of me, unscrewed the top of a bottle of red wine, and took a long swig. I gasped and stared at him. Up close, his porcelain skin had a pale, fragile translucence. His long blond hair softly framed his face, and his eyelids were shaded with baby-blue powder. I didn't use the term lightly, but he was angelic. He paused drinking to take a breath, looked directly at me without seeing me, then put the bottle back to his lips. When he'd drunk half of it, he wiped his mouth and crossed the road to the Tube station.

"Excuse me," I said as I followed, but he was already walking into the ticket hall.

I hesitated. I'd lived in London for decades, but I'd always had a pathological fear of the Underground. Not for the trains themselves—for the actual underground and its awful connotations of death. I would rather spend hours traveling on several buses than step onto an escalator leading down into those deep, dark Hadean pits. Up ahead, Sebastian was walking through the barriers, and if I was to catch him, I would have to move my feet. He joined the escalator and began to sink from view. *Move my feet.* I sniffed in a deep breath and took a step, and another, and several more until I was standing in front of the barriers. Other people were touching their travel cards, making the barriers open. I patted my pocket and groaned. I couldn't go on even if I wanted to, because my travel card was in my wallet, and my wallet was in my jacket pocket. Sebastian was halfway down the escalator. Even if I shouted, the ticket hall was too crowded and noisy for him to hear.

Suddenly, I was forced through the barriers by a large man who'd touched his travel card behind me. He didn't acknowledge what he'd done but pushed past me to the escalators and, as if he'd cleared a blockage, a stream of people rushed after him and I found myself caught up in the surge.

"No, no," I said as I was swept along. "No, no, no." But no one heard me. Few were even aware of me. At the last second, I wrenched free, staggered to one side, and leaned a hand against the wall to breathe. It was unbearable having to face all my phobias at once, intolerable.

Without warning, a deafeningly loud roar accompanied by a sustained blast of wind funneled through a tunnel and rushed up the escalators. I opened my eyes wide in astonishment as wind whipped around me, billowing my shirt and lifting my hair. In trepidation, I peered down to the lower level, expecting to see smoke, or flames, or worse, but the area was deserted, apart from Sebastian, standing alone, swigging from the bottle. It was a surprise to see him. I took a few steps forward and stared at the escalator shifting and pulling away, the flat platform morphing into steps, the jagged edges teeth-like, and felt nauseous. I knew that if I took hold of the handrail, it would drag me down whether I was ready to go or not.

Alighting passengers from the train that had just arrived trickled into the hall. If I was going to get his attention, it would have to be now.

"Sebastian!" I called as a baby screamed. "Sebastian!" as an announcement boomed out of the loudspeakers. He glanced toward the train, tipped back his head to drain the dregs, stood the empty bottle on the floor, and dashed down the steps to the platform. Too late. I was too late. Once again, the deafening roar and swirling wind rushed up the escalator as another train arrived, and I threw my arms wide and swayed backward as if blasted by the foul breath of Cerberus. Then something extraordinary happened: another surge of people engulfed me, lifted me up, carried me down the escalator, and deposited me onto the train. And I let myself be swept along, my mouth a small *o* of surprise.

15

It wasn't as terrifying as I thought it would be under the ground. If I disassociated myself from the concept, I could have been anywhere. Or at least elsewhere. That was what the other passengers seemed to be doing, removing themselves from their current location with headphones and phone screens. I looked at them sitting in the seats, standing in the aisle, all of them staring at their mobiles. All except one. Sebastian was sitting in the last seat in the row, his head resting on a glass partition, his arms folded across his chest, his eyes closed. I squeezed along the aisle, stood on the other side of the glass partition, and looked down at him.

I'd thought him angelic when I'd seen him earlier, but now that I had time to study him, I could see how damaged he was—how thin his body was within his clothes, how fragile and pale his skin was—and I wondered what could have happened to make him like this. The train pulled into a station, and his phone beeped with a text alert. He pulled it out of his pocket, and I had a perfect view of the screen.

Come straight back. We need your help. She keeps trying to get out. He didn't send a reply but put the phone in his pocket, slumped back against the partition, and closed his eyes again. Who kept trying to get out? Simone? Could the person who'd sent the text be her kidnapper? It was supposition, straw clutching. The text could have been about anyone—a pet, even—but I wanted to know. I was burning to know because I was desperate to find her, and right then, Sebastian was my only lead. My intention had been to ask whom he'd been talking to when he was in her flat, but my intention had changed. I was now determined to follow him to find out for myself who needed his help.

He alighted at Tottenham Court Road and turned onto Soho Square, but rather than go straight to his flat above the jazz club, as I was expecting, he went into a pub. I slowed to a stop. Before this all began, I would never have set foot in a pub. I hated them. Hated the sickly-sweet smell, the sticky tabletops, the impenetrable gloom. They were worse twenty years ago, when Mary had persuaded me to join her for a drink after work and I grudgingly agreed. Back then, they stank of stale cigarettes that clung to my skin for days. She'd laughed when I'd complained about this. I've never understood why.

The pub seemed overly full for a weekday afternoon. I was

anxious about the number of people inside but quickly realized this could be to my advantage. I stood behind a group at the bar and scanned the pub. Sebastian was farther along, knocking back what could have been a vodka shot. Three more shots were on the bar in front of him, which he drank in quick succession. He looked at his phone, then held two fingers up to the bartender. Two shots later, he put his hands in his pockets and left the pub.

There was a slight sway to his gait as he walked across Soho Square, but he didn't appear to be outright drunk, just tipsy. At the top of Frith Street, he leaned his forearm and forehead against the front window of an art gallery and became still. I stopped as well, as close to him as I dared. For a moment, I thought he needed to vomit. Instead, I heard him say, "Fuck, it didn't sell. It was good. Why didn't it sell?"

Then I remembered the easel in his room above the jazz club and wondered which of the many paintings within the gallery was his. Soon, he stood upright, squared his shoulders, shook back his long hair, and set off again with his listing gait. And I followed behind as inconspicuously as I could.

It was the middle of the afternoon, so I wasn't expecting the man to be sitting behind the tiny box office. His voice took me by surprise again as I followed Sebastian through the jazz club's side door.

"We don't open till nine. Show starts at eleven."

I turned toward him. "I'm not here to see the show."

At my words, his eyebrows lifted, and he said, "I remember you."

"Good, so you'll remember I'm only here to see a friend."

He picked up his phone. "Which friend? I'll call them, and they'll come down to meet you."

"Not this again," I cried. "I gave you fifty pounds for no reason last time. The least you can do is let me in without the interrogation."

I could feel his eyes moving over me, scrutinizing me. "Just give me a name, and you can go up," he said, by way of compromise.

I pushed up my glasses, thinking this could very well be a mistake. "Sebastian."

"Sebastian? Why didn't you say so before? He's just back from the pub. Seems a bit pissed. How do you know him?"

To bring the conversation to a swift end, I turned and quickly ran up the stairs.

The bar was deserted, and the door marked "Private" was open. Even before I'd reached Sebastian's landing, I could hear voices within his flat: a man's and a woman's, both with the same heavy accent. Every now and then, they slipped into another language that sounded like Portuguese. I stayed where I was, halfway up the stairs, not wanting to risk being discovered, and settled back to listen.

"What took you so long?" the man asked.

"Problems with the trains," Sebastian replied.

I heard a soft thump, as if someone had collapsed into a chair, followed by a heavy sigh.

"You are drunk," the woman said.

"And you're not, darling." I heard the crack of a bottle top opening. "Want a drink?"

There followed some words from the man and woman that I couldn't understand and then Sebastian asking, "Where is she?"

"In the bedroom."

My heart leaped. Were they talking about Simone?

"She heard me talking to you on the phone earlier. She knows you did not find the Nokia. She is not happy," the woman said.

"It's not my fault it wasn't there. It was probably nicked during the break-in. I found the rosary, though."

"Okay. Good. At least we have something we can work with. You have all the equipment you need?"

"Yes."

"Make sure you sterilize everything."

"I know."

"And wear gloves."

"I'm not an idiot."

There was a pause before the woman added, "Okay. We will go now. Keep an eye on her. Do not let her leave. It is too dangerous for her." Another pause before her voice again. "Hey. Do not fall asleep."

And then the man's voice. "Look at you, man. You are

wasted. *Você é inútil.* This is not a good idea. May, look at him. *Meu Deus.*"

Another pause before the man's voice again. "Come on. Wake up. You are a liability. You could screw everything up for all of us."

I heard a slap, then Sebastian shouting, "Ow! Jesus. I'm awake. Jesus."

"Do not drink anymore," the woman said. "We are relying on you."

Then there were footsteps close to my head walking toward the door, and I quickly retreated down the stairs, through the door marked "Private," and ducked behind the bar. They were talking in their language as they walked down the stairs, and when they emerged, I was surprised to see False Hellebore walking across the bar with an older woman. I frowned. What was he doing here? And who was she? At least I had a name: May. It occurred to me that the most expedient way to find out the answers to all my questions was simply to go upstairs and demand Sebastian tell me. And then to open his bedroom door to see who was behind it.

"What's the worst that can happen?" I whispered as I crouched behind the bar. "Physical violence?"

But I'd seen how brittle he was. I doubted he could do me much harm.

I was about to stand when Sebastian came tumbling down the stairs and spilled into the bar. He took a moment to right himself, then stayed where he was, swaying dangerously.

"Bas, mate. What're you doing up this time of day?" I jumped at the sound of another voice. "I thought you were a vampire."

"I'm on a ciggie run," Sebastian slurred.

He took a step toward the stairs to the street and stopped again.

"Man, you're wasted," the voice said. "Here, let me give you a hand down the stairs."

I was trapped. It could only be seconds before whoever was helping Sebastian came back. My only escape was up. Quickly, I slipped out from behind the bar and went up the stairs.

The door to his flat was wide open. I peered inside and saw the chaise longue, the mustard-colored armchair, the scruffy seagull in the glass case, and the pink velveteen throw screwed into a ball on the floor. At the rear of the room was a door that I hadn't been able to see before, and beside that, a small kitchenette. I stepped into the room and immediately covered my nose. It reeked of stale cigarettes and body odor. I retreated back into the hallway, took a deep breath, and went in again, this time making straight for the door at the rear of the room. My hand hovered over the handle as I realized, with excitement, that if Simone was indeed behind the door, I was about to become her rescuer. I savored the feeling for a moment, then pushed the door open and instantly deflated. The room was empty. I glanced at the chaos of clothes and shoes, the filthy carpet, and, beside the unmade bed, what I presumed to be drug paraphernalia—a lighter, a small tin foil package, a flask, a spoon, a syringe—and finally the open window. It opened onto a small balcony, which connected with the balcony of the neighboring building. It would have been an easy escape. I sighed. If Sebastian had indeed kidnapped Simone, then there never had been such an inept captor. I put my head through the window and inhaled deeply. This room smelled worse than the other one.

I went back into the main room and crossed to the front windows to look out for Sebastian's return from his cigarette run: he was sitting with another man at one of the tables outside the Italian café opposite. A server was placing cups of coffee in front of them. This was my chance to leave. I turned for the door but stopped when I saw the cloth-covered easel. I don't know why I felt compelled to remove the cloth. I wasn't ordinarily interested in art, but perhaps being so close to Sebastian on the train and seeing the intimate place where he slept had brought me closer to him. Just as my telescope had brought me closer to Simone. I lifted one corner of the cloth, flipped it over the top of the canvas, and gasped.

It was a portrait of Jonathan Wainwright. "How on earth?"

He was in a garden surrounded by a vine-covered fence, sitting in a rattan chair, a drink in his hand. There was a slight smile on his face. He looked at ease. I moved closer to the canvas and realized with a jolt that he had no eyes, and the places where they should have been were burn holes. Quite possibly, cigarette-burn holes. I looked at the corner of the canvas, but instead of a signature, a skull and crossbones had been scratched into the paint. I stood back and took in the painting as a whole. I wasn't educated enough to know whether it was good or bad, but it was certainly realistic. I'd recognized Jonathan straightaway, having known the younger version at the university. And it was full of detail, especially the garden. There were children's toys on the grass in front of his chair, a bottle of sun cream on a table, but it didn't look like an English garden. The plants were tropical: bromeliads, bougainvillea, cactus. Then something made me look again at the vine covering the fence surrounding the garden, and that's when I spotted the red trumpet-shaped flowers.

16

MY MIND WAS BUZZING. I WANTED TO GO HOME AND ORGA-
nize my thoughts, and I would have done so if my keys hadn't
been with Susan in my jacket pocket. Neither did I have my
travel card, so it was with heavy feet that I walked the four miles
back to Hampstead. The hill seemed steeper than usual on the
way back, the journey interminable. When I rounded the corner
onto Susan's road, I was surprised to see her still standing outside on the pavement where I'd left her, my jacket folded over
her arm. She must have been there for hours.

"Did you speak to him?" she asked as I approached.

"No, but I followed him to Soho."

"You went all the way to Soho?"

"I did. And now I need to go home. I'm very tired."

I held out a hand for my jacket, but she clamped her elbow
against her side and looked at me steadily.

"My jacket?"

"Come in a minute," she said, turning to her steps.

"Not right now. I just need my jacket."

She held it tight. "I've got something to show you. You seem the clever type. You'll know what to do."

She disappeared through her front door, and there was nothing I could do but follow her into her kitchen, where she picked up a mobile from the table.

"Listen to this. It's babble. Can't make head nor tail of it, but I have a feeling it's important."

She put the phone on the table and pressed the screen. Suddenly, distorted words blasted out, filling the room, making me leap. I picked it up but had no idea how to turn the volume down. Susan took it from me and repeatedly clicked a button on the side, but even at a lower level, it was impossible to decipher the conversation. I bent toward it to concentrate and, after a while, could make out two voices, a male and female. It was a few minutes more before I realized I was listening to Portuguese.

"Is this Simone?"

She nodded.

"You recorded her?"

"I did. I heard shouting and thumping. I was too frightened to knock on her door because he sounded like a right mean one, but I thought I'd better get some evidence in case something bad happened. She was okay, though, thank God, just had a small cut from banging her head on the doorpost. I didn't believe it for a second. More like she banged her head on his fist."

"When was this?"

"About a month back—but now that she's missing, I wonder if there's a connection." She scrolled down the screen and held the phone up for me to see. "Here's another one. I recorded it the day before she disappeared. I was worried because I saw a man waiting for her when I come home from the shops. I didn't like the look of him. He was lounging on the front steps like he owned the place, cigarette in his mouth, flicking ash into my light well. He looked like some kind of cowboy, with those boots on his feet. You know the ones, leather with heels? I give him a dirty look, but he just sneered at me. I heard 'em talking outside when she finally come home. Couldn't understand a word, but I could tell she was scared."

She pressed Play. "Can you work out what they're saying?"

I didn't know Portuguese, but I could pick out a phrase that was repeated throughout the conversation: *professor de inglês.* The English professor. When the recording ended, I picked up the phone.

"Can I borrow this?"

"Why? To give to the police?"

"Ah…no."

"Good. My Stanley was always having run-ins with the police. I don't trust 'em as far as I can throw 'em, which at my age ain't no distance at all. You're different, though. I feel like I can trust you."

In my profession, trust was assumed—part of the job description, but this was the first time anybody had told me they trusted me to my face. Hearing it caused a strange sensation. "I know someone who can translate the recordings," I said. "So can I borrow it, or do you need it?"

"Take it. Nobody calls me, and I can always check my socials on my laptop."

"Your what?"

"My social media."

I had no idea what she was talking about. She picked up the phone, repeatedly pressed the screen, and handed it to me. "There, it's unlocked now. Bring it back when you're done. No hurry."

Half an hour later, I turned onto the entrance to University College London's Senate House and paused momentarily to look up at the imposing art deco building. The sight of it inspired the same awe as it had the first time I'd seen it, sending the same shiver of realized ambition and anticipated privilege down my spine. But I shook my head, knowing these aspirations belonged to another life, and set off for the library, where I was expecting to find my Portuguese ex-colleague.

Matilde Acosta was a petite dark-haired woman in her late thirties; golden skinned, with a smattering of dark freckles across her nose. Standing five feet tall, she was fragile in appearance but fearsome in reality. When she opened her mouth to speak, her voice boomed, filling whatever space she happened to be in. It didn't take long to find her. As expected, I heard her long before I saw her, and when she saw me, she let out a loud cry, ran toward me, pulled me into a tight embrace, and kissed my cheek. And once again, I was reminded of *Lobularia maritima*, sweet alyssum—the tiny plant with a big impact.

"*Minha amiga.* What a wonderful surprise. It's so good to see you, my darling. *Meu Deus!* Your face! Have you been attacked?"

"No. I fell but I'm fine," I said, trying to pull out of her embrace.

"It doesn't look fine."

"It's nothing. Really."

Matilde moved her eyes from my face to take in my whole body and pulled in her lips to prevent further comment. After a moment, she said, "It really is wonderful to see you, Eustacia. We're missing you very much. The department's falling apart without you."

"I don't believe that for a second," I said, finally extricating myself from her grip and wiping my cheek.

"It's true. Your module had a seventy percent dropout this year."

"Seventy percent?"

"Seventy-two, actually. It's because of the new safety rules the university had to implement after the…" She paused. "…incident. The course is theory only now, the students aren't allowed to do experiments, and the new lecturer is rather dry. I'm afraid, after you, the students are finding him very dull. He doesn't excite them like you used to. No one could ever be as good as you."

I wasn't good at responding to compliments because I'd never been taught how. A simple *thank you* seemed boastful, as if I agreed with the accolade.

"I'm sure it's not as bad as that."

"It is, Eustacia. If we have the same drop-out rate again next year, the university may cancel the course." She took a step closer and said in a marginally quieter voice, "You should know, there's a group of us petitioning for your return. We need you here. Preferably before the start of term."

I took a step back. "They won't want me. Besides, I'm not sure I want to come back. I'm enjoying my freedom. My hours are my own to fill as I please."

She raised her eyebrows. "And how are you filling them?"

"My research is keeping me…" But the sentence trailed off when I remembered that my research had been destroyed.

"You can continue your research here. You'll have use of the facilities, and I know several students who'd jump at the opportunity to assist you."

I cleared my throat to bring the subject to a close. "I'm not here to talk about that. I'm here to…" I paused as I remembered that Matilde was not the type of person one could simply ask a favor of, then leave. She would want a conversation—or, as she would put it, a catch-up—to wrap around the favor. "I'm here to ask if you fancy a cup of tea?"

I knew she was beaming, even though I wasn't looking at her directly. I could feel it.

"Oh, yes, please. That would be absolutely wonderful."

᪐

We went to a café off Russell Square that a lab technician had once told me about, and I sent her to sit in the garden while I ordered. When I joined her, she was reading from a folded newspaper, her legs neatly crossed, an expensive bag left casually open on a chair beside her. I held our mugs of tea and glanced at the tree above her head.

"Can we change tables?"

Matilde looked up from her newspaper. "If you want, my darling."

I crossed to an empty table on the other side of the garden, and Matilde watched me a moment before standing and gathering her belongings.

"I like this place." She waved her newspaper expansively as she sat down. "The garden's lovely."

"It would be lovely if it didn't have a poisonous tree in it," I said.

At this, she looked around in alarm. "What poisonous tree?"

"The one you were sitting under. *Cascabela thevetia*, yellow oleander. I have no idea why people insist on putting it in café gardens. The flowers, leaves, and seeds contain digitoxin, which slows the heartbeat."

She stared at the tree on the other side of the garden. "Is that dangerous?"

"Ingesting a single seed slows the heartbeat…to a stop."

"Goodness! Should we tell someone?"

"There's no point. In my experience, they don't seem to care."

She shrugged, then turned her attention back to me, as if I'd given her permission not to care either.

"I wanted to say, I'm so glad we're doing this. I've wanted a catch-up with you for so long. After the inci—after what happened, I left so many messages on that ancient answering machine of yours, but when you didn't reply, I assumed it was broken. Or…you didn't want to speak to me."

She leaned her elbows on the table, rested her chin on her linked fingers, and stared at me. Recoiling from the intensity of her gaze, I took Susan's phone from my pocket and placed it on the table.

"Would you mind translating some recordings for me?"

Matilde looked down at the phone, then back to me. "I thought you wanted to talk about what happened." She placed her hands on the table, palms downward, and leaned closer. "I can see how much it's torturing you, my darling. Guilt can be so destructive, but talking helps and, as you know, I'm a very good listener."

I frowned. In the years I'd known Matilde, being a good listener was not a trait I would have given her. A talker, yes, but not a listener. I pushed the phone across the table.

"The recordings are in Portuguese. I'm not sure how to access them, but I'm sure you will."

She pulled back her hands, made a small head shake, picked up the phone, and rapidly touched the screen.

"All right, but you know it's not healthy to bottle things up. If you're not careful, they will explode, and then all manner of hell will—" But she was interrupted by the two voices as she pressed Play.

She clicked the button on the side of the phone to increase the volume and held it to her ear.

"It's Brazilian Portuguese. You can tell because the vowel sounds are rounder and we pronounce an *s* as *sh*, whereas they extend it to make an *ss* sound. Also, they're using *você* as the familiar form of *you*. We use *tu*. I'll start again and translate." She put the phone on the table between us. Their conversation was remarkably clear, as if Susan had had the audacity to creep into the garden and record them through an open window. "She sounds scared of him. She says...*You told me to go. To hide.* He says...*Didn't tell you to leave the country, told you to go to Ubatuba, wait for me.* She says...*Didn't feel safe, had to get away. I'm safe* here. He says…*Safe? Did you think I wouldn't find you? Did you think you could disappear? You can't disappear, too much knowledge in that beautiful head."*

At this point, there were sounds of scuffling on the tape, banging, gasping, then the male voice again.

"Stay where you are. Don't make me hit you." Matilde pressed Pause. "What is this?"

I'd forgotten that it was highly likely she'd ask questions. "My neighbor gave it to me."

"It sounds like a recording of an assault. You need to take it to the police."

"I intend to. I just need to know what they're saying first." I pressed Play. Immediately, she pressed Pause.

"It's okay," I added. "She wasn't hurt. I met her after this was recorded, and she was perfectly fine."

Matilde frowned but pressed Play and picked up the translation again.

"She's screaming at him to get out. He won't go. He says…*You've been gone a year. Do you know how difficult it's been to find you?"*

She waited while we listened to more scuffling and banging. "He's asking if she did the job he gave her before she ran away. He says…*Did you deal with him?* She says…*How was I meant to deal with him? Nobody knows what he looks like. Nobody knows his name… You know his name… No, I don't. He's just an English professor… That is his name: the English Professor."*

I pressed Pause. "*Professor de Inglês,* the English Professor."

"Do you know who it is?" Matilde asked.

"No idea. Let's carry on."

"He says...*You've found him, haven't you? That's why you're in London... No... Don't lie. Tell me his name... I don't know it... Don't make me hurt you.*" She stopped the recording. "This is making me very uncomfortable."

"Keep going. Please."

Matilde shook her head but pressed Play.

"She says...*Believe me, I'd tell you if I knew anything. I want him found as much as you do. All those people, Andreas. Five lives lost because of him. Two more ruined.* Goodness, has this English Professor killed five people? You really need to take this to the police."

I held up a hand to silence her. "Wait, what was that word? It sounded like *coyotillo.* There, did you hear that? She said it again. *Coyotillo.*"

I leaned closer to the phone, but it clicked over into a new recording.

"*Você esteve?*" Matilde said, repeating their words aloud. "*Aqui e ali.*" She closed her eyes to concentrate. "It's the same two as before, right? This must be a different day because the quality of the recording's different. Do you know who the man is?"

I pictured his face, the deep scar on his cheek, the malevolence in his eyes.

"Only that his name's Andreas."

"She's asking where he's been. Where he's staying. He's staying in Soho… Ah, here we go." She opened her eyes. "He's her husband."

Husband? The word was like a punch to the gut, making me groan and wrap my arms around my torso. Matilde pressed Pause.

"Are you okay?"

I straightened and thought of Jonathan Wainwright. "Are you sure he's her husband?"

She tilted her head and looked at me intently. "This was not what you wanted to hear?"

"It's not what I was expecting to hear," I corrected. "I thought she was with another man."

Matilde raised her eyebrows and smiled.

"Let's continue," I said, baffled by her expression. She pressed Play and closed her eyes again.

"I hear a cork pop. He's saying he feels like celebrating because…*Not only have I been reunited with my long-lost wife but also I've found the English Professor.* She's speaking but I can't hear what she's saying. There's a lot of background noise. It sounds like chopping."

All at once, I realized that I'd witnessed this conversation. Simone chopping vegetables at the kitchen counter, Andreas drinking wine. I knew all the actions and everything that was to come, and now I would know the words.

"He goes on," Matilde continued. *"But so have you, haven't you, my love? And to think, all this time, we thought he was a man."* She pressed Pause again, leaned toward me, and said excitedly, "So he's found the person who killed those people, and she's a woman?"

Matilde was no longer the impartial translator. She'd become as invested in the conversation as I was. This hadn't been my intention, but I should've known it might happen. I should also have known she'd ask questions. She'd always had a fierce curiosity; it wasn't in her nature not to.

"Keep going," I urged.

"Her voice is clearer now. She says... *How did you find her?* He says... *Easy. I followed you. To the café, to your university, to Soho. Now we're on the same page, we can work together like a proper married couple, no?* His voice sounds distant now. It's not so clear. He says... *She lives just around the corner... very next street... clever of you to take an apartment so close."*

This must have been when Andreas was standing at the top of the garden steps.

"She says she doesn't know what he's talking about. He says, *Don't you? Strange, you both looked so cozy in the café."*

"He must have been watching us," I said, as realization struck.

"She's saying something, something... I can't quite hear. Sounds like, *dresses like an old man... She's harmless... a bit of a character.* He's saying, *She's not harmless... She's an expert in poisons. People died... untraceable poison... poison from a local plant.*" Matilde gasped. "My God, Eustacia! Are they talking about you?"

"I think so. What's she saying now?"

"She's asking what he intends to do. He'll do what she was meant to. She says she'll do it. He says she's had a year. She says...*I can get close to her... I can get close to her as well. Right up close... How? On the street where you could be seen?... I won't be seen... You will, Andreas, believe me. CCTV everywhere.*"

She pressed Pause, fell back against her chair, and cried, "The police *really* need to hear this."

Her volume was drawing attention as her voice bounced off the high walls surrounding the garden. The other customers had fallen silent, but there was little point in asking her to lower her voice.

"I'm serious, Eustacia. You could be in danger."

"It's fine," I said. "This recording was made days ago and nothing's happened."

"Yet..."

"I'm fine. Everything's fine. Let's continue."

She exhaled heavily. "Only if you promise to go to the police."

"Yes, yes," I said impatiently.

Swiftly, she grasped my hand. "*Promise* me."

I made an expression that I hoped resembled sincerity and said, "I promise."

She sighed, nodded, and touched the play button.

"Okay. Where were we?" She listened for a moment. "Ah,

yes, she's saying…*Let me do it. I can make her trust me, invite me into her home.* He asks how and she replies…*She likes me. She can't look at me. She trembles when I touch her.* He's laughing. *It's true, Andreas. I felt it. I felt how much she wants me. She'll be putty in my hands.*"

Matilde looked up, one eyebrow raised. *She'll be putty in my hands.* Six words that turned the precious memory of our time together in the café upside down. No. She didn't mean it. She was trying to save me from Andreas. That's all. I undid the top button of my shirt as heat crept up my neck into my face. I was acutely conscious of Matilde's gaze. Conscious more of how exposed it made me feel. But she didn't ask questions; she didn't even smile. She just coughed delicately and continued.

"She says…*I'll make it look like an accident… I'll use one of her own plants.* He says…*Too risky. She knows who you are. Better to do the job quick with a knife.* She says…*She doesn't know who I am.* It sounds as if he's pacing on a wooden floor…"

Then Matilde's eyes flew open as she translated, "*All right, but if she isn't dead in a week, I'll kill her myself.*"

17

THERE WERE MANY EMOTIONS I DIDN'T UNDERSTAND, BUT fear wasn't one of them. I understood well the physical reactions it induced. The increased heart rate, the surge of adrenaline, the panicked and muddled thinking—but for some reason I felt none of these when I heard Andreas's death threat. It was as if my safety was of a lesser concern than Simone's. Matilde, however, turned white, and her hand shook as she held the phone, but she said nothing, pressed the screen and continued her translation.

"The voices are clearer. The subject's changed." She furrowed her brow. "She's saying something about a tutor, an English lesson, cooking a meal, she can't afford to pay him so cooks for him instead. He has a disabled wife…"

There was a silence, then Matilde whistled as a furious stream of Portuguese poured out of the phone.

"I'm sorry but I'm not going to translate this next bit. Let's just say he's angry that she's been wasting time cooking meals when she should have been doing the other job."

Suddenly, there was a loud crack, like a gunshot, making Matilde leap in her seat.

"What was that? Has he shot her? Did she shoot him?" she shouted.

I knew exactly what it was. It was my terra-cotta pot smashing on the paving stones.

"It wasn't a gun."

"It sounded like a gun."

I glanced around and saw that the other customers were no longer pretending they weren't listening. They were blatantly staring, wide-eyed, waiting for Matilde to continue. She pressed Play.

There was the sound of knocking, then Andreas speaking English with an accent.

"Wait. Can you turn up the volume?" I asked, straining forward to listen.

It sounded as though Andreas was welcoming someone, possibly the English tutor. I heard…*My wife telling me about you… Would you like wine?* A pause, followed by a different man speaking: *Thank you, but no. We can have the lesson another time.*

I gasped. It had been years since I'd heard that voice—that irritatingly confident, entitled voice.

Then it was Andreas again, *Stay. I will leave. Do not wait up,* meu amor. *I will be late getting home.* The sound of a door closing, silence, and then Jonathan's voice, louder this time, crystal clear and seething with anger: *Why's that man here? You said you'd divorced him.* Then Simone's quieter reply in English: *...will not sign the papers...being difficult...makes no difference to us...Why are you so upset? You have a wife. I have a husband...Nothing has changed.* Then there was a loud thump, as if a wall had been struck, followed by Jonathan's shout, *Everything's changed!*

Simone was talking again. There was urgency in her tone and one very clear word: *misunderstanding.* I had no trouble hearing the reply. Jonathan shouted it so loudly that Matilde had to turn the volume down.

"There's no misunderstanding. I'm not an idiot. I understand perfectly what you and your husband are doing, but you can fuck off. Do you hear me? You can both fuck off back to Brazil and leave me alone."

There was the sound of a door slamming, then footsteps on floorboards. Rapid key tones as a number was punched into a mobile phone and Simone's voice: *"Merda. Merda. Merda."* And finally, silence.

Matilde scrolled, looking for another recording.

"That was the last one," she said, putting the phone on the table. "Whoa... Jealousy, an unrequited love triangle, death threats. This is like a bad soap opera. Do you know who this Jonathan is?"

"Jonathan Wainwright."

She paused. "That name sounds familiar. How do I know it?"

"He was head of History of Art at UCL twenty years ago, but he moved to Southside Arts."

"Ah, yes. I remember him now. Liked the pretty students. No one ever really knew why he left. How on earth did this young woman become involved with him?"

"I don't know but I intend to find out. Thank you, Matilde. I'm sorry this wasn't the catch-up you were expecting, but you've been very helpful."

I picked up the phone and stood, but she followed and gripped my elbow.

"You're not leaving?" Her eyes widened, darting across my face. She seemed almost angry.

"I am. I need to think about this."

"Let's think about it together."

"I'm better on my own."

She exhaled heavily, noisily. "Are you? Remember what I said before about not bottling things up? About finding someone to talk to?"

"Yes."

"Promise me you will?"

I looked at the sky, impatient to leave. "Yes."

"Good, because I'm worried about you. And…" She stepped close. "I'm saying this as a friend, you should know that you look absolutely *dreadful*. Not just your poor face—all of you."

I glanced at her, not sure how to respond. "It's…been a difficult few days."

She nodded sympathetically, put her arms around me, and kissed my cheek.

"Even so, you lost your father over a year ago, my darling. Don't you think it's time you stopped wearing his clothes?"

18

FATHER HAD BEEN A PROFESSOR OF CLASSICS AND ENGLISH at Magdalen College, Oxford. He'd retired to a small flat in Camden a decade before to be closer to what he called his charmingly eccentric daughter, who had secured a professorship of her own at University College London. He could have named me after any number of ancient Greek goddesses but chose instead Eustacia, as a nod to Thomas Hardy. I had no memories of my mother, who disappeared unexpectedly when I was very young. A parting so sudden that Father was thereafter left in a constant state of shocked bewilderment. So sudden that he was also forced to pause his illustrious career to look after his charmingly eccentric daughter. I knew I took after him in looks and stature. That is to say, unremarkable. I'd seen photos of my mother. I knew that if I were to stand beside her, we wouldn't be recognized as kin. But what I did have, and the thing that stood me apart from my peers, was the fact that I styled my hair and dressed like an old man. Androgyny was not unusual among the students.

It was, however, for a lecturer. And so, when Matilde suggested I stop wearing Father's clothes, it felt like a judgment on my identity, one I wasn't ready to relinquish.

Her comment about my appearance hadn't been completely dismissed, however. I did have every intention of going home to bathe and change, but I couldn't shake the image of Susan standing outside on the street for hours, waiting for my return from Soho. And I couldn't ignore the possibility that she might be doing the same thing now. Her front door was on the latch when I arrived, as if she was expecting me. I knocked but there was no reply, so I walked through the house into the garden. She was sitting at the table, staring into the middle distance, as if she'd pressed a pause button, but as I approached she looked up with the vague expression of someone waking from a dream.

"Are you all right, dear?" she asked.

"Are *you* all right?" I answered.

She exhaled. "I've been with my Stanley. Sometimes I get so lost in memories of him and me that when I come to, hours have gone by." She waved a hand dismissively. "I don't want you to get the wrong impression. He weren't no angel… It weren't all sunshine and flowers, but he was mine." She looked at me pointedly. "You ever have someone special?"

I thought of my lost love and cast my eyes around until they fixed on the back of my apartment block.

"I should go home. I just came to return your phone." I put it on the table.

"Did you get a translation?"

"I did. It seems Simone didn't come here just to study art history. Do you mind?" I asked, pointing at the garden chair, forgetting I'd intended to go home, and sat heavily. "She was looking for an English Professor."

"And the angry man?"

"Andreas. He told Simone to deal with the English Professor, but he wasn't happy when she told him she hadn't found him."

"*Deal* with him?"

"That's what he said. *'Did you deal with him?'*"

"Don't necessarily mean what we think, though, does it?"

"It definitely means what we think, Susan."

It was the first time I'd called her by her name, a surprise to us both. She seemed pleased. I could tell this even without looking at her.

"I should go home," I said again. "I need to bathe."

But I didn't stand up. I stayed where I was, gazing up at the railings around my roof garden.

"Have a bath here," she said. "You can use Simone's bathroom, it's nicer than mine. Leave your clothes on her bed, and I'll throw them in the washing machine."

I was about to protest this bewildering suggestion when she cut me off by adding, "Have you eaten? You must be hungry. I'll open a tin of soup. Come down when you're done." Then she stood stiffly and went into her kitchen.

Totally thrown, I glanced up at Simone's back door. If I entered her flat again, I would be disturbing a crime scene. I stood and walked to the bottom of the steps. But Susan had been in multiple times, and Sebastian had been poking around that very day. And DCI Roberts didn't seem at all interested in preserving it for Forensics. I climbed two steps. What difference would it make if I went in one more time? Not to have a bath, of course. That was a ridiculous suggestion. Just one more time for one last look.

It felt different to be in the kitchen this time. Almost as if I'd been given permission to claim ownership of the place and the things within it. I placed my hand on the countertop, closed my eyes, and pictured her standing where I was, chopping vegetables, grinding coffee beans, pouring wine. All those ordinary tasks I'd watched her do each day through the telescope. I knew which cupboard she kept the coffee beans in, which one the mugs.

I looked again at the two embroideries on the wall beside the cupboard. Their stitches were so large there was no defined shape. Even standing back, I couldn't tell if I was looking at a primrose or a daffodil. They seemed an odd choice for an art history student. Although, what did I know? Perhaps it was their naivety that gave them their worth. I flicked off the light above the oven, went through the opening, and surveyed the front room. Sebastian had left a mess. Books and papers were scattered over the floor, and the sofa cushions had been pulled off the base. I wanted to tidy up, as if it were my own home, but I resisted and went upstairs.

In the bathroom, I caught my reflection in the mirror and snatched off my glasses. Sometimes it's easier to exist in a blurred world than to face harsh reality. I picked up a bottle of bubble bath, unscrewed the lid and smelled lavender. On a shelf beside the door was a candle and matches. I lit it and the aroma of *Simmondsia chinensis* filled the room. It wasn't unpleasant mixed with the scent of the bubble bath, although I noted lavender and jojoba would never be a combination found in the natural world. I looked down at the bath and shook my head at the thought of Susan's suggestion, then bent and turned on the taps. Quickly, I undressed and left my clothes on the bed as instructed and stepped into the bath. The water was scalding, just as I liked it. I allowed myself a moment to relish the unfamiliar feeling of water lapping over my thighs, then, holding my bad hand aloft, gradually lay back until my chest, shoulders, hair, and face were submerged, and for the first time, I experienced the peculiar sensation of Autonomous Sensory Meridian Response. Only when my lungs began to contract did I sit up and wipe the suds from my eyes.

My hand was getting worse; the skin was now cracked and peeling, with puss within the cracks. I hissed out a breath. This was what I'd been trying to avoid. Slowly, I lowered my hand under the surface, endured the searing sting of hot water on broken skin—allowing the pain to run its course—and lay back. Cradling my hand against my chest, I thought about Simone and Jonathan's conversation in the recording. It didn't appear to be a lovers' tiff or a flash of jealousy. For Jonathan, it seemed much more serious. What had he meant when he'd said he understood perfectly what she and Andreas were doing? As far as I could see, they were too fixated on finding and dealing with the English Professor to be plotting against Jonathan. I shuddered at the memory of Andreas's death threat and the fact that he knew so much about me, my occupation, my address. How long had he been following me? That day when I'd focused the telescope on him as he stood outside Simone's back door, had he known the roof garden opposite was mine? Was he aware of me watching him? I soaked for a while as I thought, and when the water was cool and the bubbles evaporated did I sit up, wash with my usual efficient speed, stand, and wrap a towel around myself.

There were a bewildering number of bottles and tubes of cream, oils, and lotions beside the sink, making me wonder what possible use Simone could have for them all. I ran my fingers over them, remembering her gently rubbing the arnica into my hand, and picked up a tube containing what was essentially just diluted beeswax. Frowning, I put it down, unscrewed the lid from a jar of moisturizer, and lifted it to my nose. It wasn't an unpleasant smell. I scooped some out with a finger, leaned forward, and stopped, my hand poised midair. This close to the mirror, I could see that my eye was still badly swollen, the skin a muddy purple. I touched the finger with the cream to my cheek, rubbed in a circular motion, and felt nothing. I prodded the rubber flesh harder, moving up toward my eye until, finally, there was pain, and the memory of falling off the ladder and hitting my face rushed back. I let out a *hmm* of relief that the injury was self-inflicted and moved away from the mirror until my face returned to a blur.

My clothes were no longer on the end of the bed, and Susan had left nothing to replace them. Annoyed, I looked around the room to see if there was anything I could borrow. A dark plain-looking skirt was lying at my feet. I picked it up, held it against my waist, saw the thigh-high slit, and dropped it again. A pair of insubstantial red leggings with white stripes on each side hung over the back of a chair. I considered them, then discarded them. I glanced at the pink padded bra. A brightly colored kimono was hanging from a hook on the back of the door. I held up its sleeve, eyeing it cautiously. It was not something I would wear even before I'd started dressing in Father's clothes. I lifted the sleeve and sniffed. It had the same heady scent as the camisole, and after hesitating for a fraction of a second, I slipped it on. Beside me was a full-length mirror. I peered at the blurred brightly colored reflection, imagining I was looking at someone else, then slowly smoothed a hand down my torso to my thigh, feeling the soft fabric against my skin, and closed my eyes.

A door clicked shut downstairs, and my eyes flew open. I tied the kimono's sash firmly at the waist, put on my glasses, and called, "I'll be down in a minute. Did you bring some clothes?" There was no reply, so I went out onto the landing and immediately staggered against the wall when I saw who was standing at the bottom of the stairs. There, in front of me, staring up with the same expression of shock I knew must be on my own face, was Simone. Straightaway, I noticed the change in her appearance— the dark-ringed eyes, the greasy hair tied in a messy bun, the once full, red lips now pale and chapped—and my mind raced with all the terrible atrocities she must have endured during her captivity. "You're safe," I gasped.

She opened her mouth, and it stayed open for several seconds before words came out.

"What are you doing here?"

"I've been so worried about you." Swiftly, I descended the stairs. "Did you escape through the window?"

She narrowed her eyes. "Is that my kimono?"

I looked down at myself. "Ah…yes. I had to borrow something. Susan's washing my clothes."

"You know Susan?"

"Yes."

Simone blinked a few times. "I don't have time for this."

She threw a quick glance at the front door, then went into the front room to riffle through the drawers of her desk, seemingly oblivious to the art books and essay notes strewn across the floor and the pulled-apart sofa. I followed and watched while she searched. All the vibrancy, the vitality, the rare qualities that had placed her on a different plane were gone. All the things I'd so admired about her, vanished. She was just an ordinary girl who looked like she could do with a bath.

"Did you climb over the balcony?"

She ignored me.

"Did you climb over the balcony?" I asked again.

"What are you talking about?"

I paused, confused for a moment. If she didn't know what I was talking about, it couldn't have been Sebastian's bedroom she'd escaped from.

"Were you being held somewhere else, then? By someone else?"

"I do not know what you are talking about."

"I'm talking about your kidnapping," I said, a little too loudly.

She glanced at me, frowning. "Why do you think I was kidnapped?"

"Because after you left my flat eight days ago, I saw you being pushed into a car and driven away, and no one has seen you since."

She made a sound that I didn't grasp the meaning of and said, "I was not kidnapped. I was staying with my friend." Then she dropped the book she'd been holding and turned to the kitchen but stopped and made a low whistle when she saw the glass on the floor. Carefully, she stepped over it, crossed to the shelves, and started taking everything off them. "*Cadê? Cadê? Cadê?*"

Thoroughly confused now, I asked, "What about the note that was left at the café? The one that said you were leaving your job?"

"What about it?"

"It wasn't your handwriting."

At this, she turned to me, her head shaking. "*Nossa Senhora!* Rose! I was not kidnapped! I was staying with a friend." Then she tutted loudly and continued clearing the shelves.

"Which friend?"

She ignored me and moved to the cupboards and drawers.

"Was it Andreas?"

Slowly, she lifted her eyes to fix me with a dark, skeptical stare. "How do you know Andreas?"

"Susan overheard you arguing."

"She knows Portuguese?"

"Not a word," I said, cautioning myself to be careful. "But she heard the name *Andreas* several times and was worried enough to mention it to me."

Her eyes still fixed on me, she stepped close and scanned my face. So close that I could smell stale sweat and cigarettes. My heart thumped. I held my breath. Eventually, she let out a *pfft* and returned to her search.

"She should mind her own business. You both should."

I exhaled and wiped a hand across my face. "We're worried about you," I said quietly.

"There is no need. I am okay."

She was bending low now, pulling out the contents from the cupboard under the sink: cleaning products, cloths, plastic bags. There was no method to the search. She was just emptying shelves, drawers, and cupboards, and leaving everything on the floor, as if she had no intention of returning to put it all away. I tried again.

"But was it Andreas?"

"No."

In the moment, I hadn't been sure it was Andreas who'd pushed her into the car. It could have been False Hellebore. It could have even been Sebastian with his hair hidden under the baseball cap. I'd been too shocked by what I was seeing to take in details, so I couldn't be absolutely sure. I hadn't even made a note of the car-registration number.

"Was it the young man with the long blond hair?"

Her hand paused above a bottle of bleach.

"The young man with the long blond hair," she repeated, straightening. "You have been spying on me."

A breath caught in my chest. "Of course not. I wouldn't dream of doing such a thing."

She dropped her head, as if it had suddenly become too heavy to support. "Susan has been spying on me."

"No. No. I only mentioned him because he was here earlier today and he let himself in with a key—so naturally, we assumed he was a friend of yours. I wanted to ask if he knew where you were. I even chased after him, but he was too quick for me."

Gently, she kicked a bottle of cleaning fluid.

"*Meu Deus*. Listen, Rose, I was not kidnapped. I have not been in danger. I was staying with my friend. You should leave now and forget we ever met."

I shook my head vigorously. "I don't want to leave. I want to help you. Just tell me what you need me to do."

This made her laugh. Not the bright, optimistic laugh that had given me so much pleasure before. This was joyless.

"You do not know what you are saying. You do not know anything."

I pushed up my glasses. "I know you're looking for a mobile phone."

A jolt seemed to run through her body.

"I know you're looking for an English Professor," I rushed on. "And I know you're terrified of Andreas."

She was staring at me now, eyes wide open.

"You don't know me," I continued. "This is only the third time we've met, but I want you to let me help you. Please, Simone."

She opened her mouth to speak. Closed it again. Opened it and eventually said, "My name is not Simone."

I didn't hesitate. "And mine isn't Rose."

❦

A loud and sustained banging on the front door startled us. "Who's that?" I gasped.

"Go to Susan's," she snapped back. "It is not safe for you here."

"No. I want to stay with you."

She grabbed my arm and pulled me to the back door. "Go. Now!"

I descended two steps, stopped, and listened. As soon as the front door opened, it was slammed back against the wall, and a shouted stream of Portuguese filled the air. I recognized Andreas's voice instantly. I tiptoed back up the steps and peered through the front-room door into the hall in time to see Simone stagger backward, clutching the side of her head, and fall at the foot of the stairs. But this didn't end the shouting. If anything, it became more frenzied. I clapped a hand over my mouth to stop myself from crying out and darted back into the kitchen. What could I do?

I was painfully vulnerable in the thin kimono, but the only

thought in my head was to protect her. I looked around wildly, saw a knife beside the sink, slipped it into the sleeve of the kimono, and, in a wavering voice, called out, "Simone? Are you okay? Susan and I heard shouting."

It was an insane gamble, but it was the only thing I had. Andreas fell silent. Simone fell silent, and, fingering the knife through the fabric of the kimono's sleeve, I stepped into the front room.

"Simone? Where are you?"

I was shaking uncontrollably, but I forced my feet to move, one in front of the other, until I neared the door to the hall. She was on the floor, staring up at me with an expression of shock, and standing over her was Andreas, his expression mirroring hers. Several seconds of numbed silence passed before Andreas snapped his head around, grabbed her by the arm—half lifting her off the floor—and shouted something in Portuguese. Then he dropped her, spun back to me, switched to English, and roared, "What are you doing here?"

I didn't have time to answer because he rushed at me, grabbed me by the neck, and shoved me hard against the wall.

"What the hell are you doing here?"

His grip was powerful, not only in the pressure against my windpipe but also his fingers digging into my skin. I tried to gasp in a breath but couldn't. Immediately, Simone was beside us, dragging at his arm.

"*Não. Não. Para com isso! Ela não é professor de inglês. Não é ela.*"

Her efforts did nothing. His hands were still firmly around my neck. I felt my feet lift off the floor, heard the knife from my sleeve clatter onto the boards. I clawed at his hand around my neck, at his face, at his eyes, but his grip didn't loosen. *Não é ela. Não é ela. Não é ela.* It was a constant stream of muffled words flowing over me while my vision pulsated with white sparks, and just as I was beginning to succumb to the creeping dread of inevitability, he released me, and I dropped heavily to the floor. But before I passed out, I saw Simone standing over me, the knife in her hand.

19

NÃO É ELA.

I knew no Portuguese, but I understood some Spanish. *Não é ela.* As I lay slumped against the wall in Simone's front room, the phrase was playing on a loop inside my head. *Não é ela.* In Spanish, *No es ella. It isn't her.* I opened my eyes and gradually became aware of my surroundings. A man was kneeling beside me, holding my hand. He smiled when he saw my eyes open.

"Welcome back," he said kindly. I had no idea who he was.

"My glasses," I croaked, and was confused by the sound of my voice. He scanned the immediate area, picked them up, and helped me put them on, and I saw that he was a paramedic.

"You've been in the wars, haven't you, poor thing. What happened to your hand?"

He wasn't holding my hand. He was examining it.

"Urushiol poisoning." Again, the strange croak. "It's infected. I need antibiotics."

He smiled as if my hand were the least of my problems. "They'll sort that out at the hospital."

I looked past him to the two figures standing by Simone's desk. Oblivious to the fact that I'd regained consciousness, Susan and DS Hannah were repeatedly pressing Play, Stop, Play on Susan's phone, filling the room with Simone's voice. *Não. Não. Ela não é o professor de inglês. Não é ela. Não é ela. Não é ela.* I let out a peculiar sound, not dissimilar to a baby's gurgle, then tried again.

"It's not her."

They turned, and Susan cried, "Oh, thank God. You're awake."

I straightened and tried to clear my throat, but the lump wouldn't shift.

"She's saying it's not her."

DS Hannah came over and knelt beside me. "Who isn't her?"

"Me. He thought I was the English Professor."

"Who thought you were the English Professor?"

"Castor. Andreas. The man in the recording. He kidnapped Simone. Although, it seems he didn't kidnap her after all."

DS Hannah exchanged a glance with the paramedic. "Casper Andrews?" he asked, jotting the name down in his notebook.

A thought bolted into my head. "Where's Simone? Is she okay?"

"She's gone," Susan said. "I called the police as soon as I heard the shouting." She glared at DS Hannah. "But they come too late."

He cleared his throat and said, "We have officers looking for her now. Mrs. Marsh kindly provided a photograph."

"Who's Mrs. Marsh?" I asked.

"That's me, dear," Susan said, smiling. "You had a photo of Simone?"

"I had a rummage around while I was waiting for the police to arrive, and you know what else I found out? Her name ain't Simone. It's Zena. Zena Sousa. She's been lying about her name all this time."

"Zena, born of Zeus," I said, sinking back against the wall and closing my eyes. Behind my lids, I watched the white sparks dancing. A flash of blue, then Andreas's face close, his eyes bulging, a vein in his forehead throbbing. A flash of blue. Then Simone—no, Zena—standing over me, the knife in her hand. A flash of blue. "Let's get her into the ambulance," the paramedic said, hoisting his bag over his shoulder.

"One minute," DS Hannah said. "Professor? Please open your eyes. I need to take a statement."

"Not now," the paramedic cut in. "She needs to be seen by a doctor, and she shouldn't be talking. Her larynx and trachea are damaged. You can come to the hospital later if you need to speak to her. Are you okay to walk to the ambulance, love? Or would you like a chair?"

"I can walk," I croaked, standing awkwardly and taking his arm. "Thank you."

Straightaway, Susan was by my side. "I'm coming with you."

"No, I'll be accompanying her," DS Hannah said.

"There's only room for one of you."

"It'll be me, then," Susan said.

DS Hannah put his notebook in his top pocket. "No. It'll be me. I need to take her statement. We can make a start on the way."

Susan fixed him with a steely gaze. "So you expect an eighty-five-year-old to go to the hospital by public transport? I don't think so. Besides, I have all her belongings downstairs. You're not going to make me drag them onto a bus as well, are you?"

"Mrs. Marsh…"

But she ignored him and called after the paramedic, "I'll be with you in a minute, dear. I'll just fetch my shopper."

I touched my throat tentatively. The emergency-room doctor had given me anti-inflammatories and an antiseptic gargle, and advised full voice rest. He'd also prescribed antibiotics for my hand, which, as far as I was concerned, was the greatest prize. Like a faithful dog, Susan had stayed by my side, and when the doctor had finished, she ushered DS Hannah out of the cubicle and pulled my clothes out of her shopper. Perplexed by the odor of washing powder and the unfamiliar softness of the fabric, I held Father's suit a moment before spreading it out on the bed.

"I've got something to show you," Susan whispered as I dressed. "That's why I insisted on coming with. I weren't sure when I'd see you again, and I didn't want them dodgy police seeing it first."

She gave the curtain a quick check, reached into her shopper, and pulled out a slim cardboard box containing a charm brace-let, several letters, a small black book filled with page after page of numbers, some dried peas, and a few photographs of Zena as a child.

"See anything important?" she asked.

I picked up one of the photographs. It was of three children standing in front of a vine-covered fence. Zena stood taller than the boys and had a protective arm around each. Two dark-haired, olive-skinned children; the other, blond and pale.

I lifted the photo closer to my face and realized that the vine was a *Mandevilla sanderi,* the same as the one surrounding my garden. The same as the one in Sebastian's painting.

There was a rustle of the curtain as DS Hannah asked, "Are you decent?"

"No," Susan shouted, snatching the photograph.

But I took it back and croaked, "Wait."

I looked again and saw a figure standing behind the

fence—the face in shadow, the arms folded across a slim waist, a hip bone jutting forward against a tight-fitting knee-length skirt.

"You've had enough time," DS Hannah replied. "I'm coming in."

Quick as a flash, Susan whipped the photo out of my hand, threw it into the box, shoved it into her shopper, and covered it with Zena's kimono. I wanted a longer, closer look at the figure standing behind the fence. It must have shown on my face, because Susan said, "Come to mine for the box when you get the chance." Then, as DS Hannah entered: "I'll have a cup of tea in the canteen before you drop me home." She pushed past him, wheeling her shopper away.

"Okay. Let's begin," he said, sitting on the only chair and opening his notebook.

The Nokia was on the bed, along with my glove, leather pouch, wallet, watch, and keys. Quickly, I sat on the edge of the bed, slipped everything into my pocket, and put on the watch. "Professor Eustacia Amelia Rose?" he said, turning my name into a question.

I ignored him and stared at a pictorial instruction poster for washing hands that was behind his head.

"Can you tell me what you were doing in Zena Sousa's flat in nothing but a kimono?"

I exhaled gruffly and shook my head. He made a smile-frown expression, which was puzzling.

"All right, let's start at the beginning. Was Zena Sousa in her flat when you first entered it?"

I knew what he was doing. He would've seen the broken kitchen-door window. He was trying to catch me out, trying to make me admit to breaking and entering. I shook my head again.

"She wasn't in the house?"

I shook my head more vigorously, pointed to my neck, and covered my mouth, reminding him of the doctor's instructions. He lifted his eyebrows and said, "Ah. You can't talk."

I shook my head.

"Not at all?"

What was wrong with the man? Why was he finding this so difficult to understand? I shook my head again.

"Okay. Let's go to the station, and you can write your statement down."

He stood to leave, but I stayed where I was. "I need to wait for my antibiotics prescription first."

"She speaks. It's a miracle," he said, opening the curtain and taking my arm to make me stand. "We'll ask the hospital to forward it to the station. Let's go."

I tried to pull my arm free, but his hold was surprisingly firm. "That will take too long, and who'll take it to a pharmacy? I need the antibiotics. My hand... It's getting worse." I held it up for him to see how blackened it had become. How cracked and pustuled. How precarious the fingernails. "Please. If I don't start the course now, I may lose it."

DS Hannah recoiled and let go of my arm. He hesitated,

weighing his decision, and finally said, "Wait here. I'll go and see what the holdup is on that prescription; then, we'll go to the station."

"You have to take Susan home first. We can't abandon her."

"She can get a taxi."

"She'll be in the canteen. Take her to the taxi rank, put her in one, and pay the driver."

The corners of his mouth dropped, so I sat down again and folded my arms. "I'll not leave this cubicle until Susan is safely on her way home."

He sighed as if I were asking him to push a boulder up a mountain, but he eventually nodded.

✒

For someone who'd spent her adult life in a laboratory, there was so much about hospitals that I loathed—the peculiar smell, the excessive heat, the bacteria, the artificial light, the incessant beeps, the stale air. Or perhaps it was because the last time I was in one, it was to visit Father. Certainly, I most definitely didn't want to be sitting on that hospital bed, listening to the awful moans coming from the patient in the cubicle next to mine or the muted yet urgent conversations of the doctors and nurses outside. But I had to force patience because I needed the antibiotics. I needed them more than anything else.

Half an hour later, DS Hannah had not only located my prescription but had also gone to the pharmacy to collect the drugs. We were now walking down a long corridor toward the exit, but as it came into view, he stopped to answer a call on his radio. When he finished, he took my elbow and steered me down a different corridor and around many corners, finally stopping outside a glass door.

"What're we doing here?" I asked, my voice hoarse. He was looking through the door. I followed his gaze.

Inside the room, I saw an eerie tableau. Three people were gathered around a hospital bed. One of them was in a wheelchair, a woman with her back to me. On the bed lay a body completely covered with a blue blanket, and I realized with a jolt that someone had just died. I looked again and was surprised to see Sebastian sitting in a chair, his head lowered over a bowl, and, standing beside him, another woman with her hand on his back.

I turned to DS Hannah and asked again, "What are we doing here?"

"One moment," he said, still holding my elbow.

I turned back just as the woman in the wheelchair was maneuvering to face the other way, and when I saw her face, my eyes flew open. It was Mary Spicer. All at once, I was flung back twenty years to the first time I saw her—the most significant five minutes of my life, forever burned into my memory. It was at a faculty meeting at the university. I was twenty-four and newly appointed as the botanical toxicology lecturer in the faculty of Life Sciences—the youngest lecturer in the department. I'd been sitting quietly at the back of the room, not drawing attention to myself, when I became aware of a strange sensation, like an iridescence creeping through my body. It was as if a shimmering light was moving from my toes to my scalp, leaving a trail of goose bumps in its wake. I had scanned the room, wondering what could be causing such a peculiar feeling, when my eyes fell on a tall, slim woman about my age, with shoulder-length blonde hair, standing at the doorway, not quite part of the meeting but not separate from it either.

Until that moment, my day had been like every other. I'd woken at dawn, had left my porridge to simmer while I took my habitually shallow bath. Had eaten at the kitchen table, chewing each mouthful thoughtfully, and then walked to the bus stop. A morning like every other. But one hour later, I found myself staring slack-jawed at a woman who was leaning against the doorframe with graceful nonchalance, one hand on her slim hip, the top three buttons of her blouse daringly undone, listening to the head of department give his weekly talk. In response to a mystifying sentence that I had assumed was a joke, the whole room laughed, and one side of the woman's mouth lifted into a half smile. I had gazed at that smile until the lights ricocheting through my body became so agitated that I was sure they must have been shooting out of my pores, sending a million spears of light into the room.

And maybe, for a split second, that's exactly what had happened, because something drew the woman's attention and made her turn her head. For a moment, our eyes met, and I'd felt mine open wide, wide, wider until I was able to see more than I'd ever seen before. Slowly, the woman's smile had spread until both sides of her mouth were lifted, and for a full minute, we held each other's gaze. Two bright lights locked together in a room faded to dark. Then the woman had winked, stepped backward through the door, and was gone, and I was left staring in bewilderment, wondering if she'd been there at all.

I put a hand over my heart. I hadn't seen Mary for twenty years. All I had of her were a few photographs and memories. And here she was, right in front of me. Older, with thin, gray hair, a sallow complexion, and deep lines on her face, but still Mary. Where had she been all this time? What had she been doing? Why was she in a wheelchair? What was she doing in this hospital with Sebastian and a dead body? So many questions I wanted so desperately to ask. Unexpectedly, DCI Roberts appeared on the other side of the glass door, and the shock of seeing him scattered my thoughts. He looked at me for a long time before opening the door and stepping through.

"Eustacia Amelia Rose, I'm arresting you for the murder of Jonathan Wainwright. You do not have to say anything, but it may harm your defense if you do not mention when questioned something which you later rely on in court. Anything you do say may be given in evidence."

I blinked, hearing but not listening, then slowly turned back to the room, a strange sensation creeping through me as I realized that it was Jonathan lying dead in the bed. That it was Jonathan who was the poison victim.

"When did he die?"

"An hour ago."

"What's Mary doing here?"

"You didn't know?" He took a pair of handcuffs from his belt. "She's Jonathan's wife."

The strange sensation increased until it was threatening to take over my whole body. My vision was blurring. I had to keep blinking. Behind Mary, Sebastian threw up into the bowl, but rather than go to his aid, she turned her chair away until she was facing the door. Facing me. DCI Roberts was putting the cuffs on my wrists behind my back. DS Hannah was pulling my elbow. I was straining away from them both, not wanting to leave, because at that moment, Mary's and my eyes were locked together. I never cried, but right then, I could distinctly feel tears running down my cheeks.

20

THEY MADE ME SIT IN THE BACK SEAT. IT WAS UNCOMFORTABLE with my hands cuffed behind my back. DS Hannah was driving. DCI Roberts was sitting in the passenger seat in front of me. I stared at his bald patch and said, "You know I didn't do it."

It was several long seconds before DCI Roberts replied. "I know no such thing."

The Nokia was in my pocket. I could feel it through the fabric of my trousers.

"I don't blame you for thinking I'm guilty," I rasped painfully. "It's a very logical supposition. I am, after all, a toxicologist, and I've long loathed the unfortunate man. I can see that you'd think I poisoned him, then destroyed my own garden and invented a burglary to conceal the fact, but I assure you, Richard, I didn't kill Jonathan Wainwright."

I coughed, and a thousand knives stabbed my throat.

"I do, however, think I know who did, and if you'll allow me my liberty for a short while longer, I'll prove it."

It was never going to happen. Murder suspects aren't given a get-out-of-jail-free pass just so they can prove their innocence. There are procedures to follow, paperwork to complete, data to be inputted—which meant a long night in solitude, trying to ignore the image of Father watching me sorrowfully as I lay curled on the holding-cell bunk. Trying also to ignore the shame of him seeing me brought so low. I couldn't shake a bitter conviction that I'd been done wrong, and if only I could find out why and by whom, everything would be okay.

With the thin blanket covering my head, I went back to the day I'd first seen Mary. I'd stayed in my seat at first, staring at the doorway, wondering if she'd been there at all; then, I'd stood up, right in the middle of the meeting, and followed her. In the corridor, I'd watched the sway of her hips as she sauntered past the seminar rooms, and, as if connected by an invisible thread—or perhaps by the enticing trail of her lily of the valley perfume—I'd followed her down two flights of stairs to the canteen. At the counter, I'd stood close behind her, close enough to be engulfed by her scent. And when she'd turned around and smiled to find me standing there, I'd simply said, "Well, now… Here we are." I rolled onto my back, stared at the cell ceiling, and remembered Mary buying us tea and listening to her talk about her PhD research project. I'd watched with fascination the way she'd cut her cake and put

THE WOMAN IN THE GARDEN   193

the delicate forkfuls into her mouth, the pauses while she chewed and swallowed. And I remembered how I'd become light-headed and needed to briefly cover my face with my hands when she told me we would be sharing a lab for the year.

There were so many memories of the year we'd spent together: swimming in the Hampstead ponds, cycling in Hyde Park, gallery visits, theatre nights, the opera, ballet at Sadler's Wells. The television nights in her tiny flat, our weekend by the sea. Each and every memory cherished. And I remembered with visceral clarity the close of the year—her research project complete, the tenancy on her flat ended—and the searing pain of separation when Mary left London to go on holiday with Jonathan and didn't return.

There was a rap on the holding-cell door, and DS Hannah came in. Exhausted, I struggled into a sitting position to take the second dose of antibiotics he gave me. I didn't like the brusque way he told me to follow him. I liked the corridor he was taking me down even less because I knew where it led.

DCI Roberts was already in the interview room when we arrived, and sitting at the table opposite him was a young woman. I eyed her silk blouse and gray cashmere cardigan with interest.

"Lamb's ears," I said with a residual rasp.

She looked up from the file she was reading, and her eyes widened as they traveled over my face and neck.

"I'm sorry? Did you say something?"

"*Stachys byzantina*, common name lamb's ears. Silver silky-lanate hairs that cover the leaves. Thrives best in direct sunlight. Do you like direct sunlight?"

She looked at DCI Roberts, then back to me.

"Good morning, Professor," he said. "This is your solicitor, Meredith Wise."

She stood and extended a hand. I ignored it.

"Mr. Bishop's my family solicitor. Why isn't he here?"

She smiled as if expecting the question. "He asked me to represent you this time because he's not a criminal lawyer."

"I'm not a criminal," I shot back.

"And it's my job to prove that to these two men."

She was still purposefully extending her hand, so I looked down at it.

"You're very young."

"Wisdom doesn't always come with age."

I guffawed at the innuendo but didn't take her hand.

"Shall we proceed?" DCI Roberts asked flatly.

Meredith Wise smiled and sat down, but I stayed where I was.

"Please sit down, Professor," he added.

I walked over to the wall, leaned against it, and patted my hair. It felt peculiarly soft after using Zena's shampoo. "I'd prefer to stand."

"We need you to sit," DCI Roberts said, indicating the camera pointing at the empty chair. I glanced at it.

"You know my feelings about this room. You agreed we'd only conduct interviews in your office."

My voice sounded very deep and unfamiliar. I tried clearing my throat.

"That was before you were arrested on suspicion of murder," he said.

Meredith Wise stood and put her hand on the back of the empty chair. "Please sit down. The sooner we start, the sooner we finish."

I looked at the ceiling. "I'll sit down if you answer my questions first," I said.

DCI Roberts shook his head. "I'll be the one asking the questions."

I touched my neck. It was painful to speak, but there was so much I needed to know. "Then I won't sit down."

He looked up from his file and sighed. "How many questions?"

"Not many."

He let out a low hum. "Go ahead, then."

But before I could open my mouth, Meredith Wise cut me off by saying, "As your solicitor, I don't advise this."

I turned to her. "If you want to stay in this room, sit down and be quiet."

Her eyes widened like they had when she'd first seen my face. Again, she looked at DCI Roberts, then back at me.

"It's okay, Ms. Wise," DCI Roberts said. "This is off the

record. The interview hasn't officially begun. I haven't started the recording. Go ahead, Professor."

I tried clearing my throat and began. "Why was that young man in the room with Mary?"

"He's her son and Jonathan's stepson."

I paused, then said, "Of course."

I didn't know why I hadn't seen it before. He looked just like Mary when she was young—the same soft skin, pale-blue eyes, the same silky shoulder-length blond hair. A thought occurred to me: that must have been why he was so upset with Zena the time I overheard them in the restaurant in Soho. He couldn't bear that she was sleeping with his father. The thought of Zena and Jonathan together repulsed me, but it must have been ten times worse for him.

"Wait. Did you say stepson?"

"Yes."

"How old is he?"

"Twenty-one."

I made a rapid calculation.

"So Mary must already have been pregnant when she left to go on holiday with Jonathan. She must have been pregnant when she was working with me in the lab. Who's the father?"

DCI Roberts shuffled his papers as if his patience had been exhausted.

"I don't know and it's not relevant."

"It's relevant to me," I said.

"But not to this investigation. Please sit down now, Professor. I've let you ask more than enough questions."

"What about the other woman in the room? Who was she?"

"I said, sit down."

I crossed over to the chair and made to sit down but did not. "The other woman?" I asked.

DCI Roberts let out a noise of impatience. "Mary Spicer's helper. Are you done now? Can we begin?"

My solicitor glanced at me, then quickly away, and I knew I'd gone as far as I could, so I pulled back the chair and sat.

DCI Roberts put on his reading glasses and looked at me over the top of them. "Firstly, may I say, I'm glad you're now able to talk."

"At this point," Meredith Wise cut in, "I'd like to advise my client that she is under no obligation to answer your questions." She turned to me. "You may answer with 'no comment' whenever you want."

"Only if she has something to hide," DS Hannah said in a low voice.

I shot him a look. "I have nothing to hide."

"Then you'll be happy to answer my questions," DCI Roberts said, inserting a disk into the recorder and pressing the red button. "This interview with Professor Eustacia Amelia Rose is being recorded and may be used as evidence if this goes to trial. I'm DCI Roberts. The other officer present is..."

"DS Hannah."

"Also present is…"

"Meredith Wise, solicitor."

"Good. Let's begin." He opened the file on the table in front of him. "Now, Professor, I have some good news and some bad news. Which would you like first?"

"Neither."

He coughed against his fist.

"I'm going to tell you anyway. It's too early for an autopsy, but Jonathan Wainwright's medical report states that he was poisoned. A puncture hole was found in his abdomen, so we also know how the poison was administered. However, the hospital lab didn't find a match between the poison in his blood and the *Karwinskia* berries you provided, which means he was killed with a poison yet to be identified. Our technicians will, of course, double-check the hospital's findings during the autopsy."

"Is that the good or bad news?" I asked.

He ignored this interruption. "Our lab is working through the samples we took from your garden, and we should have those results in a day or two. The good news is that you'll be staying here with us until we get those results. The bad news is that if we find a match, you'll be moved to Downview Prison to await trial."

I leaned forward. "So if there's no match, you'll release me?"

He reclined in his chair while Meredith Wise answered for him.

"If there's no match, there's no proof, and they'll have to drop the murder charge. You'll be released on bail while they either find the proof or find the murderer."

He gave his thin-lipped smile and said, "We can't ignore the lesser charges. The absence of a Poisonous Substances License, breaking and entering—"

I knew my croaking voice sounded small when I said, "That was Susan."

"—perjury."

"I'm not under oath," I said, regretting the words as soon as they left my mouth.

DCI Roberts hummed, reached for a large clear plastic bag, and put it on the table. Inside was my glove, leather pouch, watch, wallet and keys, a receipt, and the Nokia. I reached for the bag. He pulled it away.

"Why's my pouch empty?"

"The contents of the phials are being tested at the lab."

"But I can tell you what the contents are: three different concentrations of the vomit-inducing purge antidote *ipecac*, anti-digitoxin antibody medicine in case of *Digitalis* or *Nerium oleander* poisoning, and the phial of cream contains my own mixture of alcohol, hydrocortisone, calamine, and steroids in an aloe-base gel, which I've been using on my hand. And, of course, the *Karwinskia* berries."

I coughed when I'd finished speaking and covered my throat with a hand, then added, "Would you like me to write that down for you?"

"Thank you, Professor, but we'll follow procedure and let our lab technicians do their work. We can't have those clever barristers throwing a spanner in the works, can we?"

He pulled the receipt out of the bag.

"This receipt was among the items taken from you when you were processed last night. It's faded. Looks like it's been through a washing machine, but it seems you went out for a steak and"—he peered closer—"two glasses of merlot on the night Jonathan Wainwright was attacked."

I frowned, remembering now my uncharacteristic decision to go out to eat.

"Your urine sample came back this morning," he continued. "It tested positive for DMT."

In my peripheral vision, I saw Meredith Wise write something in her notebook.

"A Class A drug," he continued, turning to DS Hannah. "Are we adding the use of an illegal substance to the list of charges, Detective Sergeant?"

"We are, sir."

"I can explain," I said.

"Please do."

Meredith Wise lifted a hand. "You don't have to answer a question concerning a crime you've not been charged with unless it's connected to that charge."

"In my opinion, Ms. Wise, it most definitely is. It's my belief she perpetrated the crime while under the influence of DMT. I'm asking her to explain how it entered her system."

"Accidentally."

Ms. Wise frowned at me. "Professor, I advise you not to answer."

"I want to. It entered my system accidentally. After you came to look at my garden, I sat on the roof, holding the *Psychotria elata*. The plant from the greenhouse you so rudely described as 'obscene.'"

"Ah, yes. The one with the big red lips. I looked it up when I got back to the station. Did you know its common name is hooker's lips?"

At DS Hannah's smirk, I leaned forward and said, "If you looked it up, you'll know the leaves contain dimethyltryptamine."

There was that thin-lipped smile.

"As I was saying," I continued, "I sat for some time, thinking and, quite frankly, mourning the loss of twenty years of research, and as I sat there, I was absentmindedly rubbing one of the leaves and in the process, I released the dimethyltryptamine and accidentally ingested it." I swallowed painfully.

"Accidentally?"

"I licked my fingers without thinking."

I kept the fact that I'd then sucked on a leaf to myself. He didn't need this extra information.

He hummed out a breath. "You seem very prone to accidents."

"I can assure you, Inspector, that was the first time a drug has entered my body, and it will most definitely be the last."

"Accident prone and full of assurances." He picked up his pen and twiddled it through his fingers. "You've already assured me that you didn't kill Jonathan Wainwright."

"I didn't, and I believe the proof is in that mobile phone, if only you would look."

At this, DS Hannah clicked his tongue, a noise that I didn't understand.

"We've looked," DCI Roberts said. "There's nothing on it apart from a string of texts to and from the same unidentified number."

"What do they say?"

"We don't know. They're in code, apart from the last few." He sifted through the file, pulled out a sheet of paper, and read, "Where are you? I'm worried. This is Simone's phone. May I take a message? Who is this?"

He put the sheet on the table and looked at me before saying what I already knew.

"The Professor." He allowed a long pause. "I wonder who *the Professor* could be?"

"That's a rhetorical question. You don't have to answer," Meredith Wise cut in.

DCI Roberts nodded and looked at DS Hannah, who flipped open his notebook and read out a passage.

"On 26 June I was called to an address in NW3 by the accused. She reported the woman, whom she named 'Simone,' as missing and, based on some handwriting samples, had a theory that she'd been kidnapped. The accused then proceeded to encourage me to gain access to the woman's flat by breaking a door window. I refused. I informed the accused that she would receive a telephone call from the station in due course and asked for her mobile number. She said she didn't own a mobile phone and instead reminded me that she had already provided her landline number."

"Thank you, DS Hannah. You can stop there." He looked at me and repeated, "*She said she didn't own a mobile phone.* Did you say this?"

"I did because it's true. That's not my phone. It's Simone's... Zena's."

"So how did it come into your possession?"

I paused. The last thing I needed was a theft charge added to the list.

"I found it and kept hold of it until I could return it to her."

"Where did you find it?"

Meredith Wise held up a hand. "Unless this phone is linked to the murder charge, Inspector, I cannot see the purpose of this line of questioning."

He looked at her with irritation. "The Professor has just this minute told us the proof of Jonathan Wainwright's murder is in this mobile phone. If that's not a link, I don't know what is. So, I repeat the question: Where did you find it?"

"What does it matter where I found it?" I asked, rapping the table with my knuckles. "The important thing is that you break the code."

Incensed by his infuriating sigh, I stood and began to pace the room fast, back and forth, swinging my arms and punching the air with wild, erratic movements.

"Surely, you're not *all* half-wits," I shouted. "There must be one among you with a brain. Break the code, man. Break the damn code!"

No one was seeing the urgency. Nobody was listening. They weren't even looking at me. They were all staring at the tabletop in silence. Eventually, DCI Roberts said, "Sit down, Professor."

"You're all—"

"Half-wits," he finished for me. "We know, but we need to continue. Please sit down."

I glared at him, but he didn't look up, so, reluctantly, I sat.

"All right, we'll stop talking about the mobile. Let's put that upsetting object to one side for the moment and get back to the night in question." He nudged the receipt. "We've established that you went out for a late meal, which initially I had to question because I distinctly remember you saying you only ate food you've prepared yourself."

He looked at me over the top of his glasses. I said nothing.

"We know you left your flat, because we have statements from your neighbors."

He picked up a sheet of paper from his file, and so did Meredith Wise from hers.

"They heard: 'Bangs and crashes from your flat.' 'Thumps and bumps as you fell down the stairs.' 'Crazy humming as you careered along the road.' I presume this was when you were on your way to the restaurant."

Again, I said nothing.

"The time printed on the receipt is 11:05 p.m. Is that when you left the restaurant?"

"If that's what it says on the receipt."

"What did you do when you left?"

"I don't remember."

"Because you were under the influence of DMT."

"That wasn't a question," Meredith Wise said.

"No. It was a statement of fact. But this is a question: After leaving the restaurant, did you or did you not break your restraining order and go to the house of Jonathan Wainwright?" It had been a long time since I'd let myself think about the restraining order. At a loss, I let out a growl and shoved my chair back hard, scraping it loudly on the floor, and the strain set off a violent coughing fit, causing Meredith Wise to stand up in alarm and DCI Roberts to reach for the red button. "Interview paused."

They allowed me fifteen minutes to drink a tepid, over-brewed cup of tea. I shouldn't have lost my temper, but his ignorance was breathtaking. Why waste time on me when the

evidence was right in front of him? I was so tired. I wanted to
be home in bed, sleeping off this nightmare, but too soon, we
were back in the interview room with DCI Roberts pressing the
red button. "Interview resumed. The same people are present. I
trust you're feeling better, Professor?"

I kept my eyes low, but he took me by surprise by producing a
packet of throat lozenges and sliding them across the table.

"Now, where were we?" he asked, shuffling papers. "Ah, yes.
After leaving the restaurant, did you or did you not break your
restraining order by getting on the Tube and going to the house
of Jonathan Wainwright?"

"I never use the Tube."

"Why not?"

"I have a phobia of being under the ground. Even under the
influence of a hallucinogen, I would never put myself through
that terror."

"That's convenient. A bus, then?"

I looked up at him. "I'm assuming that if you have to ask how
I supposedly traveled to Jonathan Wainwright's house, you hav-
en't found me on CCTV? There's a camera on my street. Does it
show what time I arrived home?"

DCI Roberts shuffled papers.

"You mentioned a puncture hole in his abdomen," I continued. "Do you have the syringe? Are my prints on it?"

"I'm asking the questions," he reminded me.

"The professor's right, Chief Inspector," Meredith Wise cut in. "It seems you've run ahead of yourself. Murder charges can't be brought on hunches alone, and it appears all you have is a possible match between the poison that killed Jonathan Wainwright and samples taken from Professor Rose's burgled garden. A match that hasn't even been confirmed by your lab yet. So unless you have another line of inquiry"—she looked at her watch—"you have eleven hours and twenty-three minutes to either charge or release her." She waited for DCI Roberts to respond. When he didn't, she asked, "Do you have another line of inquiry?"

He raised his eyes to the ceiling. "Not quite yet."

"Then I think we're done here," she said, gathering her papers.

He took off his glasses, turned to DS Hannah, tapped the lab report request, and the officer left the room. Then he looked at me.

"Thank you for your time, Professor. You'll be escorted back to your cell now, but we'll speak again soon."

He went to the door to open it for the two officers who were waiting outside. Meredith Wise was packing her bag, preparing to leave, but there was more I wanted to talk about: Matilde's translation of the recordings, the fact that Jonathan was Zena's lover. Andreas.

"Wait," I said.

"What?" he asked.

21

I LAY ON MY SIDE ON THE BUNK, STARING AT THE WHITE-TILED wall, as countless suspects had done before me, wallowing in self-pity. If it weren't for Jonathan Wainwright, I wouldn't be here at all. I'd felt nothing when DCI Roberts told me he was dead, but now I was consumed with an emotion I knew to be hate. He'd stolen my love, cost me my job, destroyed my reputation and now, I was the prime suspect for his murder. And the worst thing of all was that I could have stopped him. Twenty years ago, I could have stopped it all.

He'd first crashed into our lives at a faculty party I didn't want to go to, but Mary said it would be fun. I had gone to please her. Everything I did was to please her. We'd arrived separately and, at first, I didn't see her, but then there she was in a corner, trapped by Jonathan, who had one hand on the wall beside her head, the other on his hip. I knew his type. There'd been many like him at the university, powerful men who exuded the confidence of a good education, good looks, good taste, and good breeding. His head had been close to hers. She'd been looking over his shoulder. He'd pushed a lock of hair off her forehead; she seemed not to notice. He'd leaned forward and spoke into her ear; she shrugged.

My stomach had clenched at his audacity to stand so close, and when he put his lips to her ear, fury exploded, making me march toward them. But before I could reach them, I was waylaid by the head of my department, who was Mary's PhD supervisor, expressing his pleasure that I'd decided to attend the party. I'd tried to move on, but he detained me with an irrelevant conversation in what seemed like a deliberate attempt to prevent me from reaching Mary. Half listening, I'd kept my eyes on them. Why was she smiling? Why was she pushing her hips forward like that? She must have had too much to drink and didn't know what she was doing. My head of department had taken my arm, steered me to the bar, and bought me a double whisky, which, in my eagerness to get away, I knocked back in one. But when I had turned around, Mary and Jonathan were gone.

It was after that party that he'd started hanging around the lab, asking incessant questions about my hallucinogenic blends. Volunteering himself as a test subject. He'd even started coming to the lab when Mary wasn't there, but the more I refused, the more he persisted, until it seemed to me he was developing an obsession. Perhaps if I'd relented, he wouldn't have taken it upon himself to do his own research. He wouldn't have invited Mary to Brazil, and he would not have returned home without her.

I thought again about Mary being pregnant before she went away with him, but what I couldn't understand was why he would go away with a pregnant woman. He wasn't the altruistic type. Why take her on? Unless he hadn't known. Perhaps he'd found out while they were away, and that's why he came back without her.

I remembered how I'd hounded him for weeks after he came back, demanding to know where she was, suspecting foul play. Many times, I'd gone to his house, but his response never varied. He'd stuck doggedly to his story that she'd extended her holiday to escape my neurotic infatuation and petty jealousies. He was a liar. Mary was my friend. She would have contacted me to say she was safe, if she was safe. But I'd heard nothing, and neither had any of my colleagues. Mary had completely disappeared.

It was at this time that Jonathan applied for the restraining order, prohibiting me from being within five hundred meters of his house. By the time it was granted, things had changed. One of my students had received a postcard from Mary saying that she was enjoying her time in Brazil and intended to stay. The fact that she'd chosen to share this news with someone other than me had stung at first, but I found solace in the knowledge that she was safe. And the restraining order? Well,

I was delighted by the court's decision to remove Jonathan Wainwright from my life.

There was a soft knock, and Meredith Wise entered my cell. She waited while I sat up and smoothed my hair before she spoke.

"How're you doing, Professor?"

I said nothing.

"May I sit?"

"When can I go home?"

She looked at her watch and sat on the end of the bunk. "A little over seven hours, if they don't come up with something new." She clasped her hands together and continued, "I'm sorry you had to go through that sham of an interview. Roberts knew he had nothing. He was just fishing. Your only crime on the night in question was the accidental ingestion of a Class A drug, and I doubt he'll pursue that. I've seen your urine results and I can tell you, the traces of DMT were almost negligible." She smiled brightly. "It wasn't a total waste of time, though. We now know what he doesn't have, and the longer he flounders, the sooner this will be over. All you have to do is sit tight and keep quiet for a while longer."

She patted the mattress on each side of her and stood.

"But I don't want to keep quiet. I want to assist Richard."

She paused.

"Richard? I advise you not to use his first name. Not until the real suspect is caught and convicted. In fact, I advise that if we're called back to interview, you only reply with 'no comment' from now on."

"But there's something I want to tell him. Something important."

"If there's something you want to say at this stage, say it to me."

There was annoyance in her tone. Even I could hear it. I shook my head. She sat back down.

"You have to trust me. My job is to help you." Very lightly, she touched my arm. "Let me do my job."

I looked at the soft hand on my gray shirt—the nails painted pale pink, an engagement ring on her thin finger—and changed my mind.

"All right, then. DCI Roberts doesn't know Zena was Jonathan Wainwright's lover. He couldn't find her when she was missing because she was using a different name. Why would the lover of a murder victim disguise her identity? Unless she was connected with his death?"

"Connected how?"

"I don't know, but I believe the answer is on that mobile phone. Once DCI Roberts cracks the code, we'll know for sure."

"I wouldn't hold your breath on that. He seems fixed on another line of inquiry."

I inhaled. "Me."

"Yes. He lost you last time. He's determined not to lose you again."

"You know about last time?"

"Of course. I've done the reading. I know all about the incident." There was that word again. *Incident.* The word that sent a wave of shame through me every time I heard it—but not this time. For some reason, hearing it from her made me feel hopeful that something could change. I turned toward her and forced myself to meet her eyes.

"Then you will have read that I deliberately contaminated my lab because I was under severe mental strain after losing my father. It will have said that I either intentionally set out to harm the students and lab technicians or it was an attempt to harm myself."

Her eyelids fluttered but she didn't look away.

"I want to assure you that I did not deliberately contaminate my lab. I don't know how it happened, but it wasn't me."

"Loss can manifest in many different ways," she said quietly.

I pursed my lips. "You asked me to trust you. I will do that if you trust me. I didn't do it. Even accidentally, I didn't do it."

She was silent, and I knew she was weighing the evidence against the word of a person who may or may not be reliable.

"I didn't do it," I said again, looking straight into her eyes.

She gave a brief smile and nodded. "Well, then, if that's the case, it's a great shame, because if you didn't do it, you took the fall for whoever did."

I sighed at her noncommittal answer and looked away.

"In any event," she said, standing again, "I think you can forget about DCI Roberts being interested in cracking that code."

"There may be another way," I said quickly, to stop her leaving. "Zena's neighbor has recordings of her conversations with a man who visited her. Andreas. Her husband. I've listened to them. A colleague translated the Portuguese for me. They speak about an English Professor and a mass murder using coyotillo berries."

"What are coyotillo berries?"

"The most toxic part of the *Karwinskia* plant."

She took a folder from her bag. "The *Karwinskia* was the plant stolen from your garden but not the one that killed Jonathan Wainwright."

"Correct, although I believe other plants were stolen, *Conium maculatum, Aconitum napellus, Brugmansia.*"

"You've lost me," she said, shaking her head.

"Hemlock, wolfsbane, angel's trumpet. All of these contain toxins that present the same symptoms as Jonathan's, and when I do my inventory, I'll know for sure."

She fell silent while she took this in. "Does DCI Roberts know about these other plants?"

"Not yet."

"Then I suggest we keep this to ourselves for now because if the lab finds a match with any of them, you'll be back under suspicion."

I looked at her. "That's withholding evidence."

"Not evidence—information."

"Perjury, then."

She smiled. "I said, 'for now.' Let's give DCI Roberts time to follow his current line of inquiry, and while he's doing that, I'm going to pay Zena's neighbor a visit."

At a quarter to ten, DCI Roberts knocked on the cell door and walked in. He looked heavy with exhaustion and stood with his hands in his pockets, leaning back against the wall.

"Time's up," he said, pulling the box of antibiotics from his pocket and handing them to me. "You're free to go."

He immediately turned to leave, but I stopped him with a question. "Did you find me on CCTV?"

He gave me the smile of a defeated man. "We did. You returned home at 11:15 p.m. You didn't go out again until I came to collect you the following morning."

Again, I prevented him from leaving. "Have the lab results come back?"

"We're expecting them in a day or two, so you may well be back."

"Even though you've confirmed my alibi?"

His head and shoulders dropped despondently. "You may well be back…to help us."

"Good," I said, standing and putting on my jacket. "I want to help. I want to assist in any way I can. I am an—"

"—expert, after all," he finished for me, shaking his head. "I'll be in touch, Professor. DS Hannah will take you to the front desk to collect your belongings."

"But you'll keep the mobile phone so you can work on the code?"

"Yes, we're keeping the phone." He went to the door.

"Wait," I said. "I have one last question."

DCI Roberts sighed and rested a hand on the doorpost.

"Now that Jonathan's dead, will the restraining order be lifted?"

Slowly, he turned around, his large eyebrows moving upward.

"I'm sure my solicitor will tell me if you'd rather not," I added. "I just thought I'd ask, as I have you here."

"As you have me here," he repeated, then let out a half-hearted laugh. "The restraining order was lifted years ago."

I frowned. "Then why did you ask if I'd breached it?"

There was that thin-lipped smile again.

"For your reaction."

22

I SHOULDN'T HAVE BEEN SURPRISED THAT DCI ROBERTS hadn't told me the restraining order had been lifted. I knew his tactics. I knew he was underhanded. But it wasn't only him. Meredith Wise was just as bad, asking me to withhold information. It seemed that the justice system was a game of poker, full of bluff and double bluff. Full of hunches and gut feelings. Full of things I didn't understand. I looked at my desk. The forensics team obviously hadn't been in here, because Zena's things were undisturbed. I stroked the camisole, thinking that there was no need for them now because, although I still didn't know where she'd been, I accepted that she probably hadn't been kidnapped and that DCI Roberts was probably right: she'd gotten into the car voluntarily and was driven away by a friend. The same friend she'd then probably chosen to stay with. What I'd seen—the forceful way she was bundled into the car—what I'd

heard—"Keep an eye on her. Do not let her leave."—was probably mistaken supposition.

Determined not to let faulty logic or mistaken supposition
get the better of me again, I pulled several sheets from a ream of
paper and wrote two names on the top one: Foxglove—Jonathan
Wainwright. Then I pinned the sheet of paper to the wall. I continued writing names until I had pinned up a rough circle of
pages: Jimsonweed—Sebastian. Castor—Andreas. Psycho—
Zena. False Hellebore—? Helper—? Then I wrote "Mary" on
the final sheet and added it to the circle.

I took a ball of string from my desk drawer and connected
Jonathan's name to Zena, Sebastian, and Mary. I connected Mary
to Helper, Jonathan, and Sebastian. I connected Zena to Jonathan,
Sebastian, False Hellebore, and Andreas. I connected Andreas to
Zena, then I stood back and was struck by how many lines of string
there were. How many connections among this group of people.

The sudden sound of the telephone made me jump. I waited
for it to go to the answering machine, but as soon as I heard the
voice, I picked it up.

"Professor? It's Meredith Wise. I hear you've been released.
Are you okay?"

"I'm perfectly well." I cleared my throat. My voice still
sounded strange. "Did you get the recordings from Susan?"

"I did. That's why I'm ringing. She said there's a recording you
haven't heard yet. The one she made the night you were strangled?"

I remembered DS Hannah and Susan listening to a recording when I came to, after Andreas had attacked me. It must have been this one.

"I got everything translated and transcribed," she continued. "But because you've been released without charge, I'm no longer acting as your solicitor, so I thought I'd hand them over to you. I would've emailed them, but I couldn't find an address. I had to go old-school. The hard copies are being couriered to you now."

"Shouldn't you give them to the police?"

There was a pause.

"I suspect DCI Roberts may just put them at the back of the file. I'm going to leave this with you. Give them to him if you feel you must. Or don't."

"You're asking me to withhold information again?"

"I'm not asking anything. I'm no longer your solicitor. All I'm doing is giving you the transcripts to do with as you will." She paused again. "Whatever you decide, though, Professor, I wish you the very best of luck."

❦

When they arrived, I spread the translations over the kitchen table. There was only one I was interested in—the recording of the night Andreas had attacked me. In particular, his and Zena's conversation after I'd passed out. It began with a stream of swear words from him because Zena had cut his arm to make him let go of me. She was telling him to go to hospital to have it stitched. He was telling her not to be stupid. I shuddered at the thought that he could have been at the hospital at the same time as me. Maybe even in the next cubicle. I turned the page. He asked her where she'd been. She said Sebastian's. She hadn't wanted to be there, but they'd told her Andreas was dangerous and she had to stay away from him.

So, she *had* been at Sebastian's. She *had* escaped through the window. I didn't understand why she hadn't said so when I questioned her. It was as if she hadn't listened to a word I'd said. I turned the next page and found what I was looking for. Zena was saying that I wasn't the English Professor because she knew who it was—she'd known all along. He was demanding she tell him. She wouldn't. She was asking him to trust her because she had a plan. It appeared they left the house then, because the transcript ended with the words "front door slams."

I walked down the hall to my desk, wrote another name on another piece of paper, and pinned it to the wall in the middle of the circle. The English Professor—? I connected this name to Zena and Andreas and sat down.

I'm not sure how long I spent staring at the wall, but it was dark by the time I yawned, stretched my arms wide, and stood up. I was tired. It was late, but still, I went up to the roof. There was just enough light to see the boundary railings and the shadowed humps of scattered vegetation. Carefully, I walked to the greenhouse—taking care not to touch any plant matter—to water the seed tray containing the broke-back root cuttings and was disappointed to see that there were no green shoots.

On the floor in front of the canvas chair was the *Psychotria elata*. I went to it, sat down, and nudged it with my foot.

"The trouble you got me in," I murmured.

The telescope was still angled toward Zena's house. The forensics team would have seen it, may have even looked through the eyepiece and seen whose house it was trained on. The word voyeur sprang to mind, making me cringe.

Way off in the distance, somewhere high above the Heath, a summer storm rumbled, but the sky above was clear. I sat in the canvas chair, staring at the stars, waiting for the first drops of rain, and when they finally came, I carefully made my way down the ladder. In the kitchen, the porridge I'd abandoned on the day the forensics team came was still in the saucepan. I scraped the congealed mess into the bin and went through to the bathroom to see the inch of water still in the bath. I pulled the plug and watched it drain away. How long ago that morning now seemed. How much had happened since.

I took off my glasses and moved close to the mirror. The bruising around my eye had subsided to a dull brown, but, lifting my chin, I could see there were still red marks on my neck from the pressure of Andreas's fingers. Briefly, I wondered where he was now. And where was Zena?

Too tired to go to bed, I wandered into the front room and stood at the window.

"Long gone, I hope," I said, looking out into the deserted street. A movement caught my eye. There, at the bottom of the road, near the lamppost, a figure was hunched at the edge of the pool of lamplight. My breath caught in my chest at the sight of it, and I lifted a hand to my throat, but then a large adult fox stepped forward, its tail down, its ears pricked up, and scampered across the road and through the gate into the communal gardens. I sensed a benign presence nearby. It whispered in my ear with Father's voice.

Don't be afraid of shadows, Eyebright. Grasp them tight and pull them into the light, and you'll see they're nothing but dust.

It made me run a hand across the back of my neck and mutter, "Exhaustion...or insanity."

On the way to my bedroom, I stopped in front of the photograph of Father and looked at him sitting there, quietly reading his book.

"You'd've had this whole thing solved in a jiffy, wouldn't you?" I knocked the glass above his face with a knuckle. "You old rogue."

In the bedroom, I pulled the curtains, then carefully folded Father's suit and placed it on the wooden chair beside the door. "Don't be afraid of shadows," I said, and as the digital clock clicked over to midnight, I fell into a dreamless sleep.

23

WHEN I WOKE THE NEXT MORNING, I DIDN'T BEGIN MY USUAL routine but stayed where I was, listening to the trills, whistles, and chirrups of a black bird in the communal garden, appreciating the complexity of its song. Dawn was breaking through the gap between the curtains, sending a cleansing wash of luminosity across the carpet. I'd never noticed the clarity of this light before. The digital clock read 5:00 a.m., but I lay dozing for another hour, dipping in and out of sleep. At six, I rose and opened the window, drew a breath, filling my lungs with fresh air, and looked out over the street.

There was movement behind the windows of the apartment block opposite, early commuters preparing for work, families waking their children for school. The neighbors beginning their morning routines. I watched a young couple emerge from the front door of their block, kiss, then go their separate ways. A little farther down the road, a smartly dressed woman with a briefcase carried a steaming mug to her car, a piece of toast in her mouth. For the first time, I didn't see these people as mere subjects for an observational study. I now appreciated that they were individuals with their own stories, relationships, problems. They were real people living their lives.

At six thirty, I changed into overalls, collected sample bags and a fresh notebook, and climbed the ladder. In the daylight, the garden looked pitiful, but I didn't pause for reflection. For three hours, I carefully catalogued each salvageable remnant before sealing it in a bag and storing it in the greenhouse; then I meticulously disinfected every inch of the roof with cotton swabs, taking care to neutralize any residual toxicity. And finally, I burned the contaminated swabs and remaining vegetation in my brazier. It was arduous work, and after I'd finished, I sat on the canvas chair to study my notes. It was as I'd suspected: the three plants that caused the same symptoms as the one that killed Jonathan Wainwright were missing. I'd have to cross-check in greater detail, but it also seemed that one or two others had been stolen as well. I stood and made my way down the ladder. It was imperative that I tell DCI Roberts straightaway.

He wasn't at the station when I arrived. The duty officer made me wait in the lobby even though I'd told him I was assisting with a very important case and should be allowed to wait in his office. I eyed the other people waiting with me. There were too many of them. They were making me uncomfortable. Half an hour later, he finally arrived but didn't seem particularly pleased to see me.

"I have the list of the other plants that were stolen from my collection," I said as we went into his office.

He put an evidence bag on his desk. "And I have something I'd like you to look at as well."

"Oh?"

He took off his jacket, hung it on the back of his chair, and sat heavily. "I've just been to see Mary Spicer."

"Oh?" I said again, my pulse quickening.

"We had an interesting conversation. No, interesting's the wrong word. It was more an *evasive* conversation. She didn't seem too keen on answering my questions. A bit like you," he said, and smiled.

"What did she say?"

"Witness statements are confidential. I just need your help with some plant-matter identification." He waved a hand at the bag on the desk. "Mary found this hidden in the garden shed. It'll go to the lab, but as you're here, I could do with a first impression."

I gave him a cool look. "I'll be happy to do that for you, right after you've told me what she said."

For some unfathomable reason, he laughed and leaned back in his chair.

"I'm now assisting with this case," I reminded him. "I should have full disclosure of all the facts."

He didn't speak for a long time but sat with his head tilted back against his chair, looking at me down his nose. Eventually, he straightened.

"You're right. Who knows, a fresh pair of eyes might be just what we need."

He took his notepad from his jacket pocket and turned to a page.

"Okay, so we started with the night of Jonathan Wainwright's attack. She was in bed at the time and had just fallen asleep. She said she was woken by the sound of someone knocking on the front door. She checked the time. It was 9:45 p.m."

He flipped the page.

"She couldn't get out of bed to answer the door because Jonathan had left the wheelchair too far away for her to reach when he'd helped her to bed. He was asleep on the sofa in the next room. Actually, she said he was 'passed out' on the sofa because he was 'stinking drunk.' It took several more knocks before he roused himself enough to answer the door—or, in her words, 'stagger to the door.' She said she heard a muted conversation and assumed he'd gone into the front garden to talk to the visitor. She then heard a crash as if the dustbin lid had been knocked off, and several thumps as if someone or something was being thrown against the front door."

"There was a fight?" I asked.

"Yes, sounds like he put up a fight. She then heard him come back into the house and go into the front room—she assumed to go back to sleep on the sofa. She thought he was fine and went back to sleep. She said it wasn't until her helper found him unconscious the next morning that she realized something was wrong. That's when they called an ambulance."

"What time did they do that?"

He flipped another page. "Ten o'clock."

"So the poison was in his system for over twelve hours before he reached the hospital."

I turned my head to look out his office window.

After a pause, he asked, "If he'd got there sooner, could he have survived?"

"Possibly. It depends on the toxin."

He riffled through the papers on his desk until he found the one he was looking for.

"His autopsy was yesterday, but I don't have those results yet. I do have the toxicity report, though. Here."

He handed me the page and I scanned it quickly.

"Abrin. The poison found in the seeds of *Abrus precatorius*, common names jequirity bean, deadly crab's eye, rosary pea—depending on which part of the world you come from." I looked up. "This is a highly toxic concentration, but yes, he could have survived."

"There's an antidote?"

"Yes."

He let out a rush of air and rubbed his face with both hands. "Let's just… Let's just keep this to ourselves for now."

He didn't seem in any hurry to continue, but I was impatient to know about the bag on the desk.

"Tell me about that," I said, pointing at it.

"Ah, now, this comes with a bit of a story. Mary has a theory that Jonathan may not have been poisoned by the mysterious visitor but that he brewed up some kind of potion with the stuff in that bag, injected himself with it, and accidentally overdosed."

"Then where's the syringe?"

"She couldn't explain the lack of a syringe."

I shook my head. "Why does she want to make it look like an accident?" Then I considered this for a moment before adding, "To protect the murderer?"

He made a humming sound. "No, I don't think so. I've seen this before. It's a coping mechanism because she can't accept the fact that he was murdered."

A coping mechanism. I'd never heard of the term. It certainly wasn't anything I'd experienced. I adjusted the cuffs of Father's suit jacket and asked, "Did she say what was in the bag?"

"Samples he'd collected during his travels around South America. He was obsessed with naturally occurring hallucinogens. She said he went on a plant-finding trip every summer, usually with a student. He was going to write a book about it but never got around to starting. She said he'd planned a trip for this summer but had had an argument with the student he was going to take, so canceled it. Apparently, the argument made him so depressed that he'd started drinking heavily. She told me she thought he was having an affair with the student." He inhaled deeply. "I got the impression there wasn't much love in that marriage."

The image of the two shapes in Zena's bed moving rhythmically, the glimpse of her perfect breast, flashed across my mind. I shook my head vigorously to get rid of the revolting thought.

He didn't speak for a while, and I knew he was watching me, but eventually, he pushed the bag across the table and said, "Here, open it. Take a sniff. Tell me what you think's in it."

"I beg your pardon?" I gasped, appalled by the suggestion. "You want me to expose myself to the toxin that might have killed him?"

"That's just Mary Spicer's theory."

"And if she's right?"

He gave his thin-lipped smile. "Fair enough. We'll leave it to the lab technicians. Listen—his funeral's tomorrow afternoon. Will you come with me?"

24

IT WAS A WHILE BEFORE I NOTICED THE FLASHING LIGHT ON my answering machine. I'd been too absorbed mulling over DCI Roberts's suggestion of accompanying him to Jonathan's funeral. He'd worked at UCL a long time. There were bound to be many people attending who would know me. It crossed my mind to go in disguise, to forego the suit just this once, but perhaps there would be so many people that I could blend into the background. Hide in the periphery. It was only when I was about to go up to the roof to water the root cuttings that I noticed the answering machine. I pressed the button.

Tonight, usual time, usual place. Payment as arranged.

With all that had been happening, I'd completely forgotten about this purchase. Not so long ago, the sound of the courier's voice would have sent trills of excitement through me, but I no longer had a plant collection. All I had were a few root cuttings that may or may not take and the plant remnants I'd rescued when I'd cleared the garden. What was the point of adding to something I no longer had? Good sense was telling me to ignore the message; the demon inside was saying the opposite. I let out a growl of indecision, walked away from the answering machine, and climbed up the ladder.

It was a shock to see the roof swept bare, even though I knew it would be. There was no longer any need for overalls, gloves, or protective footwear. No more use for the spray bottles or propagation brushes. I glanced at the greenhouse. It was unlikely any of the salvaged plant remnants had survived, but if they had, I decided I would begin again. If not, I wouldn't. I slipped on a pair of gloves and began to open bags. The samples inside the first three were black and shriveled, but in the fourth, one bud deep within a nest of dead roots appeared to be plump and white. I scooped a peat and horticultural sand mix into a pot, snipped the root, and dipped it in hormone powder, carefully cocooned it in the compost mix, and dampened it with distilled water. The chances of it surviving were slim, but it was enough to make my decision. I took off the gloves, closed the greenhouse door, and went downstairs for Father's waxed overcoat.

At the pergola, I waited for the courier to leave; then, with the package safe in my pocket, I headed back to the path. After fifty meters or so, I became aware of a tingle of apprehension. I was usually at ease with the snaps and rustles around me, but something felt different this time. Something felt threatening. My senses sharpened. I inclined my head to listen. The sounds of disturbed undergrowth were not diminishing as I walked away from the Heath, and every now and then, I was sure I could hear soft footfalls. Someone was following me.

With a racing heart, I stopped walking. The sounds behind me stopped as well. Slowly, I turned around, but the path was deserted. I stood still, staring hard in the direction I'd come until my eyes watered from the effort. All was silent. Whoever was following me must be standing as still as I was. By a stroke of luck, a cloud moved across the moon, plunging the path into darkness, and I took the opportunity to make a dash for the relative safety of the lit road.

Halfway down the hill toward home, I felt the prickle across the back of my neck again. I turned around. No one was there. I stepped into the center of the road for a better view—there, movement in the trees lining the pavement. I squinted and focused on that point, but there was only a dense tangle of brambles and the overhanging leaf-laden branches of a copper beech tree.

I inhaled deeply through my nose, said aloud, "Don't be afraid of the shadows, Eustacia," and continued walking.

Seconds later, a hand clapped over my mouth, an arm circled my chest, and I was dragged down onto my back. Eyes wide with panic, I looked up at the man kneeling over me, his head swathed in moonlight.

There were places to get a drink in Hampstead after midnight if one knew where to find them; restaurant lock-ins, basement bars. The kinds of places one only frequented if one knew the manager. The Brazilian manager, say.

This one was in the basement of a large stucco-fronted residential house, on a quiet road off the high street. Its signage was subtle, and from the staircase down to its unassuming front door was covered with ivy. There were few tables inside and fewer customers: a couple in a corner absorbed with each other and oblivious to their surroundings, a man talking quietly in another language to the bartender, and me in Father's waxed coat, sitting alone at a table against the wall. I was uncomfortable. I felt incongruous. My eyes were darting back and forth, judging the distance between my table and the exit. It was warm inside the bar, but I didn't take off the coat, and I repeatedly touched the outside of the pocket containing the package, like a nervous tic.

Andreas finished talking to the bartender, placed a glass on the table in front of me, took off his baseball cap, and hung it on the back of his chair.

I looked at the glass. "What's this?"

"What you asked for: water," he replied.

"I asked for sparkling water."

He shrugged, sat down opposite me, and filled his glass from a bottle of red liquid. "Water is water."

My body tensed at the proximity. This man had attacked Zena, had strangled me, and—real or imagined—had been occupying the shadows that had haunted me for weeks. I flicked a glance at the freshly healed scar that ran from his temple, across his cheek, cutting through the stubble to his chin. He exuded a dark menace, the stuff of nightmares. Yet here I was, having a drink with him.

"I asked for sparkling water," I repeated.

He lifted the bottle.

"You want some cachaça?"

I thought of the double whisky my head of department had bought me at that party twenty years before. The drink that had prevented me from reaching Mary in time to stop Jonathan from stealing her from me. The drink that had made me vow I would never touch alcohol again.

"No. The last time I had a drink, something bad happened," I replied flatly.

For some incomprehensible reason, this made him roar with laughter.

"You are funny," he said, signaling the bartender to bring another glass. "It is the same for us all. We are jolly when we begin but mean by the end. The trick is to know when to stop, no?"

I made to protest, but the bartender was already on his way.

He winked at me as he put the glass on the table, which was puzzling. Andreas filled my glass from his bottle and saluted me with his own. I took a sip of water.

"You've been following me. Not just now. You've been following me for a while," I said.

"Yes. At first, because I thought you were someone else, and then because I was curious about you. I wanted to know why Zena was interested in you, and now I do. You are a very unusual woman. Very cool."

"Cool?"

"Yes, cool. The way you speak, the vintage suit, your hair… the Rolex. You are very stylish."

I tugged down my coat sleeve to cover Father's watch. "I have no idea what you mean."

I was nervous. Or perhaps unnerved. I picked up the water, took a large gulp, and absentmindedly touched my neck.

"I apologize for that," he said, waving a hand in front of his own throat. "I lose control when I am angry. I am—how do you say it—*hot-headed*. It was lucky Zena was there to stop me."

With an unpleasant shiver, I thought that if only that tiny shred of root had not been alive, I could be at home now, my front door safely closed and bolted. But there had been something about the way Andreas knelt over me, as if he was praying or making an offering, that had made me agree to go to the bar with him. And he *was* making an offering of sorts—the offer of an explanation. I glanced at him quickly. He was watching me, a small smile playing on his lips.

"Well?" I said, shifting uncomfortably. "I haven't got all night. You brought me here to tell me something."

He leaned forward, rested his elbows on the table, and laced his fingers.

"I did, but nothing comes for free. I give you something, you give me something. That is how it works, no?"

An arm of his sunglasses was tucked into his shirt opening, and the weight of it revealed his chest hair. I averted my eyes.

"I have nothing to give you."

"I think you do."

I tugged my sleeve farther over the Rolex. "What could I possibly have that you would want?"

He paused before answering. "Zena."

"Zena?" I asked, eyebrows raised. "I don't have her."

The table moved as he leaned forward. I lifted my eyes and fixed them on the wall behind his shoulder.

"You know what I mean. Where is she?"

"How should I know?"

He shifted his chair so that he was in my sight line. I shifted my gaze.

"I can assure you, I don't know where Zena is, and I don't know if she's with the English Professor either."

At this, his body jolted upright. "What do you know about the English Professor?"

I chose my words carefully. "Only that it's not me."

He sank back in his seat, tutting and mumbling, and I kept my eyes fixed on the wall.

"You are a tricky one," he said. "You show nothing. What is the expression in English? *Poker face*? Yes, you have a poker face. So difficult to read. So dangerous."

"I'm no threat to you. I'm nobody."

"Nobody. Ha! You are funny."

I finished the water. "If I was Zena, I would've gone home to Brazil. If you want to find her, you should do the same."

"It is not so simple," he said.

"Surely it's as simple as getting on a plane?"

"No. They will not allow me back."

"Why?"

It was several seconds before he answered.

"Oh... What the hell. Why not? Okay, I will tell you." He leaned forward again and inhaled deeply. "Zena and me, we are from São Paulo. When I first saw her, it was like, *wow*—an explosion, you know? She was so beautiful. I fell for her totally, but she was not so into me. She was getting over someone else and not looking for a *relacionamento de recuperação*. She was into wellness. Yoga, meditation, detox. That kind of thing. She set up a wellness center on the coast, and it took up all her time. It was not my thing, but I wanted to see her, so I trained as a meditation therapist and asked for a job."

I let out an unexpected guffaw.

"I know what you are thinking. How can an angry man teach meditation? You have to understand, I was not always like this. I was not always so angry." He shook his head. "Anyway, Zena took me on because my English is good and she wanted more foreign clients. For a long time, we worked together, and slowly the business grew. People came from all over the world: Australia, America, Canada, Britain. Everything was going well. Then Raul had this fantastic idea to make more money, and Zena said yes and that was—how do you say?—*the beginning of the end*."

"Who's Raul?"

"Zena's brother. Have you heard of ayahuasca?"

"Of course. I'm a botanist."

"Raul said he had a friend from Peru who knew someone who would supply the leaves for below market price. Someone called the English Professor. He said his friend had shown him how to make the tea and lead the sessions. He was so confident, so convinced this was going to make us rich. I did not want anything to do with ayahuasca. I did not want the shouting and the crying and the vomiting. I wanted the center to be a calm, quiet place."

He finished his drink and stared at the empty glass.

"Go on," I said, sliding my untouched cachaça to him.

"So, just like that, Raul becomes an ayahuasca shaman, and he holds his first session using the brew from the English Professor. Nothing happened at first. Nobody hallucinated. Nobody cried, nobody shouted or vomited. We thought he had been scammed. The clients thought *they* had been scammed, so Raul upped the dose and upped the dose again until people started to get sick. Ten. We had ten people sick. And then…five of them died." He dropped his head and said in a cracking voice, "I tried to talk them out of it. Believe me, I really tried. But they did not listen." Then he slumped back, wiped an eye, and lifted his hand. "I need one minute."

When I was a child, Father had made me aware of the wide gamut of emotional states so I could learn to simulate a suitable response. Some I understood: hate, anger. Others were a mystery. Remorse belonged in the mystery group. I waited one second, then asked, "What were their symptoms?"

He sniffed deeply.

"They could not move. It was hard for them to breathe. They could not fill their lungs. Eventually, five of them stopped trying. Of the rest, two were paralyzed and three recovered. Zena closed the business, but it did not stop the lawsuits from the victims' families, or the legal letters from the legitimate ayahuasca retreats, or the threats of violence." He touched his scar. "It was a bad, bad time. I told Zena to go stay with the English family while I sorted out the mess, but by the time I was ready to join her, she'd already left to come here."

"The English family?"

"A woman and her son. They were staying at a house in Ubatuba. I never met the kid's father. He was only there in the summer." His shoulders slumped. "Anyway, until I clear my name, I can't go back."

"What about Raul's friend from Peru?"

"Disappeared. Puff. Just like smoke."

"And he didn't tell Raul who the English Professor was before he disappeared?"

"No." He picked up the bottle and looked at the label. "You know something? For a while now, I have been thinking maybe this English Professor does not exist. Maybe he is just a phantasma."

He put the bottle back down and sighed, and a wave of anger pulsed through me.

"If you don't think he exists, why bother stealing plants from my garden and destroying the rest?"

He looked up. "*Que?*"

"The vandalization of my garden. The decimation of my collection—which, by the way, took twenty years to build."

"Your garden has been destroyed? The one on the roof?"

"At least you're not denying its existence."

"I knew it existed. I did not know it was destroyed. Who did it?"

I looked at him pointedly, looked away, looked back again.

"Oh yes, I forgot. It was me." He shrugged one shoulder and

continued, "Why would I steal your plants? I am staying in a tiny room, in a cheap hostel above a seedy cachaça bar in Soho. Where would I put them? What would I do with them?"

I made a sound of incredulity. "Are you stupid? They're highly toxic. You'd murder someone with them."

Anger flashed across his face at the insult. "I would not use a plant to murder someone. There are easier ways. Anyway, I am not here to kill."

I thought of his death threat, of his hands around my neck.

"I just want to find the English Professor. Clear my name and get my life back... Get my wife back."

At my cringe, he said, "You think I am too old for her, don't you? You think I am too ugly to be with someone as beautiful as Zena. Believe it or not, I used to be very good-looking. I was very popular with women...before all the trouble."

He shook his head sadly, gathered his glass with both hands, and deflated back into his chair. "You think I am tragic, don't you? Tragedy can look like comedy from afar, no? You are probably laughing at me right now."

I sat very still, my hands clasped together, too preoccupied with my own thoughts to pay much attention to what he was saying. I knew a murderer wouldn't give an honest answer to the question I was about to ask, but I asked it anyway.

"Did you kill Jonathan Wainwright?"

Without a flicker of reaction, he replied, "Who is he?"

"He was…"

I paused. I'd assumed he must have found out about Zena and Jonathan, and that was why he'd been so angry with her on the night he strangled me. Subtlety was not my strong point. Neither was tact, but I knew about discretion.

"…a lecturer at the university Zena attended."

A light switched on behind his eyes as he made the connection.

"The guy she cooked meals for? The one with the disabled wife?"

"Yes."

"Someone killed him? Man, that is tough. Poor guy."

I had no reason to believe him. He was a violent man, and yet he seemed genuinely surprised.

"How did he die?"

"He was poisoned."

Andreas narrowed his eyes. "Oh, I get it. I stole the plants from your garden and used them to poison some guy I only met for two minutes. Why would I do that?"

"I don't know. You tell me."

"Listen, it is like I told you. I am here to find the English Professor and clear my name. I am not here to kill some guy Zena cooked pity dinners for because his wife was not giving him any at home."

He paused to absorb the words he'd just spoken, and when comprehension hit, the light behind his eyes burst into flames.

Seething with rage, he slammed both fists on the table, jumped to his feet, kicked over his chair, and threw his glass across the room. Straightaway, the bartender rushed forward and grabbed his flailing fists, and in the midst of the shouting and the struggling, I stood calmly and left the bar.

25

THERE WAS A CONSTANT STREAM OF PEOPLE WALKING UP the path from the carpark to the church for Jonathan's funeral, most of whom I presumed to be his Southside Arts colleagues but also many I recognized from UCL. I was standing in the graveyard, hiding underneath a yew tree, waiting for DCI Roberts. Mary and Sebastian were already inside the church. I'd seen them arrive with Mary's helper. They didn't see me.

"You're here," DCI Roberts said, suddenly appearing beside me, stating the obvious.

"Isn't it a bit soon for the funeral?" I asked. "He only died a few days ago."

"They requested he be buried straight after the autopsy, and the coroner gave the go-ahead. They did seem in a bit of a hurry, though. Shall we go in?"

I put a hand on his arm to stop him. "Not yet. Let's wait till the last minute."

He looked down at my hand, his eyebrows raised, so I snatched it away.

"Your hand looks better," he said. "Your face too." Again, he was stating the obvious.

The final trickle of guests entered the church, and as the usher was about to close the doors, I said, "Come on. Let's go."

I felt a chill the moment we stepped inside, and not because it was cold. It was the muted light through the stained-glass windows, the dusty, ancient smell, the ethereal organ music. We found an empty pew right at the back, from where we could see the whole congregation. Mary was sitting in her wheelchair in the aisle at the front. She must have felt uncomfortable, sticking out from the crowd like that. She must have hated all those pitying eyes on her.

She looked so frail, hunched over in her chair. Nothing like the straight-backed, confident woman I'd known. I took in her drab black trouser suit, contrasting so severely with her gray hair, and thought that she would never have worn anything so dour when we were young. She'd always worn skirts, dresses, pretty blouses in bright, optimistic colors. I'd tried my hardest to emulate her. I couldn't, of course. Even though I wore my hair in the same style, did my makeup the same way, and bought my clothes at the same stores as her, I couldn't, because she was beautiful and I wasn't. I patted my hair, smoothed the front of my jacket, and fixed my eyes on the vicar high up in the pulpit. It was a simple service. Sebastian's eulogy brought tears and laughter, even though he was patently drunk. He did a fine job of listing Jonathan's failings while appearing to reminisce about the good times. He dressed Jonathan's long absences when he was a child as opportunities to misbehave and get away with it.

Jonathan's compensation gifts when he finally showed up were invitations to exhort even more, and the emotional blackmail he'd piled on Jonathan for never being around as schoolboy japes. I wasn't surprised that he was drunk. Nor that he was wearing the same brown corduroy trousers and purple T-shirt I'd seen him in before. I was surprised, however, when he said he'd only just found out Jonathan was his stepfather after spending his entire life thinking he was his son. His voice sounded flat when he said this, as if he didn't care. But I think he did. And judging by the strange noise Mary made that echoed around the church when he said it, I think she did too.

Perhaps the shock of this news was the reason he drank so much for someone so young. Perhaps it was also why he'd burned out the eyes in his portrait of Jonathan. I thought of the time on the Tube when I'd been standing on the other side of the glass partition, looking down at him, and remembered how vulnerable he'd seemed. How fragile.

Father told me about sympathy and empathy. They were

certainly concepts I understood intellectually but had never felt emotionally. However, watching Sebastian at the lectern, pretending he didn't care about the words he was saying, made me feel something unfamiliar. Something sorrowful. What was even more curious was that, when Sebastian returned to his seat, DCI Roberts leaned toward me and asked in a low voice if I was all right. He asked again as we slipped out of the church early to find a discreet place to stand near the grave. I ignored him both times.

While we waited, I bent to pick up a soft red yew-tree berry and held it in the palm of my hand. The black seed within the red pulp contains taxine glycosides, the cardiotoxic chemicals that cause heart failure, and a memory popped into my head of putting one in my mouth when I was a small child to suck off the sweet-tasting red pulp and Father slapping me hard on the back of the head to make me spit it out. I squashed it between my thumb and forefinger, popping out the seed, and wiped my hand on my trouser leg.

It took a while for the pallbearers to slowly carry the coffin to the graveside and longer for everyone to gather. Mary and Sebastian were closest to the grave. They looked pale and ill. I let my gaze drift over the crowd and, with a shock, found someone I wasn't expecting to see. There, at the back, was Zena, looking as vibrant and beautiful as the first time I saw her through the telescope, her sleek black hair hanging loose, the corners of her full red lips slightly turned down to reflect the occasion. My breath caught in my chest. I hadn't seen her since the night Andreas had strangled me. I wanted to rush to her, drop to my knees, and thank her for saving my life. I took a step forward to do just that but stopped when she moved to rest her head on the shoulder of the man standing next to her. *False Hellebore.*

When I saw them together like this, it was blatantly obvious they were related, and straightaway I knew False Hellebore was her brother, Raul. The one who had killed those people in Brazil. But he was so young. Strong-looking and muscular, sure, but with the lack of stubble and in the white shirt and tie, he could have been a schoolboy in uniform. I couldn't believe he was capable of doing those things Andreas had said.

I don't know why I didn't point them out to DCI Roberts, but something kept me from speaking. Perhaps it was because I didn't want him crashing in before I'd had a chance to think. In any event, he was moving away to find a place closer to Mary so that he could wait at a respectful distance for the other mourners to trickle away before approaching her. I stayed where I was, hidden beneath the tree. I didn't want Mary to see me. I wasn't ready.

She remained alone by the graveside long after everyone had gone, sitting so still that a robin flew down and perched on Jonathan's gravestone less than a foot away. DCI Roberts stood motionless as well, a few meters away. The bird began to sing, and this must have roused her, because she gripped the wheels of her chair and tried to turn them, but they were caught in a rut of freshly turned soil. Straightaway, DCI Roberts was by her side.

"Hello again, Mrs. Wainwright. Can I help you?"

"Please," she said, without looking up. "This damn chair."

He took hold of the handles and pushed her over the uneven grass and onto the path, then tipped his head at me, indicating that I should follow. I kept my distance, but not so far that I couldn't hear their conversation.

"It was a lovely service," he said.

"Was it?"

He pushed her awhile longer, then added, "I'm very sorry for your loss."

She let out a sigh, as if she'd heard the platitude too many times. "That's kind of you to say. You don't have to push me anymore. I can do it myself."

He glanced back at me, then moved up to walk beside her, his hands jingling the coins in his pockets. Soon, they reached the path leading to the church entrance and stopped, and I ducked in close to a knapped flint wall to listen.

"It's a good turnout," he said, waving his hand toward the milling crowd.

"I only recognize a few of them. Some are so young. Must be students."

"He was popular."

"It appears so."

They fell silent, and she was about to move away when he stopped her by asking, "Who are they?"

"Who are who?"

She looked in the direction he was pointing, to a small group standing apart from everyone else. I looked at them as well. It was Sebastian, with Zena and Raul. I looked back to Mary, keen to hear what she would say.

"That's my son."

"Yes, I know your son. Who are the other two?"

A few seconds passed before she answered. "I don't know. I guess they're his friends."

"You don't know them?"

Again, she paused. "No."

"You're sure?"

She looked away. "Yes."

"Perhaps you could take another look?"

"I don't need to. I know I don't know them."

"That's strange, because they're staring at you."

"Everyone's staring at me." She gripped the wheels, angled her chair away, and added, "You must excuse me now, Inspector. I need to find my helper so we can lead the way to the wake. Will you be joining us?"

"Thank you, but no. I need to get back to the station." He inclined his head. "Please extend my sympathies to your son. It's very hard for a young man to lose a father at such a vulnerable age."

"Stepfather," she corrected. "Kind of."

"Kind of?"

"Jonathan and I weren't married."

I gasped, loud enough for DCI Roberts to shoot me a warning look, and I ducked out of sight.

"I'm sorry. I didn't know," he said.

"There's nothing to be sorry about." Then she turned her head away from him but toward me, and said as an aside, "I wouldn't have married him if he'd paid me."

"What was that?" DCI Roberts asked.

She moved her chair a few feet away and said, "I really must go now. Thank you for taking the trouble to come."

"It was no trouble at all Mrs. Wain—Ms. Spicer…"

But she was already wheeling away.

Outside the graveyard walls, I walked with DCI Roberts to the carpark, and when we reached his car, he surprised me by saying, "Get in."

"No, thank you. I'm getting the bus."

"I'm not offering a lift. Get in."

He took a monocular from the glove compartment and put it to his eye. This was behavior I understood. I opened the car door and got in. He put a photograph of Zena that I assumed was the one Susan had given DS Hannah on the dashboard.

"Now, then. Let's see if she really doesn't know them, shall we?"

Sebastian was standing by Mary's chair. They were deep in conversation. Mary's helper approached, adjusted the blanket covering Mary's knees and took hold of the wheelchair handles. I looked at her. There was something about her I recognized. Not only from the hospital room—also from somewhere else, but I couldn't remember where. I turned my attention to Sebastian. He was scanning the people mingling outside the church, then made a beckoning gesture. I couldn't see who he was beckoning to, so I took the monocular out of DCI Roberts's hand and put it to my eye. I panned across the crowd, landing on Zena and Raul walking toward Sebastian. I moved the monocular back to Mary and focused on her helper's face, and now that I could see her clearly, I immediately remembered where I'd seen her before. She was the woman leaving Sebastian's flat with Raul in the jazz club bar—May. But why had she been there? It made sense she should know Sebastian. He was her employer's son. But what was her connection to Raul?

Just then, Zena and Raul arrived, knelt down in front of the wheelchair, wrapped their arms around Mary's legs, and rested their heads on her lap.

"What on earth?"

"What? What's happening?" DCI Roberts asked.

And Mary opened her arms and embraced them like the Messiah gathering the little children, a beatific smile on her face.

26

ON THE WAY HOME FROM THE FUNERAL, SO MANY QUESTIONS were ricocheting around my mind that I thought I'd develop a migraine. I understood Zena would want to go to Jonathan's funeral to say goodbye to her lover, but why be so blatant? Why approach her lover's wife afterward? Why kneel before her? And why would Mary embrace the student Jonathan was having an affair with? Unless she didn't know the student was Zena. As I got off the bus, a thought struck me, making me turn off the high street and head to Susan's house. I wanted to find out how Zena, Raul, and Mary knew each other, and I suspected the answer was in the cardboard box Susan had brought to the hospital.

With the box under my arm, I ran up the stairs to my flat. In the front room, I emptied the contents onto my desk and riffled through the photographs until I found the one I was looking for. There was Zena, with her arms around the two boys and, on closer inspection, I thought the blond boy could have been Sebastian. He had the same fair complexion, the same pale-blue eyes. But it was the figure in the background I was most interested in. I opened my desk drawer for Father's magnifying glass, held it above the photograph, and focused on the figure. I could see folded arms across the slim waist, a hip bone jutting forward, wisps of shoulder-length blond hair, but however hard I squinted, I couldn't see past the shadow to the face. I exhaled. Andreas had mentioned sending Zena to stay with an English family in Ubatuba. The family could have been Mary, Jonathan, and Sebastian. Or it could have been another family entirely.

I went to the pages pinned to the wall and wrote "Raul" next to False Hellebore, then added strings connecting Zena and Raul to Mary and stood back for a broader view. With all the strings connected, the pages looked like a wheel. I cut one more length of string for Raul and connected it to the name in the middle: the English Professor.

The telephone rang, making me jump, but instead of waiting for it to go to the answer machine, I picked it up.

"Yes."

"It's DCI Roberts. You've probably only just got home, but Jonathan's autopsy report's in, and I thought you might like to see it. I'll be in my office till seven, but I can wait if you think you'll be later."

"I'll be fifteen minutes."

It had been so long since anyone had stood up when I entered a room that I'd forgotten the response etiquette.

"Thanks for coming, Professor. Take a seat."

Eyeing the revolting chair, I crossed the room and sat.

"Before we begin, I have something for you." He passed me an evidence bag. "The lab technicians have finished with your phials, and I've taken the liberty of including a copy of their report. They were very impressed with your antidotes. In fact, the word 'genius' was used."

I wasn't the least bit interested in the report.

"Where're the *Karwinskia* berries?" I asked, looking in the bag.

"The lab kept them. It's all in the report."

I was disappointed. It'd been my intention to use them for propagation, but I didn't say this out loud. A thought occurred to me.

"Did you crack the code on the mobile phone?"

"Not yet."

"Do you mind if I have a go?"

He gave his thin-lipped smile and took the phone out of a drawer, but as I reached for it, he pulled it back and said, "You do realize, if you crack the code, I'll have to press-gang you into joining the police?"

I paused. "That was a joke?"

"Yes. That was a joke."

He laughed, and I waited patiently for him to finish.

"Okay, let's get to it," he said, sliding a folder across his desk.

I picked it up and looked at the first page. "Where's the autopsy report? This is the tox."

"Turn it over."

I turned to the next page and scanned it. "They found two puncture wounds, the second deeper than the first."

"Yes. It looks like it took two attempts to get the poison into the right vein."

"You said there was a fight. Maybe Jonathan defended himself. Maybe they had to subdue him before they could inject him."

"Possibly. The toxin concentration was low surrounding the first puncture wound but much more concentrated around the second. The assailant may only have injected a small amount before Jonathan stopped them the first time."

I turned to the blood results. The same ones I'd read the last time I was there.

"Abrin. The poison found in the seeds of *Abrus precatorius*."

"You said if he'd got to hospital sooner, he could have been saved."

"That's right."

"So the assailant knew he wouldn't get there in time. They knew his wife wouldn't be able to help him." He took a piece of paper from the file. "This is the list you gave me of the plants stolen from your garden. *Abrus precatorius* isn't on it."

"Because it wasn't stolen. It was destroyed but not stolen."
I thought a moment, and added, "The toxin's also in the peas.
They could easily have taken some without my knowledge."

He leaned back in his chair and folded his arms over his belly.
"So we're confident we know *how* he was murdered. We just don't
know *why*. Why would anyone want Jonathan Wainwright dead?"

"Are you asking me, or was that a rhetorical question?"

"Read the last page."

I turned to it and said in surprise, "This is the toxicity report
from my laboratory contamination last year."

"Yes."

"Why's that here?"

"Because traces of the poison that was on the door handles
and counters in your lab have been detected in the bag of vegetation Mary Spicer found in her garden shed."

I looked up from the page in confusion. "I beg your pardon?"

He handed me another piece of paper. "This is the report for
the contents of the bag. As you can see, it's heavily padded with
culinary herbs, some marijuana, but also *Banisteriopsis caapi* and
Psychotria viridis."

"Both hallucinogens," I said. "I've done a lot of research into
these plant combinations."

"I know. I've read your publications."

"You have?" I asked, stunned.

He smiled. "The question is, how did the *Karwinskia* toxin

found all over your lab end up in a bag of narcotics in Jonathan Wainwright's shed?"

Totally at a loss, I shook my head.

"This is where detective work comes in, Professor. This morning, I paid a visit to the lab technician who first reported the contamination. She wasn't forthcoming to begin with, but when I told her Jonathan was dead, the floodgates opened. She said he talked her into getting him a copy of the specimen-cabinet key by saying that if she didn't do it, he'd leave her. Apparently, she loved him, so she stole the key from the key store, made a copy, and put it back before anyone noticed."

I knew my eyes were wide open. I could feel the shock on my face. I knew which lab technician he was talking about and couldn't believe she would do something so dangerous.

"Jonathan—presumably wearing gloves; otherwise, he would have gotten very sick—went to your lab, opened the specimen cabinet, rummaged around, disturbed the container of *Karwinskia* toxin, took what he was after, and, in the process, contaminated your lab in his clumsy attempt to cover his tracks."

I was astounded by what he was saying—horrified. But I also couldn't help feeling vindicated.

"He took my *Banisteriopsis caapi* and *Psychotria viridis* samples," I said. "I told you there was a theft when you arrested me. I told you again and again, but you wouldn't listen. No one would listen."

"I know, and I apologize for that, but you were—how can I put this?—very unstable at the time. Your behavior was unpredictable, and you were often quite incoherent."

"I was upset. I'd just lost my father."

"Indeed. It was a difficult time for you." He paused. "But you know what this means, don't you?"

I considered, then gasped because I did. I knew exactly what it meant. At once, my vision blurred. My throat constricted. I couldn't breathe. I put a hand to my chest and felt my heart pounding through my jacket. I thought it would explode out of my chest. I looked wildly around, desperate for an exit. I thought I was dying—I was. I was dying. But then DCI Roberts was by my side, holding my hand, tapping my back. Telling me to breathe one, breathe two, breathe three, breathe. Telling me not to cry. Telling me I was brave. I was very brave.

✑

I don't know how long I sat perched on the chair, leaning forward with my head hanging between my knees, but it was long enough to feel embarrassed to be sitting like that in front of him, because it had been a year since I'd last had an episode, and it had also happened in front of DCI Roberts. I felt dizzy when I finally straightened. I felt like I might vomit. I felt like my head no longer belonged to my body. The realization that the lab contamination

hadn't been caused by my negligence, deliberate or accidental—
that I should not have lost my job and my reputation—was a
stab straight into my heart. I clamped my teeth together as I
realized that the bitter conviction I'd felt for the past year—that
I'd been done wrong—had not been imagined. It was real. I *had*
been done wrong. And the irony that the wrongdoer had been
Jonathan Wainwright was almost laughable.

"Are you okay now?" DCI Roberts asked, handing me a paper
cup of water.

I tried to stand, but my legs wouldn't support me.

"Whoa, there," he said, grabbing my elbow. "Don't stand up
yet. Just stay there. You've had a shock."

My mind was racing. "Why did he take those particular samples? What did he want with them?" And then, as if it could be
the only answer—the only one in natural, factual existence—I
knew. "Because he was the English Professor!"

"Who?"

"That's why he was always hanging around the lab, asking
questions about hallucinogens all those years ago. And that's why
he was always disappearing off to South America. He was plant
collecting, experimenting, perfecting his blend. Twenty years
later, I bet he couldn't believe his luck when he discovered his
new girlfriend was a botany technician at UCL. He would have
known exactly what she had access to from back when he worked
at the university. She was an opportunity that couldn't be missed."

I thought of the recording of his and Zena's conversation on Susan's phone. He'd said he understood perfectly what she and Andreas were doing, because he thought they knew he was the ayahuasca supplier. He thought they were on to him. I looked at DCI Roberts.

"It was a revenge killing. Jonathan made an ayahuasca blend using the specimens he stole from the cabinet and sold it by proxy in São Paulo. But I don't think he had any idea he'd contaminated the leaves with *Karwinskia* toxin. The ayahuasca was bought by the owners of a wellness center. They thought they were buying it cheap. They were anticipating a huge profit. They had no idea they were buying a poisonous concoction. They gave Jonathan's brew to their clients, and five of them died and two were paralyzed. I think the people who bought the ayahuasca came to London in search of the English Professor and found him."

DCI Roberts was staring at me. "How do you know this?"

"Because one of them thought *I* was the English Professor at first, and that's why he tried to strangle me."

He flipped through his notebook. "DS Hannah wrote down the name you mentioned that night. Casper Andrews. Is this the man?"

"Andreas, not Andrews. He's Zena's husband, so possibly Andreas Sousa."

He wrote this down. "And an address?"

"He's staying at a hostel in Soho. I don't know which one. The bartender might know."

"What bartender?"

"The one who works at the bar in Hampstead. I don't know the address, but I can show you. It doesn't open till eleven, so pick me up tonight and we can go together."

DCI Roberts was staring at me open-mouthed, his large eyebrows raised, wearing an expression that, for the life of me, I couldn't read.

27

It was too cruel that once again it was Jonathan Wainwright who was responsible for throwing my life into turmoil. I looked at the circle of names on the wall.

If I'd known he was the one who'd contaminated the lab, my name might very well be pinned up there with the other suspects, and DCI Roberts's decision to arrest me would have been perfectly reasonable. The fact that he'd evaded justice was galling. Knowing that he'd continued to teach and live his life as if nothing had happened when I'd lost my job and been ostracized by my peers was even worse. I already detested him, but what I was feeling now was a whole new level of hate. My only consolation was that he wouldn't be able to hurt me ever again. I took the Nokia out of my pocket, pressed the messages button, and looked at the top text—*The professor*—and reminded myself that they could take away my job and my reputation, but they couldn't take that. I was still a professor. I was still a member of MENSA, and if I was these things, I could also be a code breaker. I pushed up my glasses, pulled out a fresh sheet from my ream of paper, and opened Zena's small black book of numbers.

Several hours later, I was still at my desk, surrounded by pages of number and letter combinations. Sheet after sheet of failed attempts, each one leading to the next and the next. Even with a Portuguese dictionary, this created gibberish when forward, backward, every second letter, every third, fourth letter of the alphabet was matched to the numbers in the book. I was beginning to wonder if I was totally on the wrong track, that perhaps the black book had nothing to do with the code that would unlock the texts. I was beginning to think that the key must be somewhere else entirely.

I threw down my pen in frustration, picked up the photograph, and looked again at the figure behind the fence. There was something so familiar about the stance, but I couldn't see the face, so I couldn't be sure. With a start, I realized I must be having what DCI Roberts called a gut feeling. A hunch. Was this what it felt like? An imprecise suspicion? A nebulous notion? What I did know was that the only way to confirm or deny such a feeling was through logic-based investigation. So I picked up the photograph, scooped up my jacket, and left the flat.

I hadn't been to Jonathan Wainwright's house since the night I'd banged on his front door so hard I'd broken a pane of glass, but that afternoon I felt not a shred of ill intent as I exited the train station. Emotions I couldn't put names to simmered silently as I left the gift shop and walked toward Grange Road, but rather than let this trouble me, I accepted them for whatever they were and left them alone. When I arrived at number 32, I didn't hesitate but straightaway stepped forward and knocked briskly on the front door.

Several minutes passed before I saw a shape through the glass, slow moving and low to the ground. It inched forward and the door gradually opened until I was able to look down upon Mary in her wheelchair, her eyes wide with surprise, her mouth hanging open. She inhaled but it was a long time before she spoke.

"My God, Eustacia. You look just like your father."

I lifted the corners of my mouth. "Thank you." Then I held out a gift-wrapped box. "I brought you a present."

In the kitchen, Mary offered me coffee, and I felt a pang of disappointment; she'd forgotten I didn't drink it. I watched her insert a small pod into a machine to make coffee for herself, place a cup below it, and press a button, each action methodical, as if she needed time to process what was happening. I was in no hurry. I'd waited twenty years. I sat quietly at the kitchen table, the sound of the sputtering machine loud in the room. Up close, I could see the slight paralysis in her face. The droop in one half of her mouth, her left eye partially closed. Her skin was heavily lined, and with the thinning gray hair, it was hard to recall the woman she'd once been. I sniffed in a breath and reminded myself that I no longer looked like the woman she'd known either.

For a few minutes after the machine finished, Mary stared at the cup, not picking it up, so I held out the present again. When she didn't respond, I unwrapped the box, took out the bottle, and showed it to her.

"Lily of the valley perfume," I said. "Your favorite."

She glanced at it. "I haven't worn that scent for decades."

"No?" I asked, spraying it in her direction. "I love it. It reminds me of you."

She twisted her face away, then twisted her chair away. "I find it sickly."

I chose to ignore this and said instead, "It's good to see you after all this time." I wanted to tell her that she hadn't changed, but that would have been a lie. "I heard Jonathan died recently. I wanted to offer my condolences."

She didn't answer but wheeled her chair out of the kitchen. I took this as an invitation and followed, but on the way I paused to look through a door into what I assumed was her bedroom. A hospital bed was pushed against the wall, a pressure-relief machine fixed to its frame. Next to the bed, a lift hung from the ceiling. I stepped to one side. In the corner was a small space containing a hand-held shower beside a plastic chair. A low sink, a low mirror, and a toilet, and beside it, an industrial-sized pack of moisturized wipes and incontinence pads.

The walls of the room were covered with framed embroideries. The kind that came with color-coded instructions: simple, bold, the stitches large enough for failing eyesight or small children. I'd seen something like them before, but I couldn't remember where. A paperback lay open and face down on the bedside table, its spine cracked. A shawl was on the bed beside a tartan lap blanket and an old-fashioned dressing gown. It looked like a room in an old people's home. It looked like Father's room in the hospice. I shuddered, then turned and followed Mary into the front room. She'd positioned her chair in front of the windows facing into the room, the light behind her throwing her face into shadow. She was holding a half-finished embroidery in one hand and a needle in the other.

"Here's your coffee," I said, putting it on the table beside her. She said nothing, so I sat on the sofa and watched her. I didn't like the haphazard way she was stabbing with the needle.

It was unsettling.

"Did you do the embroideries in the other room? The ones on the wall? I saw them when I was walking down the hall. They're very good."

Unexpectedly, she threw the embroidery and needle to the floor.

"They aren't good. Stop talking rubbish. At least I don't have to do them anymore."

Puzzled, I looked at her, waiting for an explanation. None came.

"I would have come to visit you sooner, but I was under the impression I couldn't. You know...because of the restraining order. But I recently discovered it was lifted a long time ago, so here I am."

She didn't respond.

"I was wondering..." I continued. "I mean, when I saw you at the hospital, I was wondering how you ended up in the wheelchair."

Again, she said nothing.

"What happened to you, Mary?"

Perhaps it was the sound of me saying her name, but something made her soften. She looked at me.

"I had an accident in Brazil."

"What kind of accident?"

"I don't talk about it."

"What are your symptoms?"

"Eustacia," she said abruptly. "I don't talk about it."

She was upset. I had upset her, although I didn't know how. I was asking perfectly reasonable questions. I took the photograph out of my pocket.

"I wanted to show you something."

She'd turned her chair away from me, so I stood and laid it on her lap. She glanced down at it, then looked up sharply.

"Where did you get this?"

"From a friend."

"A friend?"

"A neighbor. Is that you, standing behind the fence?" I pointed to the figure in the background.

Mary's brow furrowed. "Did Zena give this to you?"

I hesitated, then pushed on with a lie. "Yes."

She looked at me, then back to the photograph.

"That's Zena and her brother, Raul," I said. "And I think I know who the other boy is."

Mary made a strange noise. "How do you know this?"

I'd told one lie. I could tell another. "Zena told me."

"Zena told you?" she asked, her voice rising. Then she let out a bitter laugh. "Well, if Zena told you, I guess it's okay." She handed the photograph back. "Yes, that's me in the background, and the blond boy is my son, Sebastian."

"You knew Zena and Raul in Brazil?"

"Yes, Sebastian and I lived with them. The children grew up together."

I remembered what Zena had said in the café. So Mary was the woman who had cooked and cleaned and taught her English. Mary was the maid.

"Jonathan was around as well. He used to spend his summers

with us. We didn't invite him. He just kept coming back because he thought Sebastian was his son. I didn't have the heart to tell either of them that he wasn't."

"Then who's the father?"

She paused before answering. "David Heath."

I gasped. "Our head of department?"

The memory of Mary standing in the doorway at the faculty meeting—leaning back against the frame, the top three buttons of her blouse undone, listening to David Heath talk—rushed into my mind. Mary sighed heavily.

"I've never told anyone before. You're the first. Well, apart from David, but he was married with kids. He didn't want anything to do with it. He just wanted me gone."

I thought of David Heath at that party, leading me to the bar, preventing me from breaking Mary and Jonathan up. Had he known she was pregnant then? Was he hoping Jonathan would take her off his hands? Did Mary need a father for her unborn child, and Jonathan was right there in front of her?

I rubbed my face and said through my hands, "You didn't go to Brazil for a holiday. You were running away."

She let out a huff of air. "It was impossible for me to stay at UCL. David made sure of that. I knew I'd have to move to another university if I wanted to continue my PhD. But I didn't know whether to start looking for another placement straight-away or wait until after the baby was born. I didn't know what to do. I was in a state. Then, when Jonathan invited me to go on holiday, it felt like an answer. He felt like the answer."

After a moment's silence, I asked quietly, "What about me?"

"You?"

"You didn't think about me when you ran away? You didn't think what it would do to me?"

She raised her eyebrows. "We said goodbye. We went for that drink the week before I left, remember?"

Was that our goodbye? A glass of warm Coke in the filthy pub that had made me reek of stale cigarettes—was that all I was worth to her?

"But you said you were just going on holiday. You said you'd be back in a couple of weeks."

"I didn't tell you because I knew you'd be upset. I knew how sensitive you were, and I was firefighting. There were so many decisions to be made. So many problems to resolve before I left."

I turned away from her and stared at a side table on the other side of the room.

"I thought Jonathan had done something to you when he came home alone," I said. "For a while, I thought you were dead." I never cried. At least, I never used to, but these past few weeks had been, well…difficult. For twenty years I'd mourned my lost love and had hated Jonathan for stealing her from me. But now I knew Mary had never loved me. May not even have liked me. I was just a lab colleague whom she called upon to do activities with because she didn't know anyone else in London. I thought of all the wonderful things we'd done together over that year, and I thought of our perfect weekend by the sea. And I realized the significance I'd attached to these precious moments was utterly worthless. I shook my head and closed my eyes as a profound sadness enveloped me.

"I'm sorry, Eustacia. But you could have stopped this." She thumped her thigh. "All of this."

I thought of the double whisky and sat heavier in my seat, my body suddenly seeming double its weight. "I know."

"Then why didn't you? Why didn't you tell David I couldn't use your lab? It was a restricted facility. I was a student. I shouldn't have been allowed to use it, and certainly not unsupervised, but you left me in there alone all the time. You even gave me my own key."

I looked up, thrown by what she was saying.

"If you'd done the right thing and refused me access to your lab," she continued, "I would have looked for another facility in another university. Then I wouldn't have started a relationship with David. I wouldn't have become pregnant. I wouldn't have been forced to give up my PhD. I wouldn't have gone to Brazil with Jonathan, and I would not be in this wheelchair."

"I…" But I had no words.

All this time, I'd blamed David Heath's offer of the double whisky for losing Mary, but it wasn't his fault—it was mine. Long before the whisky, the blame was mine. I took a slow, deep breath as I remembered the pot of tea we'd shared in the canteen the first time I met her. It was when she'd told me David Heath had agreed we could share my lab. That was the moment, the precise moment, I should have refused, but when I'd hesitated, she'd laid her hand on mine and said, *Let me in.* And I did. I opened the door and let her in, utterly and completely.

Mary was still talking, but I couldn't hear her because I was staring at the side table, lost in dark thoughts of culpability when, unexpectedly, something caught my attention. I stood up.

"What's this?" I asked, picking up a chart from the side table.

Mary exhaled heavily, perhaps relieved by the sudden change of subject.

"It's an embroidery color chart. Each shape on the canvas has a number printed on it. You find the same number on the chart, and it shows the color you need for that shape."

And suddenly, I remembered where I'd seen the embroideries before.

"Can I borrow it?"

"No. I'm using it."

"I'll bring it back tomorrow."

"No, I'm..."

I made for the door.

"Wait, I'm..."

But I was already outside in the front garden, walking away quickly.

28

I OPENED ZENA'S SMALL BLACK BOOK AND HELD FATHER'S magnifying glass over a page. At first, I wasn't sure where to find what I was looking for, until I bent the spine outward, fully opening a double page. There, at the inner edge, almost in the binding, was a small dot of color. I felt a thrill of excitement. I looked at the numbers written on the page and their corresponding color at the inner edge: 303—orange, 148—blue, 1015—red, and stopped. This wasn't what I was expecting. I picked up Mary's color chart and ran my finger down the columns until I found 303. The word beneath the brightly colored orange square was "Amber." The corners of my mouth lifted. I checked 1015. Crimson. A B C. Then I picked up the Nokia, scrolled to Zena's last message, and decoded it.

J knows A is in London. We need to act now.

I thought back to the last recording on Susan's phone, the one of the conversation between Zena and Jonathan, and recalled how angry he'd been to see Andreas. Then I remembered her soft voice saying *Merda, Merda, Merda* and the dial tone sounds as she sent a text. This text.

I scrolled to the previous message and decoded it.

It will work. Trust me.

And the one before that.

I've spoken to M. She says it's too dangerous.

And then the one before that.

I met someone. She is clueless. She has a garden full of poisonous plants. I have a plan.

I put down the Nokia, touched my mouth with my fingertips, and looked through the window. It was Zena after all. I'd discounted her before because I thought she'd been kidnapped. But now I knew it was she who'd destroyed my garden, my precious collection, my life's work...and all for a handful of *Abrus* peas.

My door intercom buzzed, making me start. I checked my watch. It was 11:00 p.m. I stood stiffly and went to the door.

"Are you ready?" DCI Roberts asked.

≈

I waited in the car while he went into the bar, the windows wound down to mitigate the stench of wet dog. He was surprisingly quick. He must have used the word "perjury" to get

Andreas's address out of the bartender so fast. It seemed only a matter of minutes before he was back, squeezing his large belly behind the wheel.

"Off to Soho we go, then," he said, winding up his window. I thought we'd go straight to Andreas's hostel, but DCI Roberts stopped instead in a doorway across the road from the hostel's entrance and folded his arms.

"What are we doing?" I asked.

"Waiting."

"For what?"

On the other side of the road, Andreas emerged through the hostel door.

"That," DCI Roberts said.

Andreas was careless. He didn't pull the main door to the hostel closed behind him properly. It bounced open, then slowly swung, without the lock engaging. He didn't go far, just into the cachaça bar underneath the hostel. We watched him talk briefly to the bartender, then sit at a table with his back to the room. After a while, the bartender set a bottle of red liquor and a glass on the table in front of him, patted his shoulder, and retreated. We watched him knock back one, two, three shots before I asked, "Why are we still waiting?"

DCI Roberts stepped out of the doorway. "Stay here. He could be dangerous."

"I'm coming with you."

"No. He tried to strangle you. Stay here, and don't move."

He crossed the road, entered the bar, and sat at a table a fair distance away from Andreas. Soon after, the bartender brought him a pint of beer. I couldn't believe what I was seeing.

"What? I have to wait here while you have a pint?" I scoffed.

In my peripheral vision, a man in a black tracksuit crossed the road beside the bar. The peak of a baseball cap poked out from beneath his hood, and I knew who it was—the man from the bottom of my road. And the man who had pushed Zena into the car. I watched him go through the door into the hostel, then glanced through the bar window. Andreas was hunched over the table, cradling his glass, and DCI Roberts was drinking his pint. So I crossed the road and slipped quietly through the hostel door.

Inside was a lobby with painted woodchip walls and a dirty linoleum floor. There was a huge corkboard opposite the stairs covered in posters, ads, Post-it notes. The place smelled foul. I heard a sound coming from upstairs, like wood splitting, and followed it. At the top, I leaned around the corner and saw the man force a door with a small crowbar and go through it. I hesitated, then tiptoed to the door and peeked in. The room was small, containing only a thin wardrobe and a single bed beside a low cabinet. The man was standing in front of an open drawer of the cabinet and took something out of his pocket. It looked like a necklace. He held it above the drawer, snapped it, let the beads drop in, and mixed them around with the other contents. Then he closed the drawer and turned toward the door, toward me. And froze.

I could have backed away, but our eyes were locked. I was as frozen as he was. Finally, he took a step forward and I took a step back, then another and another until we were both outside in the hall, our eyes still fixed on each other. I was standing at the top of the stairs, blocking them. His eyes flicked past me, then back to me again. My heart was pounding. He only had to reach out a hand, and I would be falling backward. But instead of doing that, he said, "*Por favor, senhora?*" and I found myself stepping to one side.

I waited until I heard the door close downstairs before I sucked in a deep breath, filling my empty lungs. The eyes I'd been looking into, the soft brown eyes, were Raul's. They weren't the eyes of a killer. They were the eyes of a boy. Moments later I heard the door open and looked over the banister to find DCI Roberts looking up at me.

"I told you not to move," he said.

"I didn't see why I had to wait for you to drink a pint of beer."

He began his slow ascent of the stairs and was puffing loudly by the time he reached the top. I could smell the drink on his breath.

"I wanted to make sure Andreas was properly settled in down there before we took a look around his room. We don't want him walking in on us, do we?"

"I didn't think the police were allowed to drink on duty."

"I went off duty hours ago. So now you know everything's above board, shall we continue?"

I didn't think entering someone's place of abode without permission was above board, either, but I didn't say so.

"Let's see, now," he said, pulling his notepad from his pocket and flipping it open. "Room 3."

I knew which room it was, but I let him find it himself.

"The door's been forced," he said. "Police. Anyone home?" At the answering silence, he said, "This is Detective Chief Inspector Roberts. I'm coming in."

I waited in the doorway while he stood in the middle of the room, his head turning back and forth. Without moving his feet, he opened the wardrobe door. It was empty, apart from a heavily worn leather jacket on a hanger. He checked the pockets, but there was nothing. He looked down at the cabinet, then sat heavily, making the bed creak. He opened the drawer, sifted through the contents, and made that humming sound.

"What do we have here, then?"

He shook out his handkerchief, spread it over a palm, and filled it with the beads Raul had shaken into the drawer moments before. I looked closer. No, they weren't beads. They were bright-red peas with distinctive black dots. Rosary peas. Raul had snapped a rosary over the drawer. I thought back to the day I'd followed Sebastian to Soho. He'd taken Zena's rosary, the one I'd seen hanging over the corner of her mirror, and had given it to Raul when he got back to his room.

"See this?" DCI Roberts said, holding out his hand. "*Abrus* peas. Containing the same poison that killed Jonathan Wainwright."

This was when I should have told him what I'd witnessed while he was drinking his pint. Instead, I kept my mouth shut. He was tying the corners of his handkerchief when we heard the downstairs door slam, followed by the sounds of someone stumbling up the stairs. I went into the hall to look over the banister at Andreas coming up. Quick as a flash, I dashed back into the room and stood behind the door. The last thing I wanted was to come face-to-face with that man again. DCI Roberts looked at me, and I put a finger to my lips, then peered through the crack between the door and the frame. "*Que foda?*" Andreas said when he reached the door.

"Are you Andreas Sousa?"

"Who are you?"

"My name's DCI Roberts."

"Police?"

"Yes."

"Good. I need the police. Someone has broken my door. Look."

"Can you confirm your name, please?"

"Eh?"

"What's your name?"

A pause. "Why do you want to know?"

"Nothing to worry about. I just have a few questions for you."

Another pause.

Through the crack, I could see Andreas slowly retreat, then turn for the stairs, but although he was younger and fitter, DCI Roberts was by far the bigger man. Within seconds, he had Andreas's hands behind his back, the cuffs on his wrists, and a firm hold of his arm.

"Andreas Sousa, I'm arresting you for the murder of Jonathan Wainwright."

He began to walk down the stairs and, too drunk to resist, Andreas stumbled along beside him.

"You do not have to say anything, but it may harm your defense if you do not mention when questioned something that you later rely on in court."

At the bottom, he looked back up to me. "I'll make my own way home," I said.

He nodded and opened the entrance door. "Anything you do or say may be taken and given as evidence…" And let it slam shut behind him.

29

THE NEXT DAY, I LEFT THE TRAIN STATION AND TURNED FOR Mary's house. She was waiting for me in her front garden even though I hadn't told her what time I'd arrive. I looked at the dark rings under her eyes, the unbrushed hair, and knew she hadn't slept. She didn't greet me but immediately turned her chair and led the way into the front room. I took the color chart out of my pocket and put it on the side table.

"Thank you. It was useful."

Mary stared at it. "How was it useful?"

I placed the Nokia beside it, and she glanced at me, then quickly away, clearly struggling not to cry.

"You always were so very clever, Eustacia."

Something similar to the emotion I'd felt for Sebastian when he was giving Jonathan's eulogy passed through me, but I couldn't be sure if it was sympathy or pity. I inhaled decisively, took hold of the handles of her wheelchair, and said, "Let's go for a walk." Abney Park Cemetery was shrouded in a quiet calm. The paths were uneven in places but not enough to cause an obstruction for the wheelchair. On either side, the lush undergrowth made a picturesque backdrop for the ancient, tumbled gravestones. When we reached Mortuary Chapel, I pushed Mary to a wrought-iron bench in the shade of the soaring Gothic spire, kicked the brakes down, and sat beside her. Bloodred valerian was growing in clumps beside the bench, and in the shade of the chapel wall, herb robert, with its delicate pink flowers, softened the masonry.

I scanned the immediate area—spotting hogweed, yellow rattle, soapwort, greater celandine—and realized we were sitting in an apothecary's medicine cabinet. I bent to snap an honesty stem and gave it to Mary.

"Do you know why it's called honesty?"

She shrugged.

"Because the seed disks are round, like coins," I said. "The plant is being honest about its wealth."

She picked ineffectually at a translucent disk, trying to get to the seeds, and I watched her clumsy fingers before bending to snap another stem of delicate blue flowers.

"This one's speedwell. If you sew it into your clothes, it protects you from robbery on a long journey. But don't take it inside, because if you do, your mother will die."

She took the stem from me.

"That one over there with the tiny white flowers is eyebright. Father used to call me eyebright because he said my eyes were always bright with curiosity. Also, because its Latin name is *Euphrasia nemorosa. Euphrasia* sounds like Eustacia."

Mary didn't speak. I pushed up my glasses and leaned back against the bench. I was in no hurry. I was prepared to wait for as long as it took for her to start talking.

Eventually, she threw down the stems.

"You know everything, don't you? You found it all on that mobile phone."

I waited a beat. "Not everything."

"Go on, then," she said, her voice rising. "Tell me what you do know."

"I know Jonathan was responsible for the deaths and injuries in Brazil. I know he sold the contaminated ayahuasca to the dealer who sold it to Raul, and Raul gave it to those people at the center—"

"No," she interrupted sharply. "That's not right. This has nothing to do with Raul. He was just a boy, still at school. It was a man called Andreas Sousa. He bought the ayahuasca and gave it to those people at his wellness center. Not Raul."

"His center? I thought the business was Zena's."

"No. It was Andreas's. Zena just worked there."

It shouldn't have come as a surprise that Andreas had lied.

Even so, I couldn't help feeling irked by the deception. "And they were married?"

Mary made a strange sound. "God knows why. I think she did it to spite us."

"She must have been very young."

"Only just twenty, and he was much older. Rough-looking. More like a gangster than the owner of a wellness center. And it turned out he was the jealous type. Liberal with his fists, you know? I hated him. We all did. We all do."

"What happened after the accident at the center?"

She took her time with her reply.

"The time immediately afterward is a bit of a blur. Zena came home for a while. Andreas disappeared. The business went bust. The lawsuits started pouring in, and because Zena was his wife, the lawyers began pursuing her when they couldn't find him. Her life was destroyed. She was meant to stay with us until everything blew over, or until Andreas came out of hiding, but within a fortnight, she was gone. We didn't know where. Three weeks later, she called to say she was in London.

"At the time, we didn't know Zena had discovered the ayahuasca had originally come from Jonathan, but when she told us, I wasn't surprised. He was always collecting ingredients when he visited us, always experimenting with blends. She said she remembered Jonathan listening in to her arguing on the phone with Andreas about money. He'd had the idea of introducing ayahuasca sessions to the center to attract rich Western clients, but she didn't want to go down that route. She thought she'd shut the subject down. It turned out Jonathan had other ideas. During his visit last year, he found a proxy dealer from Peru who sold his ayahuasca blend to Andreas. Andreas never knew the provenance, just that the dealer had gotten it from someone calling themselves the English Professor."

"So then you followed Zena to London."

"Yes, but not straightaway. It took a while… My recovery… I was in hospital for three months."

"What do you mean?" And then I knew. "You took the ayahuasca. You're one of the injured. That's why you're in the chair."

She passed a trembling hand across her face.

"Andreas persuaded me to try it. He didn't have to try very hard, because I was curious. All of us at the center were. We'd all heard such amazing things about the life-changing benefits ayahuasca can bring. We were willing participants. Every one of us."

She dropped her chin to her chest.

"But something was wrong. Horribly, terribly wrong. People started to get sick. Not sick like you're supposed to with ayahuasca—they couldn't move. Couldn't breathe. Then they began to die. One by one. Right next to me. I suppose I was one of the lucky ones." She thumped her thighs. "Because I survived."

I watched her, hunched over in her chair, one side of her face in palsy, barely resembling the vibrant woman I had known.

"And when you left hospital," I said, "you came to London and moved in with the man who almost killed you."

Her voice was small. "Yes."

"Why?"

"He didn't know I knew he was the supplier. When he asked about the wheelchair, I told him I'd had a riding accident. At that time, he still thought I was the mother of his child. I guess he felt some kind of obligation, so he let me stay."

"I still don't understand why you'd want to live with him."

"We were waiting."

"Who's 'we'? You keep saying 'we.'"

"Me, Gabriella, Sebastian, and Raul."

"Gabriella?"

"Zena and Raul's *māe*. One of my old lecturers from Edinburgh. I looked her up after Jonathan left Brazil. I was pregnant. I had nowhere to go. She took me in... Saved me. Me *and* Sebastian. She does everything for me. I don't know what I'd do without her."

"May?"

"Yes. *Māe*. It means mum in Brazilian."

I thought of the texts I'd decoded on the Nokia. M. May. *Māe*. Mum. The woman I'd seen leaving Sebastian's flat with Raul. The woman I'd seen in the hospital room next to Jonathan's bed. The woman at Jonathan's funeral. May was Gabriella. Mary's helper. "What were you all waiting for?" I asked, already knowing the answer.

"The plan was that I watch Jonathan and report to Zena. I wanted to give up and go back to Brazil so many times. I hated living with him. I despised the fact that I was so reliant on his help. But Zena kept texting me, telling me to hold on, that an opportunity would come along soon."

I thought of Zena and Jonathan together in bed and wondered if Mary knew how far Zena was willing to go for that opportunity.

She exhaled heavily. "It took nine miserable months for the opportunity to arise, and when it finally did, it turned out to be you."

At these words, Zena's text rushed into my head. *I met someone. She is clueless.* I stood abruptly and walked to the entrance of the chapel, keeping my back turned. Perhaps I had been clueless. Perhaps I'd been so beguiled by Zena that I'd lost my reason. Certainly, if I'd resisted, she would never have set foot in my garden…and Jonathan would still be alive.

"Zena could've just taken a handful of *Abrus* peas," I said. "She didn't have to destroy the whole garden."

Mary kept her tone level. "She didn't destroy your garden."

"Who was it then? Raul?"

"It wasn't Raul."

I let out a cry of frustration, threw my arms in the air, and spun around to face her.

"Correct me if I'm wrong, Mary, but as far as I understand, someone unknown broke into my flat, stole several poisonous plants, and destroyed my garden to cover their tracks. This unknown person then gave Zena peas from one of the destroyed plants, which she used to murder Jonathan."

"Zena didn't murder Jonathan," she said in the same level tone.

"Who then, Raul?"

"No."

"Gabriella?"

"No."

"Sebastian?"

"No."

I glared at her. "Was it you?"

She made an expression that was like a smile but not. "Of course not, Eustacia. Look at me."

I looked at her thin legs, the muscles atrophied from lack of use.

"Well, he didn't murder himself, did he?"

When she didn't respond, I clasped my head with both hands in exasperation.

"Oh, I see," I cried. "It was all of you and it was none of you."

Mary kept her eyes fixed on mine. "It was Andreas."

At this, the air in my lungs rushed out in a loud whoosh. "Oh, come on. We both know it wasn't Andreas."

"Why not? Didn't you wonder why he's here and not still hiding in Brazil? He came here to find Jonathan and to kill him." She leaned forward, her tone softening. "Zena told me he tried to strangle you. He could have killed you as well. If you want someone to blame, if you want justice for what he did to you… If you want me back in your life, make it Andreas."

I stared at her. "I beg your pardon?"

She smiled a lopsided smile and repeated, "If you want me back in your life, make it Andreas."

I blinked several times, hardly believing what I was hearing. She was making an offer. Mine for the taking—in exchange for a miscarriage of justice. But I could have everything I'd ever wanted on my own terms. I knelt in front of her and looked into her eyes, and all at once, I remembered an image from our weekend by the sea: sand on Mary's cheek, a sprig of sea milkwort behind her ear, the sky reflected in her pale-blue eyes. That moment on the beach, when we'd sat side by side watching the lapping waves, was saved in my memory as a time when I was truly happy. And I could have this again. Over and over again.

I pursed my lips, weighing my decision, then stood and kicked off the wheelchair brakes.

"You're tired. I'll take you home."

30

THERE WAS A MESSAGE FROM DCI ROBERTS WHEN I GOT home, asking me to go to the station. I knew it was about Andreas. It couldn't have been anything else. I was still undecided about Mary's offer because I couldn't forgive her for what she—what they—had done to my garden. It felt important that someone be punished and, although I despised him, it felt unfair that it should be Andreas. I didn't mind him taking the blame for Jonathan's death, but my garden was another matter. I needed to go up to the roof to think.

Halfway along the hall, I remembered the package in Father's overcoat from my last delivery the night Andreas waylaid me, and I admonished myself for forgetting it. It had been expensive. A cutting from a borrachero, or devil's breath shrub, from Colombia, the seeds of which, when ground into a powder and put through a chemical process, contained a substance similar to scopolamine, the compound that causes a lack of free will. I'd read that unscrupulous criminals were using it to empty their victims' bank accounts by blowing it into their faces and walking them to an ATM. I found this fascinating and, once I'd brought the cutting to maturity, planned to replicate this in a controlled scientific setting.

I crossed the roof quickly, trying to ignore the eerie emptiness, and took the package straight to the greenhouse. My hopes for the cutting's survival were slim after so many days in Father's coat pocket, but I still felt excitement as, holding my breath, I peeled away the many layers of cotton wool. And when a green stem was finally revealed, I let out a whoop.

The propagator was on the shelf above the bench. I took a breath of anticipation, opened the lid, and found three green broke-back shoots. The Yunnan cuttings had survived as well. I was overjoyed, ecstatic, because these tiny scraps of life could be the tentative beginnings of a new collection. Taking great care, I potted the Colombian devil's breath stem and put it in the propagator with the others. And buoyed by these small seeds of hope, I thought of Mary and nodded to myself. I had made my decision.

As I was leaving to meet DCI Roberts, I caught sight of the paper-and-string wheel on the wall in the front room. It was redundant now, but even so, I went to it and wrote "Gabriella" next to Helper, then, rather than write Jonathan's name next to the English Professor, I moved his page into the center of the circle and saw how the strings from all the names connected to him, like the spokes of a bicycle wheel. It was then that I realized they all had a motive. Any of them could have done it. Even Mary could have been the one to empty the syringe into Jonathan's abdomen. With help, perhaps, but it was possible, and following this logic, Andreas was as culpable as everyone else. So why not make it him? I shook my head and began to dismantle the wheel, one length of string at a time.

At the police station, the duty officer told me DCI Roberts was busy in the incident room and asked me to wait. I looked around the packed lobby for an empty chair.

"Why's the station so busy?"

The officer gave a small head shake. "We had a postcode dispute last night."

"A what?"

"A rival gang fight—a bad one. Two stabbings, both critical. Ten arrests. It happened outside a busy pub, so there're lots of witnesses. It's taking a while to process the statements. The custody suite and interview rooms are overflowing. DCI Roberts is busy, but I know he wants to talk to you. Take a seat. I've told him you're here."

There was no free seat to take, so I went and stood by the entrance and watched the interchange of people waiting to be interviewed with others who were free to go. Forty-five minutes later, he appeared, haggard and distracted.

"Sorry to keep you waiting so long." He waved a hand around the lobby. "As you can see, we're snowed under today."

"I can come back."

"No. Come with me."

He led the way to his office and steadied himself with a hand on his desk, which still bore the remnants of his lunch: a chocolate-bar wrapper, an empty crisp packet.

"You'll notice I have a new chair. I stole it from the secretaries' office, and I'm relieved to say there've been no reprisals yet."

These words made him chuckle, although I didn't see the humor.

"Take a seat," he said. "I want to show you something."

He turned the monitor of his computer to face me, pressed a button on the keyboard, and a frozen picture of the interview room filled the screen. He and DS Hannah were in their places. Andreas Sousa was sitting opposite them. There was no solicitor. Two evidence bags were on the table between them. He pressed another key, and the interview began.

Andreas was looking around the room as if he was pleased to be there.

"This is nice. *Muito espaçoso.*"

"Can I get you a coffee?" DS Hannah asked.

"*Sim.*"

"Milk and sugar?"

"*Sim.*"

He was still very drunk. He was swaying in his seat. He seemed to be fighting to keep his eyes open. After a few minutes he lifted his shoulders in a high shrug.

"My coffee?"

"It's coming."

DCI Roberts pressed the red button on the recorder. "The time is 1:15 a.m. This interview is being recorded and may be used as evidence if this case goes to trial. Present are Mr. Andreas Sousa and DCI Roberts. The other officer present is…"

"DS Hannah."

"We appreciate you joining us, Mr. Sousa. We know it's very late, but we need to ask you a few questions." He slid an evidence bag containing a handful of berries across the table. "Do you know what these are?"

Andreas picked it up and made to open it.

"I wouldn't do that if I were you, sir," DS Hannah said quickly.

Andreas put the bag down. "These are coyotillo," he replied.

"Are you sure?"

"Yes, I am sure. I know these things. I know all about the natural world. Nobody knows the natural world better than me."

I saw the two officers exchange a quick glance.

"Are you a religious man, Mr. Sousa?" DCI Roberts asked.

Andreas shrugged.

"Catholic?"

"Do not assume I am Catholic just because I am Brazilian."

"But are you?"

Andreas turned his face away. "Of course I am."

"So you have a rosary?"

"*Sim.*"

DCI Roberts pushed the other bag across the table. "Made from these?"

Andreas glanced at the bag, then looked from one to the other of the officers. "Why are you asking me about berries?"

"Another name for *Abrus precatorius* seeds is rosary peas. In some countries, including yours, people make rosaries from them."

Andreas shrugged again. "I still do not know what you are asking."

DCI Roberts cleared his throat. "We're investigating the murder of a man poisoned with abrin extracted from the seeds of the *Abrus precatorius* plant."

Andreas let out a puff of air. "What do I know about it?"

"That's what we're here to find out, Mr. Sousa. Does the name Jonathan Wainwright mean anything to you?"

At these words, Andreas snapped to attention. Seemingly suddenly sober, he lurched forward and thumped the table.

"Do not say that name!" he shouted. "That man, he was screwing my wife. I saw them. A young, beautiful woman and that old man. Disgusting." He pushed back his chair and spat on the floor. "I kill him. Do you hear me? I kill that man."

DCI Roberts glanced at DS Hannah.

"We hear you, Mr. Sousa. Interview paused." He pressed the red button. "Let's continue in the morning. DS Hannah, will you find Mr. Sousa a bed?"

He pressed the keyboard, and the image on the monitor froze; then, he turned to me. "I've done some research into those rosary peas we found in Sousa's room. All he had to do was boil a few in water, mash them, strain the pulp, and suck the liquid into a syringe. Frighteningly easy."

I nodded.

"He then went to Jonathan Wainwright's house, lured him outside, and stuck him with the syringe. He had motive. He was angry that Jonathan was sleeping with his wife, and we both know his tendency toward violence."

I touched my neck and reminded him, "He also thought Jonathan was the English professor responsible for the deaths at his wellness center."

He leaned back in his chair.

"Yes, also that... Probably mainly that, but that part of the investigation has been taken out of my hands."

"What do you mean?"

"As we speak, two of my Brazilian counterparts are on their way here. They're charging him with the deaths at the wellness center, plus the two life-altering injuries. They want to extradite him and, frankly, I don't want a tug-of-war. I've got enough to deal with here. You've seen what's going on outside. If the Home Office agrees to Sousa's extradition, I won't object."

"You'll let them take him back to Brazil?"

"I *want* them to take him back to Brazil."

"But what about Jonathan Wainwright? Who'll be charged with his murder?"

"Sousa."

"How?"

"It'll be a pending charge. Once he completes his sentence in São Paulo, he'll be returned here for his court case. But I can't see that happening anytime soon, can you?"

I frowned.

"Anyway, whatever happens," he continued, "I'm satisfied we found our murderer." He cleared his throat. "And I wanted to see you today to tell you that we couldn't have found him without you." He held out his hand for me to shake. "So...thank you, Eustacia."

I stared at his hand, which, after a minute, he dropped to his side with a sigh that was more like a groan.

"I know what you're thinking. You're going to tell me you don't think it was Sousa." He sat down heavily. "To tell you the truth, I have my doubts as well."

He took the photograph of Zena out of his drawer, held it upright, and tapped its bottom edge on the desktop. "Border control has informed me this young lady has returned to Brazil."

I felt a pang of regret at this news. I would have loved to have seen her one last time. Not from a distance or through a telescope but up close, face-to-face, like the time in the café when we drank tea together.

"Do you know how big Brazil is?" he continued, lifting his large eyebrows. "It makes our country look like a province. A small one. If I couldn't find her here—"

"Zena didn't kill Jonathan," I interrupted.

"No?"

He leaned an elbow on the table and rested his chin in his cupped hand, and I waited for him to ask how I knew this. Instead, he said, "Are you sure?"

"Yes."

After a moment of contemplation, he said, "Well, then... Andreas Sousa will have to do."

"But..."

"But?"

I hesitated before saying it. "Is this justice?"

He let out a heavy sigh and rubbed his face, and I realized that he seemed smaller than he had the day he first came to my flat to see the destroyed garden. He seemed diminished somehow, sunken into himself. The skin around his eyes darker, his face and hands sallow and puffy.

"Ah… This may come back to bite me," he said. "But, hopefully, by the time it does, I'll be blissfully retired in a cottage by the sea with the wife, kids, and dog… Or I'll be dead."

I couldn't hide my surprise. It hadn't occurred to me that he might have a life outside the police station.

"You have a wife and children?"

His eyebrows lifted and separated.

"And a dog," he said with a boom of laughter.

I wrinkled my nose, not at all surprised about the dog.

ONE MONTH LATER

IT HAD TAKEN A WEEK TO SET UP THE LAB. EVERY SURFACE and piece of equipment had been scrubbed and disinfected.

The empty specimen cabinet was sterile and ready for the phials of toxins, and the start of my poisonous-plant collection, now independent seedlings with their own root systems, were under cloches in the lab cold frame. And, finally, my research assistant, Carla, was fully trained in all the safety protocols. After my year-long hiatus, I was up and running again. I was on top of the world. On my desk, in pride of place, was the *Psychotria elata* with its improbable glossy red bracts. Hooker's lips. I smirked at the memory of DCI Roberts's and DS Hannah's juvenile reactions when they'd first discovered the plant's common name. But that wasn't the only memory I treasured. Every time I looked at the plant, I was reminded of the young, beautiful woman I'd known called Psycho, then Simone, and then Zena.

It was late afternoon. We'd finished for the day. I pulled the laboratory door closed and locked it.

"See you in the morning, Carla."

"Yep. Bright and early. Have a good evening, Professor."

I watched her run up to a group of fellow students and link arms with them before I turned and walked to the stairs. That morning, I'd given my first lecture, and although I'd been fore-warned by Matilde, I was shocked by how few students had elected to take my course. The lecture hall must have been only a quarter full. After years of teaching at capacity, with students even sitting in the aisles, I had to admit, today's attendance was disheartening.

On the stairs, I was passed by a student, who stopped when he saw me and said, "Great to have you back, Prof."

"It's great to be back," I said, continuing on my way.

He changed direction and followed me down the stairs. I knew who he was. He was the tall postgraduate student with the huge hands and gangly gait, whose application to be my research assistant had been unsuccessful. I also remembered that when he was an undergraduate, I'd found him so irritating that I'd named him Giant Hogweed, *Heracleum mantegazzianum*—a tall, willowy plant with huge leaves and a nasty bite. I glanced at him, willing him to go away. I didn't like him and neither did the other students. There was something desperate about his manner that put everyone on edge. It meant he was always either alone or picking a fight.

"How does it feel to be back?"

I frowned. "Different. The lab feels empty without plants, and the teaching's dry without experiments. I tried to keep the students engaged today with anecdotes and cautionary tales." I held up my gloved hand. "But it's not the same as before."

He was silent, then suddenly said with urgency, "You have to make it the same as before. I need it to be the same for my work. I can't complete my research without experimentation." Unexpectedly, he grabbed my shoulder. "You need to talk to the dean."

I stopped walking and looked down at his hand on my shoulder, which he quickly removed.

"I'm sorry. I'm just very anxious. I really need access to poisons for my research."

"Then you may need to rethink, I'm afraid." I continued walking, but he stayed with me.

"I don't know if you're aware, but I've requested you as my PhD supervisor."

"I wasn't aware," I said, frowning.

He overtook me and walked backward in front of me. "No? Oh, well, I'm sure you'll be told at the next faculty meeting."

"Asked," I corrected.

He laughed tightly. "Yes, of course. But I think you'll say yes. I think you'll find the subject very interesting. Do you want to know what it is?"

We reached the foyer, and I headed for the main doors. "Not just now."

"I'll give you a clue—murder," he said in a loud voice. "Murder by plant-based poisons."

My body flinched, and I cast around to see if anyone had heard him. He was being deliberately provocative in a misguided attempt to pique my interest. But I'd had my fill of plant-based murder and intended never to encounter it again. Not even in a PhD thesis. Besides, I had enough to do to rebuild the department without taking on the additional work of supervising a PhD student. Especially one as needy and irritating as Giant Hogweed.

I pushed through the doors, left the building, and cut across the plaza, but as I was entering Russell Square, I heard a voice calling my name and turned to see Matilde running toward me. I accepted her embrace and the kiss on the cheek because I had a lot to thank her for. If it weren't for her work behind the scenes, I may not have been reinstated, even with the exoneration for the lab contamination.

"Welcome back, my darling," she said, beaming at me. "Look at you! You look so much better than the last time I saw you. What have you done to the suit? Have you had it tailored?"

"I think it shrank in the wash."

She laughed long and loud at this, and I waited patiently for her to finish.

"Well, you look great. I can actually see your waist now. This is a much better style for you."

I looked down at myself, trying to see what she saw. "Listen, I happened to see you in the lobby just now with that PhD student—what's his name?"

I had no idea. I only knew him as Giant Hogweed.

"Anyway. You know who I'm talking about." She stepped closer.

"I just wanted to give you the heads-up that he's having a few problems at the moment. His mental health is a bit unstable. He's being seen by student well-being services, but there's only so much they can do. I just wanted to make you aware in case you were thinking of becoming his supervisor. I know he's very keen for it to be you. I'm sure he's brilliant and his thesis is probably right up your street, but you've only just come back. I think he may be a bit too intense for you right now."

"I've already decided not to do it."

"Good," she said with relief. "I think that's the right decision." She stopped talking and smiled, and as the silence stretched, I was reminded of the time I met Zena on the street before I took her up to my roof garden. I'd felt an awkward tension then, and I was feeling it again now. I pointed across the square.

"I need to catch my bus."

"All right, my darling. I'll see you soon."

The bus was approaching, so I hurried to the stop and noted, with a sinking heart, how full it was. Not so long ago,

I would have let it pass rather than subject myself to the horrors of central London rush hour. But now, I hitched up my satchel and squeezed on board with everyone else, trying to ignore the hot soup of odors. In front of me was a large man with a broad chest, the buttons of his jacket open, a stain on his shirt. I pulled my satchel in front of me, trying to create a small space between us, but the queue behind was long and impatient, and more people pushed their way on until there was only an inch between us, my nose next to the stain on his shirt. I couldn't help but inhale, only instead of smelling sweat, I detected *Origanum vulgare, Ocimum basilicum, Salvia officinalis*, the Italian herbs used in whatever he'd eaten for lunch.

At my stop, I alighted and walked briskly toward home. Up ahead was a street bin. Without breaking stride, I reached into my satchel, took out the Nokia, and dropped it in, but after ten paces, I stopped and turned back. There was one more thing I wanted to do. One last act to rid myself of the weight of the past few months. I pulled off the glove and looked at my hand. The scarred skin on the back was discolored, and the blisters and cracks had healed to a texture like leather.

"Bomb-disposal experts have survived worse," I murmured, walking back to the bin and tossing in the glove.

Above me, the leaves of the London plane trees were just beginning to change into their autumnal colors, the bark splitting, ready to shed. I was relieved. Over the past few months, I'd discovered that spending a hot summer in a tweed suit was not ideal.

There was an envelope waiting for me on the doormat when I got home, covered with Brazilian stamps. I felt a thrill of excitement, hardly daring to believe who it could be from. Inside was a letter folded around a photograph.

Dear Rose,

I have been feeling bad about what Andreas did to you in London. I am happy that I stopped him hurting you too much, but it still should not have happened. He is a bad man who now is in prison here in Brazil, so we can all feel safe again. I wanted to send you this photograph so you can see we are happy and doing well. This is me with my mother, brother and my friend Sebastian—the young man with the long blonde hair, as you called him. We are standing at the entrance of our new wellness center. It will be open by the time you get this letter and we will NOT be offering ayahuasca treatments! I am glad I met you, Rose. I can tell you are a good person and I hope we will meet again one day. Tchau. Zena x

P.S. Please send my greetings to Susan.

There was no mention of Jonathan's murder or the destruction of my garden, but what did that matter now? I looked at the photograph of Gabriella, Zena, and Raul pointing to a large sign at the entrance of their wellness center. Coiling across the sign was a painting of a slender vine with long, pinnate leaves and brown pods peeling back to reveal bright-red peas, each with a distinctive black dot. And standing on a ladder beside the sign—in a paint-splattered purple T-shirt, pink bandanna, and orange sunglasses—was Sebastian, holding a paintbrush aloft and smiling for the camera. I brought the photograph closer to my face and saw that a tendril of the poisonous vine had been extended to form a word, too small to read. I picked up Father's magnifying glass and read *Spicer*. Maybe Sebastian had simply signed his painting, or perhaps he was putting his name to something more sinister. I thought of the items I'd seen on his bedroom floor—the lighter, the small tin foil package, the flask, the spoon...the syringe—and wondered if they really were drug paraphernalia or something else. I let this thought sit in my mind while I considered what to do with it, then shook my head vigorously, making it dissolve.

I scanned the letter again, and an unfamiliar feeling came over me when I saw the kiss after Zena's name. I knew such an addition at the end of a letter wasn't necessarily a declaration of love, but it was one of friendship. I turned the envelope over, and yes, there was a return address. Zena had liked me, still liked me, and was inviting me to begin a correspondence. All at once, I knew what this feeling was. It was the same one I had when I'd opened a freshly delivered package in my greenhouse. It was an excited expectation that something good was about to happen. I used to experience this feeling alone, but it didn't have to be that way anymore. I had someone to share these moments with now; so, letting out a whoop, I dropped my satchel on the floor and hurried out of the flat.

The door was on the latch when I arrived. I didn't even knock but walked straight through to the garden. There was Susan, deadheading a rosebush, a pair of secateurs in her hand. When she saw me, she tossed the cut stems onto a compost heap and smiled.

"How was your first day?"

"Mixed," I said, sitting down. "There's a lot to do, but we'll get there. Carla's turning out to be an absolute gem. I don't know why I resisted having an assistant for so long."

"I do. It's because you thought you could do everything yourself," she said, sitting opposite me. "You're one of them micromanagers. Delegating ain't a weakness, you know."

I took the envelope out of my pocket.

"I've got something to show you," I said, passing it to her.

She pulled her reading glasses from her housecoat pocket and took the letter out of the envelope.

"It's from Zena. Oh, look, she mentioned me. There's a photograph 'n all. Who're them other people?"

I moved my chair so that I was sitting next to her and leaned
in close.

"That's her mother, Gabriella," I said, pointing. "That's her
brother, Raul, and that's Sebastian, the young man with the long
blond hair who I followed to Soho that day. And they're standing
outside their new business."

"They look happy, don't they? What does that say? Abrus
Wellness Center," Susan read, squinting at the sign. "What's an
abrus?"

"It's a plant with a pretty purple flower, like sweet pea."

"That's nice. Maybe I should get one for my garden."

I shook my head vigorously. "No. That's not a good idea."

She turned to face me and patted my hand. "This calls for a
celebration, don't it? Fancy a cuppa tea?"

"I can't. I've got to go home to get ready."

"What for?"

I lifted the corners of my mouth. "I'm going on a date."

It occurred to me when I got home that now Zena was no
longer my neighbor, I needed to close my observational study
of her. I sat at my desk, took her notebooks from the drawer,

opened the most recent one, and turned to a blank page. Here I wrote the words:

Termination of study Conclusion satisfactory

I placed the forged letter to the café, the note with Jonathan's address scrawled across it, Zena's telephone number given to me by Susan, the translations from Meredith Wise, and the decoded messages from the Nokia in the center pages and closed the book. I then put this with Sebastian's, Raul's, Andreas's, and Jonathan's notebooks and tied them together with string. I doubted I would include this study if I ever pursued publication, because I had not achieved a clear and absolute result. There were still too many unanswered questions. I knew "conclusion satisfactory" really meant "conclusion hazy" because I hadn't solved the mystery. From my group of suspects, I hadn't definitively known who had destroyed my garden or put a name to Jonathan's murderer but, surprisingly, it no longer seemed to matter.

I was about to put the bundle of notebooks back into the drawer when I spotted Zena's camisole. I'd completely forgotten about it. I took it out and lifted it to my nose, but it had been too long away from its owner. It had lost that heady scent that had first intoxicated me. I considered putting it in my pocket. Instead, I folded it neatly, tucked it under the string holding the notebooks together, put everything into the drawer, and closed it. I didn't feel sad about the finality of that action because, although I knew Zena had had a hold over me—as powerful as if she'd blown devil's breath powder into my face—the hold was now broken. She was no longer an obsession. She was now a friend.

In my bedroom, a shaft of low-evening sunlight from the window cut across the carpet to the wardrobe and, as if directed, I opened the door and looked at the clothes hanging inside. I stroked the fabric of the sky-blue dress I'd worn on my weekend by the sea with Mary. A full-length mirror was fixed to the inside of the wardrobe door. I pulled the dress across my body and stared at my reflection, but I didn't recognize the woman looking back at me. Whoever she was didn't exist anymore. I let the dress go and smoothed down Father's jacket. I could see now that Matilde was right: the suit did fit me better. The sleeves were shorter, the cut tighter at the waist. I pushed up my glasses and looked again. There I was, Professor Eustacia Amelia Rose, head of Botanical Toxicology at University College London.

In the bathroom, I sprayed my head with a misting bottle, applied Brylcreem, slicked back my hair, and reinstated the side parting with Father's tortoiseshell comb. I leaned in close to the mirror and saw that the residual bruising around my eye had completely gone, and so had the red marks on my neck. It was as if the injuries had never happened. As if the events of the past few months had never happened. Physically, I had returned to normal. However, everything else had totally changed. I had my job back, and with it, the facilities and funds to rebuild my collection. I had the respect of my peers back and the exclusive use of a world-class laboratory. And I had people in my life. People I called friends. I felt truly blessed. I put on my glasses, sniffed in a breath, then did something I'd never done before. I smiled at myself in the mirror.

The bar was quieter than I'd expected, which put me at ease. It was, however, festooned with tropical and arid plants on every shelf, ledge, table, on the floor, and hanging from the ceiling, and so many of them were poisonous that I lost count. I felt I was entering the Temperate House at Kew Gardens as I approached the reception desk, but there was little point alerting the server to the dangers she and her customers were in, because I doubted she would believe me. Instead, taking great care to dodge any protruding leaves and overhanging tendrils, I followed as she led the way to the table where my date was waiting.

As expected, I heard her long before I saw her. She was talking very loudly to a waiter as he poured two glasses of champagne. I'd only had champagne twice in my life: once with Father when I was first employed as the botanical toxicology lecturer at UCL, and again with Mary on the first night of our weekend by the sea.

Both celebrations. I didn't know a date was a celebration—but then, I didn't know anything about what a date entailed. All I knew was that I'd been invited on one and I'd accepted.

The waiter left me a few feet from the table, but before I took another step, I paused to process what was about to happen. I was about to eat a meal that had been prepared by a complete stranger and converse with someone about inconsequential, perhaps even nonsensical, matters, possibly for hours. And there was a high probability that I was going to enjoy it. I cleared my throat, and she looked in my direction. Then she jumped up, ran toward me, wrapped me in a tight embrace, and kissed my cheek, and much to my surprise, instead of trying to extricate myself or wipe the wet smear of the kiss away, I put my arms around her, looked into her deep-brown eyes, her golden skin, and the smattering of dark freckles and said:

"Well, now, Matilde… Here we are."

PLANT GLOSSARY

BRUGMANSIA ARBOREA: ANGEL'S TRUMPET

- Family: Solanaceae
- Genus: *Brugmansia*
- A highly toxic flowering shrub rich in scopolamine. The powdered seeds, called devil's breath, cause amnesia, delirium, and psychosis.
- Fatal

EUPHRASIA NEMOROSA: EYEBRIGHT

- Family: Orobanchaceae
- Genus: *Euphrasia*
- A small herbaceous flowering herb used in traditional medicines to treat eye infections.
- Nonfatal

PSYCHOTRIA ELATA: HOOKER'S LIPS

- Family: Rubiaceae
- Genus: *Palicourea*
- A tropical South American shrub, notable for its distinctly shaped red bracts.
- Nonfatal hallucinogen

RICINUS COMMUNIS: CASTOR BEAN

- Family: Euphorbiaceae
- Genus: *Ricinus*
- A highly toxic flowering perennial native to Eastern Africa and India; contains ricin.
- Fatal

DIGITALIS PURPUREA: FOXGLOVE

- Family: Plantaginaceae
- Genus: *Digitalis*
- A highly toxic herbaceous perennial native to Europe, Asia, and Africa; used as a heart medicine.
- Fatal

DATURA STRAMONIUM: JIMSONWEED

- Family: Solanaceae
- Genus: *Datura*
- A weed native to Central America, used in medicines and drug abuse as a hallucinogen.
- Fatal hallucinogen

VERATRUM VIRIDE: FALSE HELLEBORE

- Family: Melanthiaceae
- Genus: *Veratrum*
- Native to East, West, and North America; high levels of toxicity in all parts of the plant.
- Fatal

AMBROSIA ARTEMISIIFOLIA: RAGWEED

- Family: Asteraceae
- Genus: *Ambrosia*
- Common weed native to Europe with a huge pollen count; highly allergenic, severe irritant.
- Nonfatal

RUDBECKIA HIRTA: BLACK-EYED SUSAN

- Family: Asteraceae
- Genus: *Rudbeckia*
- Flowering perennial native to North and Central America; coarse hairs are a mild irritant.
- Nonfatal

DICENTRA SPECTABILIS: BLEEDING HEART

- Family: Papaveraceae
- Genus: *Dicentra*
- Spring-flowering perennial with heart-shaped blossoms; entire plant contains toxins.
- Nonfatal

STACHYS BYZANTINE: LAMB'S EARS

- Family: Lamiaceae
- Genus: *Stachys*
- Perennial herb with thick leaves densely covered with soft, silver fur-like hair.
- Nonfatal

LOBULARIA MARITINA: SWEET ALYSUM

* Family: Brassicaceae
* Genus: *Lobularia*
* Small low-growing annual with sweet-smelling flowers; found on sandy beaches and dunes.
* Nonfatal

HERACLEUM MANTEGAZZIANUM: GIANT HOGWEED

* Family: Apiaceae
* Genus: *Heracleum*
* A phototoxic flowering perennial, causing blisters and scarring; a dangerous irritant.
* Fatal

CONVALLARIA MAJALIS: LILY OF THE VALLEY

* Family: Asparageceae
* Genus: *Convallaria*
* A highly toxic woodland flower due to its dense concentration of cardiac glycosides.
* Fatal

READING GROUP GUIDE

———

1. Eustacia Rose is extremely passionate about her plant collection. How does her relationship with her plants define her as a character? Then, think about your own passions. Do you have any activities, studies, or hobbies that you take as seriously as Eustacia does her plants?

2. Besides plants, Eustacia likes to watch her neighbors through her telescope. What did you think about her habit of spying on people? Have you ever taken part in people watching? If so, what was that experience like?

3. Eustacia takes Simone to see her garden, even though she has never let anyone see it before. Why do you think she did this? Like Eustacia, do you have any special places that you like to keep to yourself? Discuss.

4. We eventually learn that Eustacia was fired from the

university she was working at. What big event happened that got her in trouble? Do you think she deserved to be fired for what happened? Discuss how that past event relates to the position she finds herself in with the poisoned man and Simone's disappearance.

5. Eustacia is a unique character with a distinct voice. Do you think she's a reliable narrator? If not, give some examples as to why. In general, would you rather read a story from a reliable or unreliable narrator? Explain your preference.

6. Eustacia wears her father's clothes throughout the novel. How does her grief over his loss play a role throughout the story? Is wearing his clothes a way for her to cope, or is it something else? What are some ways you have coped with loss in your own life?

7. Discuss the interview that Eustacia must endure after being accused of murder. What evidence does DCI Roberts have against her, and did you find it convincing? If you were in Eustacia's position, how would you have reacted to this questioning?

8. This story is filled with toxic plants from around the world and even uses them as the main murder weapon. Did you learn anything new about plants and their potential uses? If so, what did you learn?

9. Did you guess the identity of "the English Professor"

before the end of the book, and if so, what clues led to your conclusion?

10. This story is filled with twists and revelations, especially at the end. What was your favorite twist, and why? Did you see any of them coming?

A CONVERSATION WITH THE AUTHOR

———

Eustacia Rose is a unique character. What was it like to write from her perspective?

Originally, *The Woman in the Garden* was written in third person, but in a later draft, I changed the POV to first person and this was when Eustacia Rose came alive. In third person, I found there was too much distance, making it harder to understand her, identify with, and even feel sympathy for her. I also had to explain all her misunderstandings and quirky reactions, which after a while came across as quite labored. Once I was inside her head, I could dispense with all of the extra explanations and just let her be her gloriously eccentric self.

After a while, Eustacia became very easy to write because she has such a unique character; I knew what her responses would be in any situation. It was as if she was a real person telling me what to put down on the page. I love that what she thinks is happening isn't what, in fact, is happening, and I hope readers pick up on this very quickly and realize they are reading more than one narrative: Eustacia's and everyone else's.

The use of toxic plants is key to the novel's plot. Why did you choose poison as your main murder weapon? What kind of research did you do to write this novel?

I'm a huge Agatha Christie fan. In fact, I'd go so far as to say, I'm a superfan. Christie wrote more than eighty books. Almost half included poisons, and about a quarter of those were plant poisons. *Hyoscyamine* from henbane, *nicotine* from nicotiana, *ricin* from the castor oil plant, *asprin* from willow trees, *aconite* from monkshood, *morphine* from poppies, *taxine* from yew, and *belladonna* from deadly nightshade feature in books such as *A Pocket Full of Rye, And Then There Were None, Dead Man's Folly,* and *They Do It with Mirrors.*

I've always loved plants and gardening. So much so that I did a degree in ornamental horticulture and design. Although my studies weren't purely focused on poisonous plants, I was fascinated by this subject—the history, folklore, and mythology. That fascination always stayed with me and became the inspiration for the book. The research was the fun part. I have hundreds of books about plants, so it was just a case of poring over them, writing notes, then delving deeper. I also made many visits to gardens—the famous Temperate House at Kew Gardens, in particular.

What does your writing process look like? Are there any ways you like to find creative inspiration?

Most of my ideas pop into my head during the night, so I make sure I jot them down into my phone before I forget them. The next day, I'll go to a noisy, busy café and expand those phone notes into a notebook. Then, in complete silence, I'll transfer the notebook work into the draft on my laptop. This way, the words go through two edits, and the ideas are fairly well-developed for the first draft. It usually takes two or three more drafts before the manuscript is ready for publication.

I'm lucky enough to live by the sea, so when I'm feeling stuck with my writing, I go to the beach and watch the lapping waves or stare at the horizon where the vast sky meets the ocean, and often inspiration will come. If it doesn't, I will have at least cleared my head and blown away the cobwebs so that I can work on a particular plot point with a new energy.

What do you hope readers experience while reading this book?

I would like readers to experience two things.

Firstly, to follow a character arc that shows the transformation of Eustacia Rose from a bitter, distrusting recluse to an open and engaged person who can interact and even thrive in society. It's a tough journey for her with many obstacles, but I really hope that after a while, readers find themselves rooting for her and wishing her well.

Second, I'd like readers to learn a little about poisonous plants but not in a lecturey way, not in an "Oooo you need to be careful" way, but more because poisonous plants are incredibly interesting.

What are some books you've read that have influenced your writing?

An awful lot of Agatha Christie! I've also read most of Iris Murdock's books. My favourite is *The Sea, The Sea*. I love both Christie's and Murdock's clear writing styles and paces and hope I've been able to achieve something similar in *The Woman in the Garden*.

What are you working on nowadays?

I've just finished the first draft of the second Professor Eustacia Rose mystery. It has many of the same characters, plus a few new ones. It also has a new plant poison murder for Eustacia to solve, along with her long-suffering sidekick, DCI Roberts.

ACKNOWLEDGMENTS

My heartfelt thanks to my first readers—Casper Palmano, Su Woods, Jackie Thomas, and Maria Cardona—for your excellent criticism. The book is all the better for your wise words.

Thank you to my Faber Academy classmates Paul Gould, Neil Alexander, and Kate Taylor for a decade of steadfast friendship and encouragement.

Thank you also to the incredible agents at Pontas Literary and Film Agency—Clara Rosell-Castells; Carolina Martínez; and, in particular, my agent, Anna Soler-Pont—for your stalwart belief in me and my character, Professor Rose. You truly are the best cheerleaders a writer could have.

Huge thanks to the utterly brilliant Carla Briner. The way you chopped up the first draft of this book and put it back together again was beyond inspiring.

Thank you to Campbell Brown and Alison McBride at Black & White Publishing and Bonnier Books UK for taking a liking to Eustacia on your first read and then taking a chance on her on your second. I will be forever grateful for your decision to bring Professor Rose to life.

Thanks also to my eagle-eyed editor, Clem Flanagan at Black & White, for still loving the book after your second, third, and even fourth read! May we work on many more Professor Rose stories together.

I must also acknowledge my very old and very tattered copy of *The RHS Gardeners' Encyclopedia of Plants and Flowers*. I've owned it for thirty years, and I will own it for thirty more.

And finally, thank you to my children—Casper, Paris, and Belle—for being so patient with my wandering concentration while I was writing *The Woman in the Garden*. I promise you, I was listening—kind of.

ABOUT THE AUTHOR

Jill Johnson has lived in southeast Asia, Europe, and New Zealand. She obtained a BA degree in landscape design. She has previously owned an editorial cartoon gallery and a comic shop and has been involved in a graphic novel publishing house. She is a Faber Academy graduate and now lives in Brighton with her children. Jill's writing is inspired by her Maori heritage.